Nursing Adeleine

Love to you always!
xoxo

All Sw...

D1713976

A. M. Swinson

Nursing Adeleine (Shattered Darkness, Book 1)

ISBN 9798366956468 (paperback)
ISBN 9798388229182 (hardcover)

Printed in the United States of America

A Dedication

To RDW & JKW, thank you for believing in me before
I ever dared to dream.
1 Thess. 4:13-14

Grateful eternally and with all my
heart for Chattanooga, Pinnacle, and Dubuque.
John 1:12

To JCS & PDS, thank you for being the melody of my
dreams and the rhythm to my song. SHMILY.
1 Corinthians 13:4-7

Love you forever.

PROLOGUE

Grayson Manor, Gloucestershire, 1873

The giddy sound of Addy's laughter bubbled like the brook below, and Joe knew exactly where the little nymph was hiding. Walking from the stables, he headed in that direction; then just before he should have outed her, he turned with a chuckle and went in another direction. He suddenly heard a splash and a cry, and without another thought, he turned and ran toward the cluster of trees above the brook. When he saw her, she was standing over the rocks, her hair drenched and her celadon dress a muddy mess. He jogged the rest of the way down to her, finally reaching out to help her over the slippery rocks and muddy edge of the brook. Her cheeks were blazing and her eyes misty. He knew she was embarrassed. Holding back another chuckle, he said, "Addy, I believe you found the best hiding place in all of Grayson's grounds. How about we go up to the house to get ready for luncheon?"

Shaking out her wet mop, she glanced back toward the brook and motioned down to her missing left slipper. "I believe my slipper is back there in the mud," she said with eyes wide. "Mama will have a fit if I arrive without it!"

He let go of her small hand and chuckled. "Stay here while I fetch it." As he carefully leaned out over the water again, he saw just the barest hint of green satin behind the rocks and gingerly reached in to grab it. As he straightened, he found the girl had stepped right alongside him. He turned, grinning at her as he held the dripping slipper aloft.

Gazing up at him very menacingly, she said, "You give me that slipper this instant, you cad!" as she tapped her foot on the ground. Giving a dramatic sigh and shrug of his shoulders, he handed it over. She giggled as she attempted to ring the slipper out over his shoes, and reached down to place it back on her muddy stockinged foot. Looking down at her dress and muddy slippers, she held her arms out and began to laugh. Joe snorted, shaking his head, and began to laugh as well.

"My lady of the brook," he said regally, bowing low before her. She reached for his arm, and he tucked her hand safely into the crook of his elbow as they walked over the rise toward the manor. He smiled down at her, and she grinned back at him, her eyes full of merriment. He and his family had just arrived for their yearly summer visit, but this year would not be all play, kittens in the stables, horseback riding, and parties. This year, contracts would be signed and the future sealed.

Seeming to note the silence that had suddenly fallen over him, she looked up at him and said tentatively, "Joe? What is betrothed?" He looked at her, lost for words, and tried to think what the best explanation would be for her. At fourteen, he wasn't certain he completely understood it all, but he knew it meant forever between them. "Well," he said carefully, "I suppose it means we will always be friends, just as we've been these last years." He gave her his boyish crooked grin and couldn't help but notice the green of her eyes matching her dress, and their gold flecks in the sunlight. Her wet chestnut hair was beginning to dry in the warm air, and the sweet freckles across the bridge of her nose were just visible on her sun-kissed face.

At nine, nearly ten, she was an effervescent, happy sprite, always full of pranks and laughter and kindness to those around her. He'd first met her some eight years before, when their parents had reconnected after years apart, and instantly a warm place in his heart belonged to her. She began toddling after him those several years ago, calling him Jojo and spouting gibberish. As she got older, she shared favorite books with him, new interests, places at the manor, and her love of horses. Somehow, he felt his life had always included her. He supposed being betrothed could be worse, and shook off the serious air that had settled about them.

"Well, now, Addy my girl. Race you to the kitchens!" he cried as he reached out and tugged a wave of her hair, dashing away.

"You'll never reach them before me, you ogre!" she shrieked after him with laughter, as her legs stretched into a run.

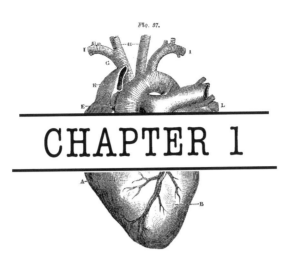

CHAPTER 1

Bourton-on-the-Water, 1887

The last rays of the December sun were quickly fading into night, and she knew it would be unbearably cold. She had all she needed, but warmth always eluded her. Her tiny room above the apothecary was clean and homey, and she was grateful to simply have a place to lay her head at night and friendly folk to share her meager life with below. John, the apothecary, and his feisty, tidy wife, Christine, had been her rescue many years ago, when she was orphaned and alone. They'd found her wandering the streets leading her horse, disoriented and barely able to speak. They'd taken her in and treated her as their own. She'd earned her keep running medicines to the village folk and by helping to garden and gather the precious herbs that healed. Now as John and Christine slowly aged, she acted in as many ways to help them as she could. She knew every medicine, every dosage, every home in this tiny village. She dreamed of becoming a nurse, if she ever had the courage to leave. As if it was possible.

She lay across her bed caught in memories from long ago, wondering at how life had shattered so quickly. That last sweet summer, after the joyful, idyllic days had come to an end, she remembered the kind embraces of their friends, the whispered promises of Christmastide in London, and watching them leave in their carriages. She'd had no idea that the melancholy that day would quickly be overshadowed by the deepest grief she'd ever felt. She yawned and wrapped herself in her dense but whisper-soft wool blanket.

The insistent banging on the door would have surely pulled it off its hinges had it continued another moment. The messenger's fist was raised to strike the wood again when the aged butler answered the furious summons and offered a gentle, "How may I help you, sir?" The messenger's hair was wild in the breeze, and as he spoke, he sounded choked for air.

"Is Dr. Ashton in? Please tell me he's in. I fear I just saw three households all at their death!"

"Wait just a brief moment. I'll find him," Robertson answered quietly. Ever sincere and ever understanding, he strode quickly from the door and, in moments, had mounted the polished oak stairs and almost immediately returned Dr. Daniel Ashton back to the messenger.

"Oh, praise be to God. Please come with me doctor!" The messenger leapt to his horse as the groom led Dr. Ashton's horse to him, and immediately they were off.

As the two men galloped toward the town, Dr. Ashton called out to the messenger. "Tell me what you saw, son, and don't skip any detail."

The messenger replied, "Mr. Gibbs was expecting me for a delivery from the smithy today but wouldn't come to the door. The horses were in the yard, and it seemed everyone was home. When he wouldn't come to the door, I finally looked in. The whole family was lying about, and a couple were moaning. They sounded restless. But, Doctor, their faces. Oh, their faces, they looked like something from hell had hold to them! I knocked at the other two cottages that share the yard with them, but they didn't answer either. I couldn't see inside as well as the other cottage, but God take me, they looked as if they were lying about the place too." His voice was ragged and cracked. He was clearly extremely upset by what he had seen. Dr. Ashton knew of only one sickness that could spread so fast and look so hellish.

Dusk was settling as they made it into the cottage yard. Things were deathly silent. The doctor gave a knock on the door and heard only moaning inside the cottage. Or was it the next cottage? He opened the door slowly and allowed the evening air to rush in before him. What he encountered inside the neat little cottage made him sink to his knees in desperate realization, having visited there just days ago. Mr. and Mrs. Gibbs lay side by side, the pox covering them both. Their hands seemed to have been entwined before their last breaths. Moans came from the bedroom portion of the cottage. Rising slowly to his feet, he made his way there. Their eleven-year-old and nine-year-old lads lay abed, one silent and still and the other kicking at the sheets and moaning weakly. Dr. Ashton wiped his face with his kerchief and went to the bedside of the kicking lad. His eyes were wild as he struggled and finally looked at the doctor. He screamed and tossed himself side to side. Dr. Ashton closed his eyes and whispered a prayer to the Lord to comfort the lad in his distress. The doctor knew the throes that preceded this death. He walked a few steps and grasped the pitcher on the bed stand. He wet his kerchief with the cool water and laid it over the lad's face. "There now, Charlie. There, there. Let this cool you. Close your eyes now, lad. Close your eyes." Walking to the front door, he saw the messenger about to step in. "Nay, don't step another pace! This house needs to be quarantined immediately. Tell me, please, lad, that you didn't come inside this or the other two cottages any days this week?" The messenger shook his head wearily and pointed to the last house.

"My Meg, she is in that cottage. I had to see her. We're to be married. She won't answer me, Doctor. She won't turn and look upon me."

Dr. Ashton walked with legs that felt mired in deepest, thickest mud, and he looked into the sky streaked with reds and blues. "Lord, be with us."

Adeleine heard the hoofbeats coming past the house. It was nigh on midnight, and her mother sat by the door wringing her hands and praying earnestly, as she had for hours. Adeleine watched through the railing as the door opened, and Papa stepped in. He'd stripped off most of his clothing somewhere, perhaps in the stables, and wore no shoes. Nor did he bring in his bag. He sank to his knees and lay his head on Ellen's lap. "It's the smallpox, Ellen. Six cottages filled with dead. The Gibbs, Hawthorns, Millers, all gone. The Gibbs boy Charlie was still fighting when I went into the cottage the first time, but on my way back, he'd gone too. The messenger, the smithy's apprentice, he'd not be moved from the Miller's dead girl Meg. He was to marry her in a fortnight. The Walkers, Ellises, and Crenshaws all lay dead. It looked as if the Ellises succumbed two days or more ago, and the new infant, she lay dead on her mother's bosom." Ellen choked back a sob and wrapped her arms around him.

"What will we do, Daniel?" she cried softly.

"First thing in the morning, we must gather everyone here. I don't know if I'll be falling ill myself or not. If we will, only time will tell. But we must prepare for the worst and hope for mercy."

Adeleine crept to bed silently. She knew she'd heard people speak of the pox that had killed in years past. But she had no idea what it meant, what they could do to stop it. She fell asleep as the dawn came, gray and full of rain, with the winds weeping as though for the villagers lost.

Everyone in the household—Robertson, Helen the cook, her daughter Clara, Billy the groom, and Jed the stable hand, and Mary and Lizzie, the spinster sisters and maids—was gathered about the table as Dr. Ashton had requested. He stood at the head of the table, and Ellen sat in her usual place with Adeleine beside her. The silence carried fear and the weight of death. Clearing his throat, Dr. Ashton looked about the table. "Last night, I answered an urgent call and found that six households were dying or dead of the pox. I removed my clothing and shoes and left my bag in the stables last night. I'd like to prepare for the worst to come here to Grayson, though I ask that you pray for the Lord's mercy on us all. I'd like the three connecting rooms in the east wing we use for summer parties to be stripped of all but necessities, the beds pulled down to sheets only. Pitchers and basins on bed stands in between. Cloths folded and ready to be used, placed between each bed. Mrs. Helen, please be sure the kitchen is stocked with things for soups and gruels, and the firewood stacked high for the stoves."

"But, Papa, why do we do this? Surely, we'll not get sick. We're away from the village a good bit, right, Papa?" Adeleine interrupted.

"Addy, we hope not to become sick. But I have been in the village a great deal these past weeks. This small pox is deadly and spreads like fire. I've not much hope that I've avoided contact with anyone I saw lying dead last night. I had many calls this week for wheezing, coughing, and the like. I never would have anticipated the pox hitting this way. Just a week past, you and Clara rode into town with your mothers. You stopped to see several folks who were sick and offer them sustenance … There's just no guarantee. We've had so much contact with those that have died. If we do get sick, doing these things will help us to fight against it and be helpful to those that don't become ill." Clara's eyes were round as saucers when she looked across the table at Adeleine. As everyone got up, they stood outside the kitchen doors, hands held tightly together.

By the time a fortnight had passed, Ellen, Daniel, Helen, Robertson, and Billy all lay abed in the upstairs rooms. The covering of pox blistered their bodies, and fluids and pus ran onto their sheets as they writhed in pain. Their glassy eyes and flushed marred faces seemed not to know one another. Jed the stable hand had run off just after the morning discussion two weeks before. Mary and Lizzie were rocking down below in their beds, burning with fever. Clara and Adeleine spent days spooning water down parched throats, putting cool cloths all over writhing bodies, and hoping for the best. But no one was coming around.

She'd washed her hands until they'd dried out, and eaten bread and broth herself until she could stand no more. The bread had started to mold. She was becoming ever so frightened. But she must not, she told herself. She must continue as Papa's good nurse.

Clara found Mary and Lizzie dead in their beds and came screaming to Adeleine's side in the sitting room the next morning, when all else was silent. Adeleine was startled at Clara's flushed face and burning-hot skin. She told Clara to lie on the sofa, that she would go check on those upstairs. First, thinking to soothe Clara, she gathered her softest, most comfortable nightdress and helped her to put it on. Starting up the stairs, she was terrified what would meet her as she entered the room.

As she quietly opened the door, her father's face was the closest. She held her breath, watching for movement. He turned weakly, looking at her as though in a daze. "Addy," he called hoarsely. "Fetch my pocket knife from my bureau, and come back to me." Frightened, she did as he asked. "Come beside me, my darling girl," he said. She took in the funny gray cast to his face, though it was angry with sores. They were raw and blistering and running. "There is a way to ward off this pox. I've known of it, but some trust it as a vaccination of sorts, and others do not. We're going to try it for you, to try to protect you." Adeleine gasped for air as she knelt beside the bed. She was desperate to flee, but her legs were frozen. He weakly motioned for her arm, and shaking, she lay her arm where he could reach her. He took hold of his pocketknife. She knew it was sharp enough to cut anything. He'd always sharpened it as he talked of his childhood in the country and of being prepared for anything to come. She cried out as he dug into the flesh of her forearm several times, but she held still. She didn't trust anyone as she did her papa, and though this seemed the most horrible thing, she knew in her deepest self he was doing something to help her. He flaked several of his angry scabs off and told her to lay the scabs over the shallow cuts he'd made.

He motioned toward the cloths lying on the bed stand and told her to wrap the strips around her arm to keep the scabs there. Weakly, he explained, "The scabs have the sickness in them. Your body will fight the sickness, and then you will be immune to the pox the rest of your life, my angel." He sighed and closed his eyes. "Lord be with you, my Adeleine. My little gem."

The next morning, all was completely still. The sky was angry with dark clouds that left a pall over the house. So little light shone into the windows downstairs it may as well have been nightfall. She looked through the house for Clara and finally found her lying between their still, silent mothers. Hot tears began to carve paths down her face as she realized no one moved. No one fought against the sheets or moaned for water. Clara lay still, looking toward the ceiling. The sores had covered her body, and though she had fresh tears on the sides of her face, she didn't respond as Adeleine called to her frantically. "Clara, please! Please don't give up! It's only you and me now. We're all alone ... Please don't leave me, Clara!" But her friend didn't move, didn't reach out to her when she reached across the bed and motioned for her hand. She only blinked hard once and closed her eyes. Adeleine left the room shaking, her nails biting into the tender flesh of her palms.

Adeleine walked through the house. As she lay on the shining oak floors that night with one candle guttering, she made up her mind. She'd leave. She'd simply walk away and never come back. She would hold vigil over them this night, and then she would go.

The following morning, she visited the sick rooms once more. There was no movement. Clara didn't breathe. None of them did. She closed the door quietly, and after leaning her head against it and choking out a single sob, she fled to her bedroom. She got out her traveling bag, the small one she could carry herself. She put in her long nightgown, her favorite crocheted blanket from mama, her brush, and an extra day dress. She dressed simply, putting on her gray wool dress, sturdy bonnet, and long cloak. Her mama had always told her there were times to dress to your finest and times to keep to simple clothing. She thought of her gentle mama. Her sparkling brown eyes and sweet smile. Her mama would stand in the kitchen kneading their bread with Cook, though others like her didn't do such things. She laughed with servants as though they were her kin and yet could hold her head up high at grand parties in London with nobility. She loved her mama. And her papa, too, for he was just the same as mama, leaving London to be a physician in the country because he wanted to heal those who had little hope and no privilege. She thought of his flashing blue eyes and tawny hair, with silver at his temples. He had the kindest face. She took up his bag from the stables and managed to saddle her small Arabian herself. She had named her Jewel. She pushed the block over to Jewel and stood high enough to mount the horse Papa had given her just weeks ago when she turned ten. She packed the saddlebag with her things and Papa's things from his visiting bag. She tied the heavy sack of food stuffs she'd found in the kitchen to the pommel and threw herself into her sidesaddle. She looped her leg like a fine lady and straightened her skirts. She pulled her cloak's hood over her head and urged Jewel toward the gates. She'd not ride into their village. She'd go the other direction and try to find the place by the water. Her papa had always told her how lovely the village there was with its cottages of golden stones on the water. Mama had always laid her head against Papa and said they must go back there someday.

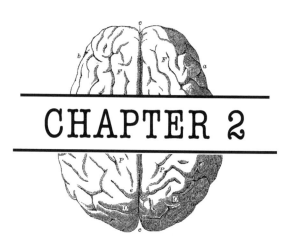

CHAPTER 2

The soft tapping on the door brought Gemma abruptly to her feet, her blanket falling to the floor in a heap. She realized she'd fallen asleep in her clothing and felt none the better for it. Her eyes burned, and she felt her muscles bunch when she stretched. The gentle tap came again, and she opened the door. Christine's kind eyes took her in, and her eyebrows shot up in surprise. "My dear girl, are you all right?" Christine began to move about the room, straightening the bed and opening the wardrobe to find a clean dress for Gemma. A smile edged onto her face as she took in the dear woman. Her Scottish brogue was a balm to her frequently over the years. "I'm quite fine, dear Christine. I've no idea how I came to be sleeping in my clothes, but, truly, I am fine," she said.

"Well, young lady," Christine said with a feigned hard look, "you never sleep past breakfast, so you gave me a fright. It's time for the noon meal now, and John is waiting for us below." Gemma's jaw dropped in shock, and hurriedly, she splashed her face and washed and got into the fresh dress Christine lay over the bed for her. "I thought maybe you were poring over some of those new medical books we bought a few months back. You'll certainly need them now." She gave Gemma a conspiratorial look and winked, and before she could ask a thing, Christine went bustling down the stairs.

Gemma quickly followed and laid a hand on John's shoulder as a good morning once she reached the small dining area. Well, good afternoon more like, she thought. He patted her hand and grinned up at her. "Well, about time you came down, girl. I thought I'd have to make medicines myself today." Gemma laughed softly. He had to wrestle her to make anything himself these days, and he well knew it. Her eyes dropped to the linen covered table. There just beyond John, near her place, was a packet that looked serious. Her interest was piqued and she quickly got into her seat and looked expectantly from John to Christine and back again. "Well open it, girl!" Christine seemed about to fizz over as she pushed the packet toward Gemma. Suddenly, Gemma felt her whole body tense. What could it be? Where did it come from?

The old familiar nervousness curled through her body as she reached toward the packet. As she brought it closer to her, she noted the St. Thomas' Hospital markings and post from London. It couldn't be. She shot Christine a fevered look, and Christine said again, "Open it, girl. What are you waiting for!" Gemma carefully opened the top seam of the packet and found a sheaf of documents. An application. She looked back up to John and said, "How is this possible? I don't understand." He seemed to take a minute to think of what to say. That was John, always so thoughtful with how his words were to be taken. He looked to Christine, and when she nodded with a smile, he said, "Well, seeing as how you've dreamed so dearly of becoming a nurse, I made inquiry of some of my old friends in London. That Florence Nightingale, her school at St. Thomas' Hospital, is all the rage. Been going twenty or more years or so now. So I asked for information to be sent here to us." He looked almost like a boy, shy and expectant, as though having just given his girl a flower. He smoothed his salt-and-pepper brown hair back and looked at Christine. She smiled back at him and looked back to Gemma. Gemma had come to love their dear faces so. She shook her head and looked over the documents. "I don't see how it could be possible. I've so little money, and it's all the way in London. Am I too old? Where would I stay? How would I live?" Christine rose from the table and went to gather their luncheon, and John reached across the table to grasp her hands.

"I believe you'll find in those documents the answers to all your questions. And you've taught and tutored in the village for a good many years, and you've learned all you could here with us about treatments and medicines. And Christine and I have saved for you for years now as well. You're a smart lass, and I've no doubt you'll be welcome there." He looked at her gently, and it seemed he struggled with what he was about to say. Looking her straight in the eyes, he finally said gently, "I do think it's time, perhaps well past time, my girl, to face your past. Only then will we know everything we need to know about getting you into that school for nurses." He gave her hands a squeeze and let go, and as Christine sat beside him, he bowed his head and gave thanks for their meal.

Gemma took some bread and cheese, but her mind was reeling, and she had no desire to eat. She looked over at the shelves of glass bottles of different colors and sizes, the herbs tied and drying about the place, and thought of how this had become home to her. She'd never told them where she came from, only that sickness had taken her whole household, and she ran away. They didn't know her papa had been a doctor, her grandpapa an earl, and her mother of quality as well, a true lady. They didn't know the disgrace of her leaving her whole family dead at Grayson Manor.

Christine noted the flush to Gemma's face and the tremor to her hands. She looked as though she might cry, but Christine knew it wasn't over the packet clutched in her arm. She was staring toward the apothecary's table and out toward the water. "Gemma?" she said quietly. "Why don't you mind the fire for me just now, and then go up to your room a while, look over everything. I'll keep your food here and come to see you in a bit. We can talk over things." Gemma looked at her without seeing her and gave a weak nod. She rose and went toward the fire, never looking to what she was doing but holding that packet as though it were a lifeline cast from a ship. She looked very much like she'd been cast into the waves of a storm.

Christine thought back to the day they'd found her. The girl had come to them hardly able to walk another step, with her forearm wrapped tightly, her wool dress muddied and starting to tear. Her cloak might have been new before she came to them, but it was rags that afternoon. She'd not let go of her horse until she stood at the steps at the back of their shop, where they pointed to their horse and promised no harm would come to Jewel.

She'd had a few things of her own in the saddlebag, and a few things of her father's. They could tell immediately her father must have been a doctor and could only speculate that something terrible must have happened to him, maybe to the girl as well. It had taken the girl a couple of weeks to start being present with them, and not trapped in her thoughts.

Christine thought back to the girl's wrapped forearm. The child had been insistent that her papa said to keep it that way. It was nearly the only time she'd ever shown any kind of temper. She'd howl and screech if they got near her, stomping her feet. It took days to get the girl to let them take it off, and even then she'd shaken like a leaf, fists clenched and tears running down her pinched face. As they put the rags in the fire, she and John had met each other's stare over the child's head. They knew this had to be variolation, they could see the healed marks on her arm, and that explained the child's weakness and look of being barely alive when they'd found her wandering into town. She'd surely been affected by smallpox. And so they'd burned most all her things to be safe, but they'd put her papa's doctoring things and a few others away in a chest. They'd heard much later some small village a ways out to the west had been nearly wiped out with the sudden onset of smallpox.

Who knew how far she'd traveled? She'd looked as if she'd walked for months. Had her papa been with her in this travel at some point? How had she gotten here? What was her full name? She'd given her name as Jim they thought at first, but one day she seemed to be working over something in her mind and told them not Jim like a boy. Gem like a fancy stone in a necklace. And so calling her Gem had turned to Gemma over the course of time, and they thought this was surely a good name, for she'd been a treasure to them. In years past, they'd wondered if they'd harmed her by keeping her. But in her nightmares that first horrible few months, she'd cried out many a time, "Everyone's dead. Where shall I go?" And when Christine would rock her back and forth and whisper sweetly in her ears, she'd curled up tightly against her and trusted her in short time. And that seemed to settle things. They hadn't the means to hire anyone to find her next of kin if everyone she knew had died.

And they loved her. So the months quickly gave way to years, and the ten-year-old they'd surely rescued had grown. As Gemma moved up the stairs as though in a trance, Christine thought how beautiful a young woman she'd turned out to be. She had a lovely figure about her. Her deep-chestnut hair hung to her waist in a thick braid. She was bright, affectionate, and kind. She drank in knowledge like a starving thing and always lifted her hands to help anyone with anything. Her expressive warm eyes were the color of honey and moss at times, and a deep sage with flecks of gold at others. Her freckles had all but disappeared at some point, but her nose was fine and straight, and her mouth full and generous with smiles. Her skin was creamy and clear, with a blush of peach. In her carriage and talk, she seemed to have been reared by quality means.

Christine couldn't fathom why no young men in the village sought her out, but in truth, Gemma never seemed to have interest in those things and said she was the happiest spinster in the village. Still, at four and twenty, Christine knew surely there was someone special out there for her Gemma. And maybe he was in London. Maybe life as they'd known it was about to change all together.

Deep in her heart, she ached for whatever pain Gemma would have to face to leave this little village free of her shadows.

CHAPTER 3

Gemma felt her emotions beginning to drag her into the mire. Like crashing waves beating down the sands, over and over. She could barely fill her lungs for the scorching tears falling and the huge lump of stone in her throat. How could she tell these sweet people what she'd done? How could anyone forgive her for running away? She'd been just a child, but surely she could have done something … somehow. But she'd had no one to tell, no one to ask for help.

She thought of what she would do now in the same situation. She'd prepare in much the same manner she had then to leave. Only she would have thrown propriety to the wind and rode Jewel astride, she thought with a glint in her red-rimmed eyes. She'd fallen asleep on Jewel's back just hours into her meandering ride that very first day and found herself slamming into the ground, confused, startled. Afraid. It seemed like it took years to gain back the air that had been knocked from her chest. Jewel had stood by her faithfully; but with no block, no fence rails, on flat ground, at just ten years of age, she had no way to get back into that sidesaddle and onto her horse. She couldn't reach. And so she'd walked.

And she'd felt badly at that. Knowing now what her papa must have been trying to do with cutting and wrapping her arm with his scabs, she could see how her body had reacted and fought the blasted pox. But she'd walked for days and days, in a stupor, afraid to sleep. What she'd heard Papa say many times was less than two days' gentle ride had taken … Well, it had taken forever. Thankfully, no one had bothered her, and truly she'd not seen a soul until walking on blistered raw feet into John and Christine's little village on the water. It occurred to her just now that was likely due to the smallpox outbreak. No one coming or going. Everyone still and dead.

Through her haze of exhaustion and recovery from sickness, the town had been like a dream. The water running happily through the village and all about sparkled in the sunlight. The stones the buildings and cottages were built of had glowed gold in the afternoon sun. She thought she'd died, for surely this was heaven, this wondrous place Mama had wanted to visit again. Mama. Papa … Clara and Cook. She felt the heaving sob through to her bones. All the others. They'd made up as much of her life as she could remember, and she'd left them dead in their beds.

She knew she'd have to tell John and Christine. It was time; there was no getting around it. To become a nurse, she'd have to use her real name. And she wanted it, to help heal others, as Papa had. But the all-encompassing fear she felt at saying her real name left her feeling like all around her had gone bright white. She wasn't sure she had any family left, and surely if she did, they'd not want her, being so vile as to do what she'd done. She felt like her head would explode with the pressure. It felt like everything inside of her were shrinking into a tight, tight mass, and she was being strangled. Gemma sat and put her hands to her temples. She attempted a huge breath of air and gave another quiet sob. Impatiently, she swiped at the wetness of her face. Looking to the ceiling, she thought to pray for strength, but she could not. The God her parents had loved and served had left her frightened and alone, no matter how Papa had prayed for mercy upon them. This same God, the same Lord that John prayed to, and Christine, what was he to her? He'd abandoned her.

Gemma shook her head and straightened her shoulders. She stood, feeling as though her body were swaying. Just as she reached for the door, Christine gave her gentle little tap. She opened the door and noticed Christine had a small chest clutched to her middle. Gemma said just above a whisper, "Let's sit by the fire. Everything I have to say, I want to share with you both together." Looking over her shoulder at her small bedroom with it's simple chest of drawers, it's tiny wardrobe she'd painted as a girl, the small bed, the tied lavender at the windows, and her small desk, she couldn't help but wonder if she'd ever be allowed back in.

Knowing Gemma must feel she was drowning by the look on her face and the rolling shallow breaths she was taking, Christine knew the time had finally come. And it was going to take all the lass had and then some.

John looked up from the herbs he was grinding on his stool for next week's needs and stood immediately when he saw the shape little Gemma was in as she reached the landing. She silently went to the sofa and sat down with a hushed sigh. He looked to Christine, and she motioned with her head to come sit at the fire. He grabbed a couple of clean kerchiefs and sat softly beside Gemma. Christine sat on the other side of her and placed the chest on the old wood table in front of them. She looked over at John, and he nodded. With a faint creak, she opened the chest in front of Gemma. Gemma seemed to still completely, then jumped out of her skin; and then she hastily moved to the floor and looked into the chest, her lips forming an *O*. Her slender fingers touched both cheeks, and as they watched, her face crumpled and her shoulders shook.

John reached to put his hand on her shoulder, but Gemma jerked away. "No!" she all but shouted. He laid a kerchief for her on the table alongside the chest.

Drawing a deep breath, Gemma began to speak with a shudder.

"My papa was a physician in London before coming to Gloucestershire. He wanted to help those who didn't have much, though his father disagreed. He built a small manor house for Mama and him and me to live in, and kept only a few servants. His father was an earl, and Papa the fourth son. When grandpapa died, Papa put away his inheritance, and we lived on what he'd made in London and whatever he made in our little village. Mama was a lady, but I don't know anything about her family. They did go to London a few times each year, and I know Mama wore fancy dresses and jewels. I think she argued with her parents whenever she went to London. I never met them that I can recall."

She paused and tried to clear her nose and eyes with the kerchief. "Our servants were like kin at the manor house.

We took meals together most of the time, and Mama did not tolerate any disrespect toward them. Our maids were old spinster sisters, Mary and Lizzie. Our cook Helen was a widow with a daughter named Clara. She was about my age but a little smaller than me." Her shoulders trembled again, and she sobbed through her next few words. "Our butler Robertson was a widower, and Clara and I were always dreaming of them marrying right out on the grounds over the brook. Dear Helen would always hush us and tell us to get out of her kitchen when she heard us chattering by the kitchen doors about her." She rattled out a broken laugh. "Our groom Billy was a kind older man, though he seemed very young, and his son was about eighteen. His mama had run off at some point, and Billy could never find her. His son was a good lad, Jed, his father said so, but they would argue about what Jed should do now that he was grown. And so you see, no one really had any family, yet we were a family together. Everyone got along, and we all loved one another."

She grew silent as she built up the will to tell the rest. She ran her hand over her face and started again. "One day, Papa received a messenger that seemed all but crazed in his hurry to get Papa to the village. Hours and hours went by that day, and my mama, she sat by the clock in the sitting room nearly the whole time Papa was gone. She'd pray and get up a while, then come back and pray and try to do her needlepoint, then pray again. This went on until nearly midnight. When Papa came in, something was terribly wrong. Mama started to cry, and he pulled her up from her chair, and they came up the stairs. I got back to my bedroom just in time that they didn't see me. I couldn't fall asleep that night, because I was so frightened. I'd never seen Papa that way. That morning, Papa called everyone to the table. He told them all several things to do to get the house ready in case we became sick. He'd seen many dead in the village the day before. And so all day everyone was so busy, and though I tried, I hardly got to talk to anyone. Clara and I sat at the kitchen door and watched everyone running to and fro, and we were so afraid we just sat silent, watching. Jed ran away that morning my father gathered everyone. Clara and I saw him saddle his horse and gallop away while we sat at the door. Things seemed more normal as the next few days went by. But then Papa went upstairs to bed one night hot with fever. Then suddenly it seemed like everyone was burning with fever, and Clara and I tried to give them water and broth, and I tried to cool them with damp cloths as Papa had shown me when I went with him on visits.

"Our maids went downstairs into their room and shouted at us not to come down. Clara went down anyway a few times, but I don't know what she saw when she did. I kept trying to feed everyone or give them water, but it seemed like they were having nightmares or their sheets were upsetting them. They would lie awake staring or sleep fitfully. Mama and Helen died first. Then Robertson. Then Billy. Clara came screaming to me one morning saying Mary and Lizzie had died, and she wanted to go check on those upstairs. But her face was bright red, and she was so hot. I told her to lay on the sofa, and I'd tend to her. So I went upstairs and checked, and no one was moving. Then Papa turned and looked at me, and he was so weak. He told me to get his pocket knife and come right back.

When I did, he told me he was going to try something to save my life. So he made three cuts and told me to put his fresh scabs on them, and I wrapped cloths around my arm as he told me to."

Again her shoulders shook with sobs, and she picked the pocketknife out of the chest. In a tiny choked voice, she cried, "This was his," running her fingers over the smooth surface. She gritted her teeth and kept going. "I checked on Clara and tried to give her water and broth the best I could, but at some point in the day, she disappeared. As night fell, I curled up in Mama's chair and fell asleep. The next morning, everything was silent. I crept upstairs hoping my papa was still with me. I opened the door, and as I stared hard at him, I realized he wasn't breathing. I heard a noise and saw Clara in the bed between our mothers. She was covered in the marks, and I could see tears on her face. I reached my hand out to her and begged her to come with me, that she and I were alone now. She wouldn't reach for me. I saw her close her eyes tight and wandered out of the room. I couldn't stand to be there any longer. I didn't know what to do with them, and I was a coward, afraid to touch them. There was no one I could tell, no one that would come help. So I wanted to run and never look back. I lay on the floor that night, thinking I was holding vigil over them all. In the morning, I looked in once more, and all was still. I got a few things and saddled Jewel somehow, and we left. And then you took me in."

She stood and turned to look at them, her face red and flooded with tears. "My father called me his little gem as long as I could remember. That's all I could think to say when you asked my name all those years ago." Her feet were restless, but she held her head high and said with all the courage she could gather, "My name is Adeleine Eleanor Ashton. My mama and papa were Ellen and Daniel Ashton, of Grayson Manor, Gloucestershire."

Adeleine turned abruptly, afraid to look into either of their faces, and fled outside to the small stable, to her beloved horse.

CHAPTER 4

The good doctor let his head fall back and stretched his long muscled legs under his desk, letting a loud sigh fill the room. He ran his hands straight back through his hair, pushing the waved hank that ever fell into his eyes back into place. His study's bay window looked out over the busy streets of London this dark and desolate December evening. The carriages, single riders, and those walking tread past the cobblestone walkway and black iron gates, oblivious to his gaze. The fire crackled softly in the hearth, and he looked about, suddenly aware that the lit tapers were the only light remaining. He'd not bothered with the gas lamps this evening.

It had been a long week. There had been a tragic death on Monday he'd been invited to view, and though he had been able to help or bind up the other passengers of the two carriages before another doctor arrived, the driver himself had become wedged between the carriage he drove and the one that veered into his pathway. Two horses out of eight had been put down due to their injuries, and the metal of both carriages had sheared and forced into each other at high speed, which would not allow them to be pulled apart. The sight had been incredible to behold from a medical standpoint, though heartrending. The man's body had been twisted and crushed, pinned between the unyielding maw of metal, but he remained alive long enough for his wife and mother to come touch him and whisper their hearts to him just once more. When the metal pinning him had finally been forced apart, he'd taken only two breaths more, and then the man had died. His life's blood had poured away out onto the streets, and he'd had to shout for someone to drag his poor wife and mother away. His wife was heavy with their first child. The doctor shook his head to clear the image from his mind and rubbed his eyes hard. Studying the man's body afterward had given much to consider and record.

The rest of the week had been busy, and as seemed to be his curse, he found himself restless even on the nights he could sleep without being awoken in the wee hours. The Christmas holiday always seemed to bring about more accidents, more illness, and, perhaps most grievous of all, more suicides. He was more often than not invited to the sites of these poor souls' demise due to his place of research in the King's College. He also sat in the House of Lords, and his fierce interest in medicine was both well-known and well trusted. He'd received encouragement and support from both to study those deceased that had no next of kin or known family to bury them. Occasionally, a family allowed a deceased loved one to be studied prior to burial as in last week's tragedy. He saw his research and study as a way to give his subjects purpose in what had been a hard world for them or a grisly death. Most of the deceased he studied were the poor and destitute, with a great deal of suicide victims. These were those bodies set to be buried in Potter's Fields, unknowns who had come to a point where they no longer had the will to breathe. He studied the workings of their bodies in his upstairs studio, finding clues to effective surgeries from their injuries and details to fill books for his shelves and those of others in the field. Life in this city came easily to the rich, but with incredible difficulty and suffering to the poor. And knowing the full difficulty of their plight as he did, his heart burned for the torturous life they led. He saw the workhouse horrors they bore, the starvation, their suicides, and their hangings. As the law of London, the undertakers, and his fellows in anatomical research at the hospitals knew they could ring the bell of his townhouse office at any hour, he rarely had a break in his business of doctoring and listening to the dead.

The fashionable townhome he employed for his medical practice sat just beside his home, the residence he now shared with his widowed mother. Their grand estate had become too much for her to manage after his late father's death shy of a year ago. With business around London booming and the busy streets and her wish for quiet, he moved her here to the townhome she and his father owned when they first married. It was still in a tony enough part of town, calm and quiet but still in style. As it happened, a developer paid handsomely to take the very grand, very opulent estate off his hands. He'd purchased the property next door to her townhome as soon as it came on the bustling market, and refitted the homes so that they could be walked between in a private manner. He'd given his mother full authority for updates and rearrangements on her side, and he'd handled his side, and, finally, the renovations were complete.

His medical practice as it were stayed under diligent lock and key from the interior of their home, as all his medical books, equipment, his laboratory studio of sorts, and his exam room for the occasional living patient who received no other answers to their suffering were here. In the lower floor of the practice, he'd fitted the back side nearest the steps down from the street with ice chambers, embalming equipment, and medical tables. Though several of the precincts had dead rooms now, he used his own, being that he researched. He typically did not involve himself in crime study, and so for his purposes, his own dead room was better, more efficient. The ground-level floor contained his study and an exam room, and a bedroom or additional office space. The second floor contained his library of medical books with a large desk set into the back corner that received the most natural light for drafting and painting his drawings and journaling his findings. The third floor contained his research lab and studio, due to its wonderful lighting from the large windows in its front and back. A custom-built lift could carry his study cadavers from the bottom floor to the top without a great deal of trouble or noise. The door leading into the hallway of his practice could only be reached from the back hallway of their home, and was kept under lock and key at all times. The door looked like any unassuming closet. Outside of that, there were no other entry points to his business residence except the back stairway down into the basement level. But the locked gates in the back of the side-by-side buildings kept that entry nigh impenetrable. He wanted the security not only for his collection of scientific treasures but also in respect for his patients—both living who'd received no good answer for their ailments, and nonliving. The blasted "resurrection men" as they were called, grave robbers, had been outlawed; and though need for study cadavers remained high and was usually met, those of questionable intent still crept about in the night. He thought about, and was deeply troubled, by these things. He felt it his duty to learn from the dead but never to take from them. In fact, many times he paid for their decent burials. Nor would he allow anyone else to take from them, which happened so often, and thus his careful security of the practice.

His butler came in each night to close it all up with him. He'd had a nurse and assistant of sorts for a time, but she'd married two springs ago and was happily making a home with her new husband. She'd been a good assistant, under-standing his purposes, of strong sensibilities, and not look-ing to waste his time with fainting or gagging or theatrics.

For the millionth time, the constant question of whether or not to take on a partner for his practice whis-pered through his mind. He shook his head at the thought even as it crossed his mind, knowing it just would not work. Even though much of England had taken a solid stand against those who didn't know a liver from a kid-ney and disavowed them, there were yet many charlatans and crooks out there claiming to be peers in the medical field. He'd seen enough leech-bearing, lance-waving mon-sters to last him to kingdom come. He'd seen patients die from being bled or sucked dry by leeches that would have improved in a matter of days if not for this mad, disgusting negligence. And he'd seen men claiming to want to heal who employed these old and defunct measures because they enjoyed watching people suffer to their deaths. No, sharing a practice was not for him. The doctor gently tugged the only bell pull in either residence to alert his butler to the fact that he was finished for the night. He sighed and began to stand as he heard Ellison's footfalls in the stairway adjacent to the wall.

He began to stand and go next door with a yawn. He was well and truly done here, annoyed by his own jumbled thoughts. The correspondence on his desk had all been responded to or thrown into the fire in the hours he'd spent here this evening. But one piece of mail remained. It bore the name Ashton, and for that reason alone, he couldn't bear to open it. Not now. Not at Advent and Christmastide. The invitations to Christmas balls and parties had all been tossed to the fire. He didn't care to be trussed up like a turkey—to be stared at and whispered about—and had no patience for meddling, matchmaking mothers or starry-eyed young chits that seemed little more than babies. He was a lord of the realm but, more importantly, a man of science and study. He had no desire for a wife. Nor a mistress. Nay, the very thought sickened him. Dr. Josiah Cairns was content as he was, and in most respects, he was happy to let the world spin as it would, long as it left him to his studies.

As the lock turned and the door between his office and home opened and his butler greeted him, he set the piece of mail against the fireplace mantle. One day soon, he told himself. Tonight, he'd have a light supper with his mother and see if sleep would come for him.

The following morning dawned dull and gray, but somehow bright. Clouds considered allowing the sun out here and there. Josiah threw his arm over his face as Ellison snapped open the curtains and fussed about the room. "Go away," he groaned.

Ellison drew himself to his most intimidating height. "For a successful and responsible son, you lie abed like a gambler or rogue that's traipsed about all night."

"If only that kept me awake nights, my good man," Josiah replied sarcastically. He sat up and ran his hand over the bristle on his face.

"Yes, sir, you do look like a wandering gypsy," stated Ellison with a twinkle in his eye. "Nonetheless, your mother is expecting you in the dining room." Grumbling, Josiah stalked from the bed. Washing up and dressing, he thought on his schedule for the day and realized not much was planned at all. He decided to take his mother for a ride round the park this morning. He stepped from his room and took the stairs two at a time, looking forward to spending the day with her.

"Good morning to you, son. Did you sleep well?" his mother said sweetly as he found his way to a chair beside her at the table.

"Well enough, Mother dear," he said. After gathering sausages, toast, jam, and his coffee, he reached for her hand and bowed his head to pray. As he said amen, he noticed his mother did not let go of his hand. With no small amount of distress, he noticed her eyes had filled and were about to run over. His mother's tears tore his heart nearly from his chest. He could study dead, cold bodies, but he could not bear her tears. Gently, he brought his other hand to cover hers, thus holding her hand between both of his. "What is it, Mother? Is something amiss?" He looked over her warmly. Every hair seemed to be in it's perfect place, she looked well, and nothing that he could think of should be troubling her. And yet he knew. Moving his chair over closer to hers, he wrapped his arms loosely about the lady. She leaned against him, and her tiny frame was small enough that her head lay against his shirt collar just below his chin. He held onto her for several moments before breaking away to look into her eyes. She had aged this past year, though she was still striking and rather lovely, he thought to himself.

"It's hard this time of year, is it not?" he said to her earnestly. She nodded her head, and a tear rolled down her cheek. "Advent and Christmas used to bear so many joys, so much laughter, with dearest friends and with our small family." His parents had only ever had him, but their home had been happy. She reached for her embroidered kerchief and daintily wiped her face.

"I miss your father so," she sniffled. "It's been somewhat hard for you for years, though, hasn't it, my boy?" she asked quietly. She didn't miss the hardening of his face.

That Christmas had come many years ago with no word from the Ashtons at all, and they'd waited months before inquiring of the family's welfare with Dr. Daniel Ashton's older brother. The shock of learning all of them had been wiped out with smallpox a mere month or two after they'd left them that last week of summer was a source of sharp, unrelenting grief. Josiah had turned fifteen and was growing into quite a handsome young man. He'd come to understand the betrothal that had taken place and, indeed, was happy with it. He cared a great deal for his Addy, as he called her. He seemed to have a depth of acceptance and kindness inside him that enabled him to see her and appreciate her for the girl she was, but also confidently look forward to the day he'd marry her.

When the news was shared with him that day in the parlor, he'd been totally silent. He'd spent hours in his rooms at their huge family estate just outside London, and when he came down later that night, he'd asked if there would be a funeral of any kind. When they'd quietly told him it had already taken place months before, he'd simply nodded. He'd never said another word about Adeleine. He threw himself into his studies and had finished at Cambridge anticipating becoming a physician. He'd finished top in his class and never stopped learning or working.

She and his father had tried to get him to enjoy balls as he reached maturity, but he hadn't the patience for it. They'd not pushed him, though they heard plenty of discussion as to his eligibility and the interest of many young ladies. Nearly a year ago—when they'd lost his father, and his place in the realm and seat within the House of Lords was transferred onto him, and his father's responsibilities were passed to him—he'd never shied away. Never stumbled. And today he was sought after constantly for his maturity in his field as well as his character. He'd earned respect; it hadn't just fallen to him. She reached again for his hand, and he took hers softly. "I'm so very proud of you, my boy. Know that, my love."

He kissed her cheek and started into his breakfast. Knowing she watched, he threw his arm over the back of his chair and leaned far back, lifting two legs from the floor. He chomped his food loudly and was delighted to pull a giggle from her. He gave her the crooked grin she'd always loved, his big brown eyes sparkling at her. She ruffled his hair and told him to behave. He rocked the chair forward with a thump and said with a chortle and his most fashionable tone, "Mother mine, we must ride about the park today in my lovely carriage so that you are the envy of all the ton. Don your muff and warmest cloak, and I shall be down at half past to collect you."

With a short burst of laughter, she warned him in her most regal tone, "You trifling rake. You *are* handsome, but don't think for a moment I won't swat you with the horsewhip!"

Sticking his tongue out at her, he gobbled down the last of his toast and ran upstairs.

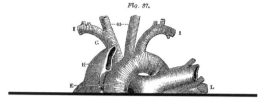

CHAPTER 5

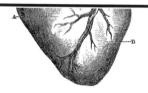

$\mathcal{J}$ohn the apothecary, or Jonathan Pierce as he was once known in London, tossed and turned in his bed, rolling first one way and then another until his Scottish bride told him she'd throw him to the dogs if he'd not stop this instant. He got up before dawn and went out to their small stable, which was really little more than lovely stonework and beams of weathered wood. He leaned against Jewel's stall and held an apple to her. She'd always been a fine mount to the girl sleeping in the steeply pitched upper room of the cottage. Gemma … Adeleine, he reminded himself, had not once acted like a lass of any means, at least any he'd been familiar with. He'd come to a serious distaste of London's so-called ladies in his youth, but Adeleine had never behaved like any of those harridans. Sure, she'd spoken beautifully, but her words had always been kind, sincere. She walked proudly and gracefully but never haughtily. She'd come to them broken yet willing to give to all freely as she could of anything she had. He'd been proud watching her grow but knew who she truly was had come from her parentage. He and Christine had only just settled in the village when they stumbled across her. And so not many folk knew enough or could have doubted them as to where the lass belonged. She'd fit herself right in with them, and they adored her. In speaking the truth of her childhood with them last evening, he was sick with the realization that she thought they'd feel disgusted by her—as though she thought they'd think ill of her for looking fear square in the eye and beating it back with bravery.

And so at daybreak, Jonathan Pierce got himself into serious riding gear, left a note for his bonny bride, and set off to Grayson Manor on his black beast of a horse, Ace. He felt shame pour over him as he considered the Daniel Ashton he'd known so many years past. How remarkable that here he'd hosted the man's dear daughter all these years. He'd been a good young man, fair, honest. He knew the man would be proud of the fierce little lady his gem had become. Why had he never looked to put things together for the girl? Fourteen years was a long time past, a long time to have kept her from any loving family she'd had left. Daniel's folk had been a good-hearted lot. It was no wonder the lass was a fine young woman.

His heart twisted in his wretched chest thinking of his selfishness. They'd been childless and simply were so grateful to have the girl. He admitted through his gritted teeth that the man had had three brothers, and therefore, she had three uncles he might have reached out to. But how could he have known? He guessed he could have pressed the child harder in those first years for names, other information. As it was now, he'd start setting things to rights sure as his name was Pierce, and take the girl back to her home so she could walk the path of healing her heartache. But, first, he had to take a look at it for himself. He couldn't stand to harm her worse than what she'd already survived. Lord only knew the shape of things there, and he'd not have her blame anything further on herself. He'd be back within five days. He prayed the Lord would guide his path and help him and Christine to leave the child with no doubt of their love. But he couldn't stand the girl feeling she'd lost everything if there was yet hope.

The time had gone quickly, and his horse had flown as if it knew John's feeling of urgency. As he found himself turning into the Grayson manor grounds, it was as though the house reached to embrace him. A feeling of comfortable ease filled him. The gardens here and there seemed manicured, the lawn attended. The manor itself was absolutely lovely—small by gentry standards but all the more pleasant for it. A warm-eyed groom strode toward him from the stables, reaching to greet him and shake his hand. "Welcome, is Ashton expecting you?"

When John shook his head and said he was there on an unexpected matter, the man boomed, "Jedediah Paulson, sir. I'm acting as groom here while my employer tries to settle the provisions of a will having to do with this property. Please let me know anything I can do for you."

"Appreciate that, thank you, Paulson."

"You're more than welcome to call me Jed, Mister ah …"

"Pierce, Jonathan Pierce. Please call me John. This horse rode harder and much faster than I expected, so I'd be grateful if you'd not mind giving him a good rubdown, some warm mash, and water of course, if things are available."

"That they are. That'll be no trouble at all." With this, Jed smiled.

"Feel free to go on up and knock. Lord Ashton will receive you, though the lord part annoys him. He prefers just mister." John chuckled and nodded, watching as the friendly fellow took his horse, while he himself headed toward the manor house. Lots of familiar names were flying; he was sure of that. This place seemed friendly, if the man Jed were to be any indication.

Squaring his shoulders, he gave the door a polite few raps and stepped back. Surprised not to be greeted by a butler, John had to collect himself quickly when the gentleman himself opened the door. He had a fine bearing, and John made his introductions and reached his hand out in good faith. The man responded in kind; and even as John noted his tawny hair color though a good deal of silver ran through it, his eyes, the set of his jaw, and more, shivers ran up his back. "I am Lord Benjamin Ashton, earl of Graystone, but please do call me Benjamin. I'm pleased to meet you." Lord or Mr. Ashton led John to a modest study, and when he offered John a seat, it was gratefully accepted. "Now, Mr. Pierce, I wonder how you may have come to pay a visit here today."

John wanted to speak carefully as was always his nature. The man was quiet, firm, and direct; and that suited John just perfectly. He noted feeling no ill will from him, just a weary sadness about the man's eyes. He brought his elbows to his knees and steepled his fingers before he began speaking. Beginning, he said, "I remember attending school with a Daniel Ashton who was youngest in his family, had three older brothers. Enjoyed the country, didn't care much for

London. We shared that opinion." He looked to Benjamin and held his peace, waiting. Benjamin ran a hand over his face and cleared his throat, clearly somewhat shaken.

"That would have been my brother." He stood, walking to the doorway of the room, leaning against the wall as if to steady himself.

"I'm here about his daughter Adeleine."

Lord Ashton turned sharply back toward John, his eyes unreadable. Peering toward the ceiling, as though he saw the past replayed there, he cleared his throat again. "Come with me, Mr. Pierce." John stood and prepared to follow. Benjamin took a walking stick from the corner and proceeded toward the back of the house. They left the house through a back door just inside the kitchens. John thought back to Adeleine's mention of this very doorway.

Walking at a leisurely pace from the back of the manor, John drank in the beauty of the place. He could hear water ahead of them. A lovely garden with stone walkways rose before them, and just below that, a line of trees sat above a melodic stream or perhaps a brook. As they continued toward the trees, a low stone wall came into view to their left. Within a few more steps, they rounded a bend and approached what was now clearly a small cemetery. Stepping into an open gate, they silently approached the middle of the yard, where four intersecting gravel paths converged. There in the center rose a grand stone monument, with a rectangular plaque set into its middle. A carved arch curved over the top, and four columns stood on either side. On the right side, a broken column stood between three that were whole, while the left side had four whole columns. The detailed six- or seven-foot-tall headstone bore carvings of eight wreaths hung over the columns and bore a crown of carved ivy over the arched top that trailed down both sides of the rectangular plaque. The monument curved gracefully down to a four-footed base, which coincided with the four paths. It was a sight to behold, the detail stunning. Carved into the center plaque was a beautifully detailed cross, strewn with lilies. Below it was carved the scripture

> I am the resurrection and the life; he that believeth in me, though he were dead yet shall he live. John 11:25

Smaller rectangular stones were set flat into the ground below the monument. At the base of the front of the monument lay one long stone reading, "Here lie Lady Ellen Ashton and Lord Daniel Ashton, loved through the storm, carried by grace to Heaven's shores." To the left, below one point of the monument's base, sat a stone reading, "Here lies Adeleine Eleanor Ashton, beloved daughter." Following the circular pattern, John came next to a stone reading, "Here lies E. Helen O'Shea, dear companion and friend," then again, around to the right, "Here lies Edward Robertson, beloved friend," then another just beside it, saying, "Here lies William Paulson, faithful friend." Then lastly he came to a stone that read, "Here lie Mary and Lizzie Stafford, dear sisters." Recorded into each stone was the birth and death of those buried there. To John's guess, these were all the staff that Adeleine had described falling to the illness, and of course her mother and father. Except, he well knew Adeleine's name did not belong. Surely, the child Clara

Adeleine had spoken of lay here. Hearing footsteps coming toward them, both John and Benjamin turned toward Jed. He had flowers in hand for each one and laid them at their stones. John recalled that Jed's father lay here as well by Adeleine's account.

Benjamin turned back to John and said in a somewhat clipped, somewhat hurt manner, "How is it that you come to ask after Adeleine? The child has been gone these fourteen years," pointing at her marker.

In reply, John simply said quietly, looking into the man's eyes, "I think we have much to discuss this evening, if you'll have me."

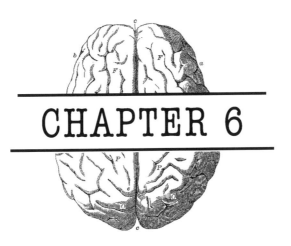

CHAPTER 6

$\mathcal{L}$ater that evening, after walking the grounds and seeing the whole manor with Benjamin and Jed, the men sat together talking quietly at a table in the kitchen. It was a very large and simply appointed room, yet there was an elegance that suited the manor well.

Windows lined most of one wall above the worktables, and two large sinks, with shelving lining the space below them, sat between the table surfaces. In a back corner, copper pots of various sizes hung from hooks descending from the ceiling. Two large double cookstoves, neatly set back into tiled alcoves and set onto brick floors, occupied another side of the room. Kettles, old cauldrons, and kitchen tools sat about ready to be used; and a roasting spit graced a short wall that also lead out to the woodpile. A tall series of built-in cabinetry matching the gleaming oak in the rest of the home, complete with leaded glass doors above and large cabinets below, ran along the back wall near the door. Various copper pie molds sat in the space between on a cheesecloth runner. The high ceilings and windows made the room feel open and airy, and the cool stone floor surely was the work of very thoughtful design. The place was spacious and bright, while lending comfortable elements to those within the home and any servants working there. A common thread of sense and comfortability seemed to weave about the home, extending to the lord and lady as well as the help.

A tall woman bustled about, having come to Gloucestershire from London along with two maids, Molly and Jane. The cook—and obvious one in charge, Ruth—was just the other side of middle age, with gray wisps of curling hair escaping her cap as she worked. Benjamin's home in London apparently had two cooks, working under Ruth's direction. If this cook moving about them was any indication, the food served by them in London must be the talk of the ton. The delicious fragrance of freshly baked bread wafted through the room, and one could hear the bubble of a simple potato and onion soup on the cookstove. Ruth brought out jars of jam, fresh butter, and cheeses. She then had Molly and Jane ladle the bowls with soup, and she herself brought the just broken bread to the table. The men thanked her, and Benjamin looked inquisitively at John and said he'd thank the Lord for their meal and the time to follow. John smiled widely, nodded, and bowed his head.

As they crunched into the warm crusts of bread and spooned the soup into their hungry mouths, the room became quiet for a time. Ruth shooed the maids out of the kitchen, asking them to take care to see that Mr. Pierce's room for the night was ready. She then excused herself, telling the men the soup would stay warm for a time and asking them to please have all they wanted. They nodded toward her as she wiped her hands, hung her apron on a hook, and walked from the room. John took care to allow Benjamin space and time to determine at what point Adeleine would be brought back into conversation. As it was, Jed mentioned her first. "I just don't quite know how the girl could be living," he said softly, giving a slight shake of his head.

Benjamin raised his head quickly and turned his eyes to John. "John, if you'd be willing, please go ahead and share with us. I can't quite fathom these things, you see. I've visited this manor several times in the last years. When we came and found them all departed, we buried each one. We laid out the garden, commissioned the monument, the stones. I just cannot fathom this, sir." He shook his head, and John didn't miss the mistiness of the man's eyes.

"My wife and I settled into Bourton-on-the-Water in the late summer that year. We'd determined to enjoy a quiet life after finding ourselves childless. London held no pleasure for us, and being an apothecary, I enjoyed the prospect of helping ordinary folk. Things were going well for us, and we were deeply attached to the surrounding village almost immediately. As September came to a close, we were finishing the last touches to our shop and living quarters, though it seemed there was still much to be done. But we were happy and felt settled. Christine and I were walking outside around our shop one afternoon, and we were startled to see a little girl leading a horse toward us. You see, our shop is nearly at the beginning of the village, and there's not much else past us coming back here your way." Benjamin nodded.

"Christine walked to her slowly, and though the child made not a peep, she stopped right in front of my wife.

Christine knelt before the child, whispering softly to her, and as I hung back, I saw tears in the child's eyes. I thought she was afraid, but the little thing simply laid her head on Christine's shoulder." John took out his kerchief and wiped his eyes. "The little sprite wouldn't dare let the reigns of her horse go, not till we turned her toward our stable and pointed out our own horse. She looked between Christine and me and laid the reins in my hand. She came inside with Christine, who gave the lass water and food. She didn't speak a word, didn't talk to us, nothing. Just looked at us with those big golden green eyes of hers."

At the mention of her eyes, Benjamin let a huff of air escape him. Looking up suddenly, he said gruffly, "Continue, John, I got away from myself is all."

"When she came to us, her forearm was wrapped in bandages. She'd not stand us to be near her if we looked like we might try to remove them from her. Finally, one day, it all started to unravel, and Christine talked her into going ahead and letting it go. We noticed the cuts healing on her arm and saw the scabs that had been there. We knew then there must be pox, and someone must have tried to help her become immune. We went through her saddlebags, and to be safe, we burned the clothing and things. We put the doctoring items she'd brought and her trinkets in a chest for her to have later. We knew out of hand her father must have been a doctor, but we didn't know where to look. The child would answer no questions of that sort and would become very upset, shaking her head vehemently, tears falling. So after some time, we just didn't ask anymore. And then there were the nightmares. We brought in our little sofa to have her stay next to our bed several months. The child would scream and cry out, sobbing. This went on for some time. My Christine would gather her close, rocking her, whispering to her, and she'd drift back off. When she seemed past these nightmares, we made a room for her in the steep pitch of our upstairs. She took to it and seemed to love it, and so we let her keep it.

She grew up almost before we knew it. She learned all we had to teach her. She tutored in town. She visited the sick. She talked of wanting to be a nurse, so I inquired with some old friends in London, and the packet from St. Thomas' Hospital came just a few days ago. We thought she'd be thrilled, but she seemed full of heartache suddenly. I held her hands and told her it may be time to tell us her past.

"Later that day, Christine went to talk to her in her room upstairs, but she said she'd talk to both of us together. Christine had gotten down the chest we'd put her things in, and she brought it in and sat it down before the girl. It upset her to see her father's old things, it seemed. After she got her composure, she told us a remarkable story about her papa being called out to homes swept with smallpox. Told us about your brother's attempt to stop things, keep them from getting it there at the manor. But she told us everyone died, and here she was in the house alone with them all. And so she packed, and climbed onto that mare of hers, and started to Bourton-on-the-Water, said her mama and papa always loved the place and had said it was little over a day away. But she fell off the horse at some point, and being sidesaddle, she couldn't get back up. So she walked and walked, and then finally, one day, Christine and I were there in front of her.

"The girl stood shaking before us just last night and told us her name was Adeleine Eleanor Ashton, that she was from here at Grayson, and that her mother and father were Lady Ellen and Lord Daniel Ashton. When we'd asked her for her name so long ago, finally, she'd just said Gem, and we ended up calling her Gemma.

"I stewed on things all last night and knew I had to find out if there was hope for her out here or just pain. And so here I am with you."

Jed stood up quietly and began to pace. "If you had Addy, who did we bury? The child had on a nightdress embroidered AEA and lay beside her mother dead when we arrived."

John shook his head. "I don't know the conditions of it all, but Adeleine told us the cook was widowed and had a child named Clara. She did tell us the child lay between Lady Ellen and the cook, Helen."

Jed and Benjamin looked closely at one another. Benjamin's face had gone from pallid to flushed to pallid again. He looked up at Jed, looked back to the table, and finally said in a hushed voice, "Please take me to my niece. I'll believe it only if I see her."

CHAPTER 7

London, January 1888

The traffic on New Year's Day was infuriating. The wind, ice, and rain, the stalled carriages, and the frustration of being locked inside his own carriage surely would send Josiah to Bedlam this day. He'd dropped his mother off at her friend's home and would likely arrive late for his meeting at St. Thomas' Hospital. The applications had come in for the new yearly nursing class starting in a matter of weeks.

He was to go over his role in the teaching of anatomy to the class with the board as well as process some of the applications. Narrowing down who would be accepted was equal halves daunting and thrilling. Nurses were needed, and good solid ones at that. As much as he fought against charlatan "physicians," he fought harder for ladies carrying on this important work. There were yet doctors against nursing as a profession, not seeing it as a vocation to be respected.

The program had been started by Florence Nightingale herself some twenty-eight years before, there at St. Thomas' Hospital. Good character was held in highest regard, and the program spanned one year. As the program came to completion, usually the good lady herself would invite her "Nightingales" to visit with her. Josiah smiled to himself. Mistress Nightingale was surely the finest nurse he'd ever met, and she held him in just as high an esteem as a doctor and researcher. He doted on the fierce little lady, and she knew it. He held many of her writings in his library, nestled between medical books and medical history tomes. He let his head rest on the seat back just as the carriage gave a sluggish jerk. He heard the crunch of ice and filthy slush as the wheels began rolling. So much for a stolen few minutes' nap, he thought.

The traffic was finally moving along, and perhaps he'd not wind up late after all. Josiah crossed his arms restlessly over his heavy jacket and waistcoat. Life felt … empty? That wasn't the right word, his life felt full, busy, with never a holiday, never a break. Could his life be full and empty simultaneously? He had his faith, his mother, philanthropy, his research. But still something was missing. It was as though he stood at a crossroads and wasn't sure how to continue yet couldn't turn back.

Staring unseeing from the window of his carriage, his mind whirled and spun and came to a stop. He saw chestnut hair, bright eyes. Heard chatter from long ago, kittens mewing. The clink of glasses and laughter in a country manor.

She came to haunt him at the most curious of times. He supposed that's why he ran from quiet, from stillness. From reflection. He briefly allowed his mind to hover over those moments that stood still and vivid in his mind's eye, the stream of quick bright flashes that once begun could hold him trapped forever. He indulged himself to con-sider what she'd have looked like now, who she would have grown into. Lovely, he was certain. Likely stunning for her differences to the typical.

He wondered if she would have understood his passion for what he did. Would she have supported him? Would she have grown to love him, to want him, as a friend cer-tainly, but as a man? A husband? And just like that, he clamped down mercilessly on the stream of thoughts, on the bleed taking place in his mind. And yet as the carriage slowed and he prepared to navigate the messy sidewalks at the hospital, he bitterly acknowledged ridding his heart so easily of her would likely never come to pass.

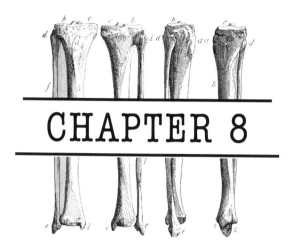

CHAPTER 8

The men had turned in early after their conversation, and supper had come to a quiet end that evening. They'd parted amiably, heading to bed, but with a great deal on each of their minds. Each mulled over their thoughts, trying to work out the snags and knots of his own torment.

Jed felt an unmistakable guilt for burying the child Clara, having set the wrong stone over her. Jed was a deep thinker, sensitive to honor. He brooded over the mistake, turning it every direction. The child had been very shy, not often seen about the place. She worked alongside her mother in the kitchen and took on tasks to help the two older maids as he recalled. The few occasions he'd seen her about, she was always arm in arm with Adeleine. How had he overlooked her? For that matter, how had he missed consideration of Adeleine's new gift, the mare Jewel? Jed remembered the frequent arguments with his father spanning that last year, over schooling, over business ideas, over Jed coming into manhood. He guessed the arguments closed his mind to much of the workings of the manor. And finding his father gone, that had overwhelmed him.

Shaking his head, he lay in bed, his thoughts too numerous to silence.

Across the hall, John carried the crippling weight of guilt for having not reached out years sooner, and, indeed, he accepted the fact that he simply hadn't wanted to face letting the child go. Here, her family had grieved the loss so deeply, and he'd been selfishly silent. Of course he'd have had no idea where to start, which direction to go. Still he felt the silent guilt coursing through him.

Down the hall, Benjamin considered the will stipulations of his brother yet to be met. He turned over and over in his thoughts the unanswered letter of two months past and in years past to Josiah Cairns, laying out in his mind the ramifications of Adeleine being alive. There were many, and they'd require her to make decisions she may not want to be encumbered with. And his heart, oh, his heart! Oh, how it ached to believe his dear little niece yet lived! He, too, thought of the child Clara, wondering why he'd found nothing of her in Daniel's detailed and exacting records.

*****

Jed had proven himself a reliable and thoughtful young man that morning when he'd galloped off to London to alert the family there of the danger. It was perhaps what saved his life. He'd mentioned it to no one at Grayson as he prepared to go. He knew Pa would have fought him doing such a thing. So he'd simply disappeared. Dr. Ashton's defeated manner that morning was so terribly opposite to his usual cheerful, hopeful manner that Jed had been pierced with fear for the family. Lady Ellen's drawn, pale pinched face and downcast eyes had sealed his decision. And so he'd made a rash but heartfelt choice and, beyond the heartache of it all, still stood by his actions of that morning. But while he was grateful for his spared life considering the incredible loss of the whole household and was grateful he'd not come back alone to face the destruction, his heart yet strained over the sudden loss of his father. It had taken him just over a week to reach London, and it had taken a matter of several more days to find and speak to Ashton—finding meanwhile that the two eldest brothers had died not long before—and nearly a fortnight to get back. In that space of just shy of four weeks, he'd known his father to be hearty and hale, and returned to find him dead and gone.

The damage to his pa's face and body had driven Jed from the room and out to the stables to retch and then weep bitterly. He'd railed at the sky that night, first bent over with hands on his knees, then with his hands pulling at his face and his hair. The remembrance of the whole ordeal set his teeth on edge.

Of course, what they'd found on arriving was the stuff of nightmares. The day yet haunted him. A chill ran through Jed's body as he recollected the dark and dank atmosphere that somber afternoon as they stepped through the wide open unlatched door of Grayson Manor. Leaves had blown through the main foyer and down the hallways, and moisture marked the walls.

The overwhelming odor had been unmistakable. The bodies were in varying stages of decline and had to be buried carefully and with haste. Jed had known enough of Mary and Lizzie to know they'd have stubbornly stayed downstairs and went looking when they weren't found above with the others. And there they lay. Eight dead, none left. The day had been bleak and bitter.

The pox had been viciously cruel to some of their faces, less so to others. Their bodies had not yet gone putrescent, and it seemed they'd been spared the invasion of insects for the most part. The cooling weather had surely helped, and it seemed none had been dead longer than a week, perhaps less. They were each gently and carefully removed from the beds, wrapped and shrouded with extreme caution, lest the smallpox be stirred to strike again. Each shrouded body was marked with a name and kept in the cool downstairs of the home until graves were dug, simple caskets built, and they could be laid to rest. Jed and Benjamin had been deeply mindful of each one's clothing, as it was the only thing to determine who was who in worst cases of the pox overtaking their form and visage. Dr. Ashton's diligent bookkeeping and attention to staff details allowed each person to be buried and a stone laid over them with their personal details. This, in part, was what confused Jed and Benjamin, though they'd not yet discussed it. How had the child Clara been overlooked in Dr. Ashton's meticulous records?

The rooms were cleared as quickly as possible, and the curtains, linens, bedding, and mattresses burned. Benjamin had sent to London for more of his staff, as well as the talented stone carver his family had employed for years.

Jed remembered Benjamin walking from the manor without realizing what he was really about the following day, grieving his baby brother, his kindhearted wife, and their lovely little girl. As he'd approached the formal garden, hands clutched before him, his head bowed, the sun shone its shifting rays down onto a beautiful spot just below the formal garden and just above the brook. Jed's eyes misted over thinking of the man's grief that day and his obvious joy and relief in finding such a beautiful area to lay out a garden cemetery.

The help of the nearby villagers who were themselves yet recovering from the blows they'd received had been incredible. They came with food, with shovels, and with intent to honor the Ashtons. Quickly, each body lay buried, with the plots arranged in a circular manner, anticipating the large monument. They'd marked the places carefully and made haste situating everything for the beautiful granite monument Benjamin had commissioned.

A funeral was planned within days, and the work that was left yet to do was taken on by the army of villagers and Benjamin's extra staff. The dulled woodwork of the manor that had been exposed to the elements was polished till it shone. The furniture was cared for, the whole manor was aired and repainted, fresh curtains hung in the upstairs rooms, and all was carefully rearranged. Renewed.

The funeral immediately thereafter was quiet and tasteful, yet poignant. There had not been time to alert anyone in London of the arrangements. Benjamin was deeply distracted and grieved, left alone, with his three brothers suddenly gone. And so with need of haste and a broken heart, Benjamin had not the will nor the time to send more messengers to London for a further delayed funeral. Only the nearby villagers had attended, lines of mourning folk intertwining to pay their earnest respects to these people who loved all equally. Within three months, the monument and individual stones were placed, and the manor was locked and left sitting lonely on the hill. It had seemed as though all had been put to rights after a tragedy and life could resume.

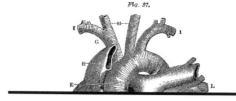

CHAPTER 9

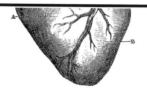

$\mathcal{W}$hen Benjamin swung his feet from the bed the following morning, he felt a sense of peace, of closure he'd not felt in the years following his brothers' passing. Though he dared not fan it, a tiny flame of hope had been struck inside him. He had a bounce to his step and a light to his eyes he'd lost years ago, and he could hardly contain his excitement this morning.

Quickly, he washed and dressed, considering all the while what he'd say to the child. Would she be pleased to see him? Would she remember the summers strolling the grounds of Grayson with her uncle Ben and her papa, the nights chasing fireflies amid peals of laughter? Her aunt Dottie, her two older cousins, would she remember them? He had no idea at all how to separate the nine-, nearly ten-year-old girl he'd last carried about on his shoulder from the woman she'd surely become. But, oh, how he longed to see her!

Mrs. Ruth did well by offering them a simple breakfast of sweet rolls and coffee, and had three sacks of food prepared for them to carry along on their short day trip.

She'd been on Benjamin's wife's staff long enough to have heard many a fond remembrance of his younger brother's family, not to mention being witness to the tears shed since their loss. At the news, she was bubbling this morning and could hardly maintain her typically stoic expression.

The morning was bitter cold, but the sky was clear. The horses were brought from the stable, and with little time wasted, the men set out. They didn't rush, as the roads were icy and somewhat dangerous. They pulled their hats low and collars high and, with their gloved hands, turned their mounts east. They shared friendly banter to fill the time, about hunts they'd enjoyed as boys, stories of first horses, first loves, and school days. The three had grown to respect one another and enjoy one another quickly, as so happens when grief bonds hearts together on common footing. Benjamin looked over at his companions and smiled quietly to himself. Surely, he thought, the Lord had orchestrated every detail, and whatever he found at the apothecary's shop this day, he felt a gentle stillness unfolding within him. And he'd not soon let that feeling go.

Before they knew it, they had arrived. As John led the men to his modest but ample stables, Christine came striding from the back of the shop. Her cheeks went pink in the brisk cold air, and her pretty blue eyes shone at her husband. John quickly introduced her to Jed, then to Adeleine's uncle Ben. Taking Christine's hand, the man Benjamin gruffly offered his heartfelt gratitude to her for caring for his niece. Christine struggled to keep the emotion from her voice as she murmured how all these years had been a pleasure and quickly turned toward the cottage, inviting them all to come in and get warm.

As they walked inside, Benjamin and Jed immediately felt warm and welcome. John inquired about Adeleine, and Christine answered that the girl had taken some various medicines to the villagers and should return any moment. Sure enough, the jangle of the bells on Jewel's bridle announced the girl's arrival to everyone. Jed stood watching at the large back window, then went and stood, somewhat hidden, with Benjamin by the fire.

Adeleine strode with purpose into the apothecary, setting down an empty basket on a nearby table. As she removed her cloak and gloves, she went to John and gave him a warm embrace. She looked into his face, without words communicating her affection to him, and laying to rest the difficulties of the last day they'd shared. He smiled fondly at her as she turned away. She then stood beside Christine, chattering and working comfortably on their afternoon tea tray. Christine looked to John, and he shook his head slightly. "That wild Percy lad managed to scrape the skin from his chin and hands just as I arrived. He must have asked me a million different questions as I bandaged him up. I was very much like him, I suppose," Adeleine said with a short laugh and a sigh. Picking up a large crock and turning to set it on its shelf, she caught movement by the fire.

Her gasp was audible. Her hand slipped from the crock, and it hit the floor with a sharp crack. She swayed on her feet, and John reached to steady her as the two men stepped forward. Jed very quietly smiled at her and said just above a whisper, "Jewel is looking mighty fine, Miss Addy."

Her sharp intake of breath was followed by her shaking her head. "Jedediah? Could that really be you?"

"Yes, indeed, Miss, and can I say how wonderful it is to see you!" He smiled his wide, unassuming grin, beaming at her. He tucked his hands in his pockets and rocked back on his feet.

When she turned her gaze to Benjamin, he couldn't help but put together every detail. Her mother's graceful bearing, the wide, upturned, beautiful green eyes with dark sweeping lashes, the pale scattered freckles, the waving, deep chestnut hair loosely pinned up … it was Adeleine all right.

He smiled at her gently, almost shyly. "Addy girl," he said, looking to the floor then back up at her. "I'm hunting for a firefly." A sob wrenched from her as she threw herself into his arms, looping her arms tightly about his neck. He rocked her gently as wave after wave of emotion washed over her. Pulling away slightly, she put her hands on either side of his face and peered into his eyes.

"Aunt Dottie? Emily and Kate?" He smiled and nodded quickly. With another soft cry, she hugged him tightly again and reached her hand toward Jed. He grasped it, smiling at her through misty eyes. "I can hardly compose myself," she chuckled. Benjamin pulled a folded kerchief from his breast pocket and gently wiped her face. "Oh, Uncle Ben," she whispered, smiling through her streaming tears.

CHAPTER 10

*M*oving in the shadows like a spectre, the man roamed the familiar streets and barrows. As though drawn to them like old friends, he turned this way and that, knowing them well enough to walk them blindfolded. Though he took note of the piles of refuse in his path, he nearly stumbled over a scrawny, starving black cat searching amongst the vermin-infested garbage for a morsel. Crouching down, he stroked the cat's rail thin back, his gloved hand gliding over the back and up through the long hair of the tail. Within moments, the cat began to purr. In a face completely devoid of expression, the man's cruel eyes gleamed. He moved as though to scratch the ears and, in a swift motion, twisted the head from the neck with a muffled crunch. Flinging the beast into the fetid waste, he continued on his way.

The hunger was pressing him, moving him. The darkness raged through him, spilling into his veins, pooling in his belly. He hated them all. The Scots and Irish, the Polish, the Jews, the English rats. They were nothing, beneath him. Unfortunates all, stinking up the streets with their toil to live. But the harlots, the whores, he hated them most.

Harbingers of disease they were, plying their filthy trade, villains of lust and suffering. It had been months since he'd rid the streets of one of the drunken mob that crawled these corners like cockroaches. He was burning with the desire, the endless hunger. The one he'd been watching for weeks was near.

The thick blackness of the squalid street enfolded the man in its depths. In the rolling fog he stood, coiled to strike, observing his prey. The disgusting woman felt the slits of his black eyes upon her and hung back, trying to bring him into the dim light of a far-off gas street lamp.

He would not be moved, and let the sound of coins entice the pathetic old wench. Her face was sickly pale, a pasty yellow, reminding him of bile. The caked-on rouge gave her a macabre look, reminding him of poorly painted death photographs. The expanse of flesh heaving over the rough battered neckline of her ruined dress was crisscrossed with the fine lines of increasing age. Her chest was ruddy and raw, bearing bruising and angry red scratches.

Her foul breath curled toward him like thick cigar smoke, reeking of ale, onions, and what he imagined to be gum rot. He watched her stumble ever closer, her boots sticking to the refuse of the street. Closer and closer, he drew her, until the blackness was so thick, the air so vile as to squeeze the very breath from the body, until he'd reached the corner of the alley.

Suddenly grasping her arms beneath the rags of her cloak, he stepped toward her as though in the first motions of a waltz. Turning her harshly, without mercy, he slammed her facefirst into the leaning brick wall. She let out a nervous, rough sob of a laugh, cursing him as she began to lift her blackened skirts. Revulsion and rage flashed through him like molten lead.

Without mercy, without waiting another moment, he dug his fingers into the back of her hair, pulling her head back sharply, and swept the knife across her throat. Staying clear of the arc of blood, he heard it hissing from her and spattering on the wall and trash at their feet. Flexing his shoulders, he shoved her limp body to the ground. He wiped clean the slender, fine blade with the bit of discolored muslin waiting in his breast pocket. He let the now filthy rag flutter down to the foul earth and released a silent sigh of completion.

Looming over her just a few moments more, he finally turned with a scrape of his heel and melted into the darkness as though he'd never been there.

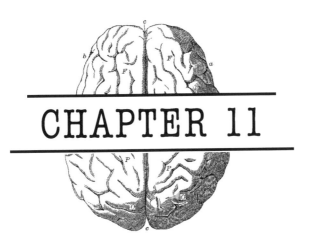

CHAPTER 11

$\mathcal{A}$deleine turned in a slow circle in the bright, airy little space that had been hers so long. She felt light, free of secrets and heartache, and knew she had John and Uncle Ben, too, to thank for it. They still cared for her, still wanted her. Loved her. She was finally able to consider her dreams in light of reality.

John and Uncle Ben had taken advantage of an unusually warm winter day and rode off on their horses some time ago. Jed had returned to Grayson. She had no doubt John and her uncle would use the time to consider her options between them, and she was excited to talk with them when they returned.

Christine was bustling about downstairs, no doubt preparing the evening meal and baking fresh bread. Adeleine would join her in just a moment; but taking in the mementos hung neatly above her desk, the quilts lying across her bed, her favorite sprigs of herbs tied with cheerful ribbon and hung across the window sash, she felt a pang of doubt. Worry tightened her face and gripped her shoulders. A dozen scenarios crossed her mind, and she briefly considered them one by one, then let them fall. No, she'd not let them crowd her mind or cloud her dreams.

If anything, Adeleine knew she finally had a future.

At times, she'd dreamed of love, of children. But no one ever caught her eye. It seemed she'd always felt older than her peers, more mature, more thoughtful, not on the same footing. And so she'd never pursued love or marriage, and now she was well past marriageable age. She'd been content with being a spinster. Comfortable.

But something had begun to nag her thoughts, a constant bother, a thorn of sorts. Yet his name unfurled like the petals of a spring bloom. *Josiah*. The name whispered through her thoughts like a summer breeze, like an embrace, welcome and warm. She eased onto the bed, turning to the side to wrap her arms through the metal rails as she gazed out the window. Even allowing herself to think his name felt like a trespass, wonderful as it was. She'd not dared to ask uncle Ben about him, nor would she.

Surely years ago, he'd married a fine lady of London. Probably had a pretty babe or two. She knew not why that acknowledgement suddenly strangled her, nor why it filled her eyes. She dashed the sudden bout of tears away impatiently. She should be—would be—glad for him. He'd been a good man as a boy, and maybe for just that reason, he had become a special girl's dream of dreams. He deserved happiness; she knew it.

Standing up, she glanced at her appearance in the oval looking glass. So dreadfully plain ... no, odd. Strange. No bright blue eyes, nor warm brown, just the strange mix of gold and green, forever changing with what she wore. Slender face, typical chin. The blasted freckles had mostly disappeared for now, but they'd return with the first kiss of the sun. She didn't blush a pretty inviting pink, more like the inside of seashells she'd seen in a trinket shop at some time. Her hair was neither straight to be elegantly swept up, nor curly for extravagant styling. No, her thick waves were unruly with an excess of cinnamon, making her the ugly goose among swans. She was over tall and neither delicately thin nor substantially plump. She was just plain unattractive. London would surely see no change to her spinster status. She turned away from the cruel glass and headed to the stairs.

Her woolgathering had gone on far too long, for she heard the men stomping into the house and the scrape of chair legs. She ran down the stairs, hoping for something still left for her to do, but skidded to a stop when she saw that everyone was seated and watching her. Smoothing her skirts, she glided to the table as serenely as she could. Uncle Ben pulled her chair for her; and as she looked into his eyes, then John's and Christine's, a scant moment passed, and they all burst into laughter.

"Addy, my dear girl, we've much to discuss!" Uncle Ben said pleasantly. John nodded across from her, and she felt she could fairly burst from the anticipation.

John started. "The first thing we'd discussed is to take you to Grayson."

Watching her expectantly, Uncle Ben said quietly, "'Tis yours, child." Adeleine's eyes rounded, and she couldn't keep the trepidation from her features as she searched for a response. Before she could speak, John reached to clasp her hand. "Your uncle Ben here was visiting Grayson considering how to put your father's will to rest when I went to find the manor days ago. It's beautiful."

She looked to him, then Uncle Ben, but could not say the words, nor ask the question scalding her throat. Christine took all this in and, in a quiet, gentle tone, said, "Fellows, if I may, the child left there having seen every loved one lying dead. You might assure her things were put to rights shortly after she came here to us." Uncle Ben's face blanched. "Yes, oh yes, assuredly! I am so sorry, how insensitive I've been. Do forgive me, Addy! Your dear parents and all the others were laid to rest there at Grayson, just above the brook. The house was scrubbed from top to bottom and brought back to its elegance and charm. It holds no shadows. You've nothing to fear, my girl. I daresay it's as lovely as ever, if not more so."

Adeleine took a deep, steadying breath. "There is more, Addy," he continued. Your papa was a frugal man. He never cared to be showy with how many horses or servants he had. When our father passed, he left a significant sum to us, but your father put his portion away to save. And he left it all to you. Your father's inheritance, Grayson, and his London holdings are yours."

She didn't know what to say, what to think. Could this be? John continued, saying gently, "From Grayson, your uncle would like to travel with you to his home in London, where you'll reunite with your family. He has offered to get you settled in for your classes. You will need new clothes and all the trimmings, and your aunt Dottie will attend to those needs of course. What do you say? Are you ready to see London?"

Staring hard at the table before her, she swallowed with difficulty and nodded. She was ready, so ready, but leaving John and Christine was almost more than she could bear. She looked over to Christine, her lips beginning to tremble.

Christine rose and went to her side. Taking Adeleine's chin in her hand, looking into her face, she said, "Don't think you'll get rid of us that easy, my lass. We will be here for all the visiting you can do, and writing you long-winded letters besides. Your dreams are here, lovey, and it'd do my heart good to see you take them up and run! You have our full support. Count on it!"

Adeleine couldn't speak for tears, so she squeaked out a soft laugh and cried into Christine's aproned bosom. After a few moments, Christine wiped her face, kissed her forehead, and said, "Now let's be eating this fine meal I cooked all alone!" The men hooted in laughter, and Adeleine laughed and quickly nodded, ready indeed to face her future.

CHAPTER 12

$\mathcal{G}$rayson Manor had greeted her in the bright winter sunlight as though knowing just who it was reaching to embrace. The neat evergreen shrubs rose joyfully into the golden light, the birds along the gravel drive seeming to cheer the visitors gently with their fluttering and diving to the lovely stairs and stately front door. The climbing ivy had increased tenfold over the years, softening the stone walls, while not taking from the manor's character. The thought of this being home trickled through her, but like water, the thought seemed ready to slip from her hands.

Adeleine held her breath stepping into the foyer, fear and thrill twining within her breast. As she turned to the right, her mother's chair sat in its place, the grand clock sitting regally in the corner just beyond it. She ran her fingers over the soft ice-blue fabric, a thousand memories assailing her. She walked further into the room, to her father's stout leather chair, another thousand memories colliding with the first. Turning back, she walked from the room and stood before the stairs. She ran her hand over the bannister, enjoying the familiar gleam and scent of beeswax. She squared her shoulders. Taking the stairs as though weighted by years of fear, heartache, anxiety, and grief, she, nevertheless, suddenly found herself at the top landing. The rails she'd often watched through stood at her right. Turning to them, she walked over and ran her fingers over the spindles. The perspective had changed, of course, but still she could look down at the foyer and sitting room. Remembering the last time she'd looked through them brought a tremble to her lips. She pressed her fingertips to her mouth to smooth it away.

Resolutely, she turned back to the left and walked bravely to the guest rooms. The doors stood open. She went to the furthest at the end of the hall; and with all her might, teeth clenched, she stepped into the room. Her jaw shifted in surprise, delight in the astonishing change from the last picture in her aching mind tumbling over her. There was no horrible death here. It smelled of lemon, lavender, and beeswax. The creamy curtains hanging at the windows lent a bright air to the room, and her papa's paintings of the grounds hung on the walls. The beautiful rug was different, as were the bed clothes. All had been rearranged. The soft blue of the room was lovely and fresh. Reaching the connecting door, she stepped into the next room. Again she could not deny the sensation of shock whirling through her. Painted a silvery pale green and hung with rich purple drapes, the room felt like a spring day. The two beds set into opposite corners were dressed all in white, crisp linens. The brass rails shone in the light, and floral paintings graced the walls. Reaching the last door, she stepped into the room where her father had lain. And yet, even as the tears began, the difference struck her. Blue drapes hung at the windows, and gleaming wood pieces stood about the room. The creamy color of paint on the walls complimented the rug's deep hues. The bed looked almost royal with it's fine linens of golds, whites, and touches of red. Adeleine shook her head. The tears were slow and steady, but not heavy as she'd anticipated. In them ran her misery, guilt, and fear, draining away bit by bit. She started to bow her head, but no words would come. After several moments, she breathed in the lovely scents, drank in the sunlight, and, for the first time in fourteen years, felt somehow whole. Unmarked. No longer shattered, and yet there was an emptiness she could not name. She left the room, lovingly caressing the doorknob on her way by. Back in the hallway, she made her way to the room Papa and Mama had shared at the other end of the corridor.

She stepped almost shyly into the room, hanging back the way she had as a girl, waiting for invitation. She drank in the familiar drapes, wood pieces, paintings. The four-poster bed stood regal and proud. She wanted to run and fling herself into its depths as she had so many times before. But Mama nor Papa were there to catch her up in their arms, she thought. Mama's favorite crocheted blankets lay together folded at the foot of the bed, and the quilt she'd toiled over for years lay softly across the mattress. The matching quilted pillows with their modest ruffles were as lovely and welcoming as she remembered. Her fingertips traced the beautiful stitching as they had so often before. Papa's bureau shone in the light from the windows. Opening its drawer gently, a giggle tumbled from her as she saw his pipe things and other mementos he'd kept over the years. It still smelled of tobacco. She gasped softly at seeing little scraps of paper she'd written notes to her parents and drawn pictures on in a careful stack in the back corner, along with an old frayed hair ribbon and an old dried flower she'd once given him for his jacket. How like Papa to keep every memento. Every sweet memory echoed in her heart.

Moving across the room, she carefully opened Mama's wardrobe. The faint scent of her perfume lingered moments in the air, then was gone. Adeleine gently ran her fingers over the varied fabrics, both fine and serviceable. One of her dressing gowns caught Adeleine's eye; and she pulled it down, hugging it to herself, quick tears falling onto the beautiful fabric. Mama had gone so quickly. The sudden memory of her mother turning her fevered face into Adeleine's palm as she'd lain a cool cloth against her cheek sent a shudder through her. She remembered the hazy expression in her mother's eyes and weak smile on her lips. It had been a last embrace, she now realized. She ran her fingers over the delicate satin and lace, then placed it back carefully into the wardrobe. Shutting the doors, she drifted slowly from the room, across the hall, and into her own childhood room.

A drawing of Jewel yet hung from the wall. A bear from Papa and a doll from Mama sat on her bed. A basket of her many attempts at needlepoint and crochet sat discarded beside her bed. She couldn't hold back a giggle. Oh, how she'd toiled over the things, and she'd hated it! She'd ever wanted to be just like her beautiful and bright mama. A sigh escaped her as she moved on. She touched the spines of her favorite books, sitting as if waiting for her in her small bookcase. She moved to a window, running her hand down the shining wood frame, and took in the grounds. It was all even lovelier than she remembered. She could see one corner of the stables to the far right, and on the left the large formal garden, the line of trees, and the sparkle of the water below. And just within her gaze, she could see the large granite monument honoring those she loved. She traced another of her drawings just by the window with her fingers and smiled softly. Touching these articles of happier times was a balm to her ragged spirit.

A gentle voice at the door said, "We couldn't bear to change this room or your parents'." She turned to see Uncle Ben leaning against the doorframe.

"I'm so glad you kept them as they were, truly, and the changes to the guest rooms are just … Well, they're just wonderful, Uncle Ben," she said with a smile and a tremor in her voice.

Coming toward her and reaching for her hand, he said quietly, "Would you like to walk down with me?" She swallowed and nodded. Walking downstairs together and out of the kitchen doors, they made the walk slowly, silently, her gloved hand tucked into his in the crook of his arm. She pulled her heavy woolen cloak firmly about her and tucked errant strands of hair behind her ears. She relished the warmth of her cloak's hood and Uncle Ben's warm hand that stayed firm over hers on his arm.

As they came to the low stone wall's gate, he held back to let her go alone. She looked to him, and he nodded. She turned and approached the monument and stood silent before it. She took in the beautiful carvings, the meaningful columns, one broken for the life cut short of a child, the evergreen ivy, the arch. Staring at the cross and scripture, a deep, intense feeling she could not name came over her. Dropping her eyes, she gazed at the stone naming Mama and Papa. Her eyes filled, and she began to move in a circle about the monument. She noted a bare place; and looking over to Uncle Ben, who still waited several feet away, he nodded. "We know now your dear friend Clara lies there," he offered. "Her stone should come before we leave." She nodded, understanding likely Jed had removed the stone that bore her own name days ago. Coming back to the front, she studied the cross and its scripture. He finally joined her, coming alongside her.

"Why this cross and scripture?," she asked.

"Well," he said gently, "your parents—the whole household, according to your papa's books—were believers in the gospel of the Bible. As are your Christine and John, and your aunt Dottie and myself." He continued, "According to the Bible, Jesus said he was the way, the truth, and the life. And not only that, but that those who believe in him shall not perish but have everlasting life."

"Well, I don't believe a word of it," she said stubbornly in a rush, her voice cold and hard. "Mama and Papa believed, they prayed, they begged for his mercy on us. And yet they did perish, them and all the others, except me. This God of theirs abandoned me, left me alone, even as Papa's last words to me were for the Lord to be with me." She ground out the words and began to move away.

"I see where your heart lies on these things, my girl. And I understand. But it is my wish that, one day, you'll perhaps see the gift He gave a childless couple in you, Addy, while providing you a home in our ignorance of your plight." At her pained expression, he smiled kindly at her.

"He has a design for our lives and brings beauty from our most bitter trials. Things often don't turn out in this life as we'd hope. There is pain, grief, tragedy. Yet with faith, we can move on with peace that passes understanding. His promises are eternal, for our souls, you see. Your mama, papa, and these others rest in heaven with him this very moment, more alive than we."

Looking into his dear eyes, so much like Papa's, she saw he truly believed what he said. She gave a brief nod and tucked her hand in his, and desperate to change the subject, she said, "I'd love to meet the people here with you. Would you introduce me?"

"It would be a delight," he replied.

He didn't miss the glimmer in her eye as she looked away, dashing the tear from her cheek, nor the turmoil rolling through her eyes as they walked back toward the manor.

Adeleine enjoyed meeting Ruth the cook, Jane, and Molly. Ruth greeted her like a long-lost friend, with tears and a deeply pleased expression. Jane and Molly had given her a bright smile, dropping into curtsies gracefully. Adeleine wished she could tell them not to curtsy just for her, but just as she went to speak, she realized this would be the way of things now. Her, a titled lady after all. She could barely contain the snort that filled her pert nose. Looking around, she was relieved no one seemed to notice.

The days passed quickly, and yet she soaked in all she could. She'd enjoyed riding over the grounds with her beloved mare, drinking in the familiar places. The favorite trees she'd climbed as a child stood even now, and the brook where she'd watched tadpoles and minnows still danced and splashed in the sun. She loved this place so. She'd delighted in taking meals with her uncle and his few devoted staff. She'd learned that Jedediah had become Uncle Ben's man of affairs years before, and so had already returned to London to handle business matters. Sitting around the table, they'd shared many conversations, and many memories, with laughter and not a few tears. Each evening was spent before the crackling fire in her mama's chair, and she slept each night curled in her parents' bed, the ruffled pillows hugged to her. Tonight, she sat with her feet tucked under her, a favorite crocheted blanket of mama's wrapped about her shoulders. A book sat in her lap untouched as she stared into the fire. The journey to London was upon her. They were to leave at first light.

CHAPTER 13

Travel to London had passed pleasantly, but Adeleine found herself strangely exhausted, stretched tight with nerves. She was anxious as could be, anticipating what London would present to her. So many details, possible shortcomings, possible embarrassment. She hoped she would be acceptable to aunt Dottie and not a disappointment. Her mother had taught her a great deal about deportment and propriety as a girl that she'd, of course, continued all her life, and she could still curtsy, though likely more practice would be needed to become graceful again. She wondered about balls and parties, if she would be expected to be here or there, or if she could simply bury herself away at nursing school.

Nursing school. It was really going to happen, and she could barely stand the waiting to get there in her excitement. Uncle Ben had made certain every detail was resolved wonderfully. How amazing the events all leading up to her enrollment there! She wondered what her room there would be like and how she'd be received.

That reminded her of the ordeal of being newly clothed, and she wondered why the bother, as she'd wear nursing uniforms more than any fancy foolish gown for the next year. She was equally nervous, begrudging, and exhilarated by the idea of her own new gowns in truth. Her slender frame and altered hand-me-downs from Christine had kept her until now from having to bother with blasted corsets. But she'd lived in a small village, using the stretched-out somewhat-flimsy corset given to her by Christine as she'd matured, and knew those days were over. The ton would disgrace her without a proper corset, the feckless lot! She knew of a more modern, comfortable wool corset available and intended to have it. If she must, she must, but on her own terms. Adeleine couldn't fathom how anyone lived in the torturous, traditional contraptions, and had no intention of finding out.

Uncle Ben had sent ahead her measurements taken by Molly at Aunt Dottie's request, and with so many ready-made fashions these days, he'd explained there would be many things waiting for her upon their arrival. Aunt Dottie would take her to her favorite modiste for any elaborate gowns needed later. They were to attend dinner this evening at the home of a widowed dear friend to Dottie, so she was grateful she'd at least be decently presentable for the occasion. Her nerves were wound so tight she truly wasn't certain she would be pleasant company. Perhaps this dinner would afford her some time to be lost in her own thoughts, with no eyes upon her.

When they arrived at her uncle's lovely estate nearing noon, a feeling of having been here before settled over her.

"Uncle, did I ever visit here as a child?" she asked as they stepped from the carriage to the neat sidewalk.

"Indeed, Addy, at Christmastide, your parents split their time between here and the home of their dear friends through the New Year." Against her will, she found herself looking into his eyes. Something passed between their gaze she could not decipher, but she could not ask anything further for the tightness suddenly at her throat. Shaking off the uncomfortable awareness of past things as he returned her gaze kindly, she put her arm in his as they reached the doorway. Suddenly, a moving, talking, laughing, bustling whirlwind of activity swooped her into the foyer and up the stairs, where she suddenly found herself being gazed at by three lovely women with a breathless laugh poised on her lips.

The older one reached for her, and she fell into a comforting and somehow deeply familiar embrace. Her aunt was still a truly lovely woman, hardly aged, and she still smelled gloriously of citrus and mint. The two other ladies standing beside her suddenly reached out and hugged her tightly, cries and sniffles mingling with laughter. Of course, her two older cousins. Emily and Katelyn, Kate for short. They were strikingly beautiful, she thought, considering her spinster status and unfortunate appearance.

They turned and began opening and reaching into boxes tied with ribbon. While her cousins were shaking out the loveliest gowns she'd ever seen and holding them up for her approval, she brought her gaze back to Aunt Dottie. Awkwardly, she blurted, "These are so much more beautiful than I ever expected! I am so grateful ... I've no idea how to repay such generosity," Adeleine said to Aunt Dottie earnestly.

"Hush, my darling girl! We are your family, and we have missed you so! Emily and Kate were always so fond of you too. This is such a joyous occasion! My stars, you've returned to us from the dead, my love. Don't worry for anything." Aunt Dottie beamed at her. Adeleine let the tears dance on her cheeks. Memories of these three filled her mind and heart. A warm comfortable familiarity settled around her like another embrace. She'd not allowed herself to remember in so long, frightened of the searing pain. But all was well, her family returned to her without constraint, without judgment, without the resentment she'd feared for so long. Kate handed her a kerchief, Emily draped her arm across Adeleine's shoulders, and Aunt Dottie was whispering furiously with dear Molly, who scurried away with a grin on her face. Within moments, she was led into a beautiful room holding a gleaming copper slipper tub steaming with warm water. Molly carried with her a brush, a robe, and towels; and the most wonderful-smelling oils were added to the steaming water. It was heavenly after the long trip to consider sinking into the deep tub.

The ladies left to give her privacy, but Molly stayed to help her. Sinking into the hot water was absolutely divine. The maid's gentle voice reached her ears from behind her. "You have the loveliest hair, like caramel and toffee, and cinnamon besides, and these waves! It'll be my pleasure indeed styling it for you, m'lady!" Adeleine turned to the darling lady's maid but was speechless for a moment considering her horribly behaved hair.

She shook her head with a smile and said, "It's only ever been a mess, so I am delighted to have you help me."

Molly beamed at her and began unfurling the thick mop to wash it. Hearing muffled voices nearby, she realized with a start this must be a suite of connecting rooms with the bedroom just beyond. Just this bathing room was well over twice the size of her bedroom with John and Christine. She hurried to finish her bath. Who knew what else would happen to shock her this day. Noting her rounded eyes, Molly whispered to her tentatively, "You are going to charm all of London, m'lady. You are a breath of fresh air and altogether beautiful." The genuine smile Molly offered Adeleine had her eyes brimming again as they locked gazes.

She laughed, feeling free, and said "Thank you, dear Molly. Let us find out what my aunt and cousins are up to, then, shall we?"

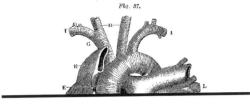

CHAPTER 14

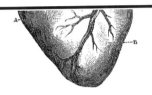

$\mathcal{L}$ady Dorothea Ashton stood talking quietly with her daughters as Adeleine enjoyed her bath in the next room. "Mother, did you see how exquisite she is? She was a darling little girl, all freckles and gold and cream, with that chestnut hair of hers, but unless I knew she was Adeleine, I don't know that I would have recognized her!"

"Emily, don't be a ninny," Kate scolded. "Those details have ever been unique to that child. How could she be looked over or confused for any other!" Both women looked at their mother and erupted into giggles.

"Here we are long married, with children besides, squabbling as we did over her when we were barely into our teen years. We are a silly lot, are we not?" Kate said with amusement in her eyes. Just then there was a gentle tap at the door. Dorothea opened it quickly and took in the dazzling child wrapped in a delicate peach robe before her, fragrant and vibrant.

Exquisite, indeed. She was four and twenty and didn't look a day past eighteen. How the Pierces had kept hold of her there in Bourton a spinster and not married to some strapping lad was beyond her. Of course, that was a fortunate happenstance as it were.

The child did have the hated and feared sprinkle of freckles, but they were pale and, indeed, charming. She was taller than Emily or Kate, but it gave her a regal air, a stately bearing not carried off by even half the silly chits of the ton. She was slender and graceful yet sturdy, substantial. Her hair was something all its own, deep-red chestnut tones lifting to caramel and threaded with gold, and hanging past her waist in thick waves. It perfectly framed her somehow ethereal face. Her fine eyebrows arched gracefully over her long dark lashes, which framed eyes as golden and green as a cat's. They were flecked with moss and shades of bronze. They could not be called brown and were anything but blue. Dorothea thought of riding through an autumn forest with deep-gold rays of sun filtering through trees and foliage. An enchanted forest nymph of fairy tales, the girl was. Her nose was pert, perfect, not regal like her bearing, but playful. Her lush mouth was wide and full, gracious and kind, generous. Her pearly teeth flashed a beautiful smile when the child was amused or unsure, as she seemed now, looking back and forth between them.

Dorothea realized with a start they'd been staring without restraint, and the poor dear's face was tingeing red. She started to speak and stammered, and Dorothea was shocked as a tear streaked down her cheek. Shaking her head, Adeleine squeaked. "I know my appearance is rather unorthodox, unattractive, but I've no intention to marry, you see. I just want to become a nurse, that is all, truly. I'd rather not even attend parties. I've just no interest." The silence was immediately broken with embarrassed apologies and assurances to the contrary. Dorothea took the child's face in her hands. It burned red.

"Please forgive us, my dear girl. No, no, what we see is quite different, and our silence was rude, staring as we take in what we knew to be a lovely girl grown into an exquisite woman. You are carved marble among whittled wood, Adeleine. Don't you see?" The child's eyes rounded and her lips parted at the words.

Dorothea started to say surely Josiah would prove to her just how lovely she was this evening, as he'd surely have quite the reaction to his lost love, back from a false grave. No doubt he would gladly take the girl for his wife, and with haste having lost so many years. He'd been gentle with her, doted on her as a child. It was well remembered among them. Her dear friend Joanna's son had grown into a handsome giant of a man, well liked and respected in London. She knew Adeleine had been so fond of him before. And he'd adored her, never mind what a cad he'd been ignoring Benjamin these years.

But she kept silent. Lady Cairns was not even aware the child was coming tonight. Maybe this element of shock was out of place, she thought. It was not intended to be out of order. It simply seemed easier than writing a cryptic note or writing a lengthy letter. The child had gracefully accepted shock after shock these weeks, Ben had told her at length. He'd been delighted to see her playful, joyous spirit emerge from time to time as he came to know his niece again, but the pain had been great and left a swath of brooding hurt and unrest within her he'd said. She doubted herself, doubted being deserving of care or affection. Ben imagined the girl almost felt she'd murdered the family and gone, not lived through a tragedy and survived. Adeleine was strong and delicate all at once, and though they worried that another such shock may be too much, Josiah and Adeleine were still legally betrothed. The boy had never responded to any of the correspondence Ben had sent over the years. It was time for all to be set right. Josiah's presence and Adeleine's this night would have to unfold with both of them unaware.

She shook herself. The hours were getting away. She and her girls had no interest this afternoon save pampering this precious girl and showering her with love, showing her in every way they wanted her, and treasured the life brought back to them. Surely, that would stay her thoughts and buoy her heart tonight.

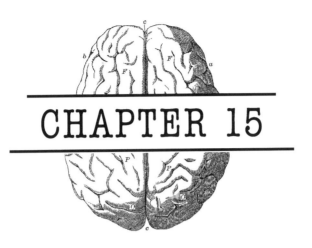

CHAPTER 15

*L*ady Cairns was delighted to have Benjamin and Dottie Ashton for dinner tonight. She swept through the sitting room and made sure all was well before hurrying back to the kitchen to check on her staff. Her mind was racing, for while she hated to set a trap for her son with the solicitor, he'd ignored the man's attempts to reach him for years. Thinking back to the summers they'd all shared together long ago, nostalgia laced with heartache filled her. She jumped hearing the doorbell and quickly drew up behind Ellison in the narrow foyer to greet her guests.

The cold blast of air as Ellison opened the door did nothing to quell her spirits. She'd sorely missed these folks. It had been years since seeing them outside of greetings at church, and she supposed the somewhat mutual heartache had just been too much to bear together. Benjamin had been deeply pained to have lost months in sharing the deaths of his brother and his family with them, and had wept bitterly the day he'd come to visit some three months after burying Dr. Ashton's household. Of course they'd not changed in their affections for Benjamin and his family, but the grief had been nigh insurmountable. And so visits had tapered off, even as affection lingered.

Benjamin was very dashing with his walking stick, his face gentle and kind as ever, and as he reached to squeeze her hand, she felt a marked difference in him. Ellison moved to take his effects, and as she wondered at Benjamin's light step, she heard Dottie's sweet voice as if she were speaking to someone behind her. As she waited in the tight foyer, Ellison and Benjamin to her left, the stairway behind her, she craned her neck to see Dottie's face. When their eyes met, they both smiled hugely and reached to embrace one another.

Her arms around Dottie, her eyes met those of the loveliest young woman she thought she'd ever seen. Releasing Dottie, she smiled into her friend's glowing eyes, waiting for introduction. Ellison helped the young lady into the foyer and took her cloak and gloves, and all went silent. She peered into the young lady's face, knowing but not knowing, seeing but not believing, filled with a strange sensation of elation and trepidation. She felt the blood slowly drain from her face. She glanced back at Benjamin; and somehow from his gaze back at the girl, perhaps in knowing that affection on his face many years ago for his daughters and one particular little girl, she knew. The breath fled from her chest, and she slumped down onto her stairs, her hand curled to her mouth. She felt her face go pale and flushed, and pale again. Shaking herself, she struggled back to her feet with Ellison's assistance. She took two steps toward the girl.

Adeleine's very blood felt as though it were vibrating her brain, buzzing through her skull like a swarm of angry bees. How could this be? She was deeply familiar with every curve of the woman's face, she knew her hair, had on many occasions held the delicate hand yet pressed to her mouth. Surely her aunt and uncle couldn't do such a thing to her. She couldn't breathe, couldn't squeeze her eyes shut, couldn't move. The face staring back at her had been so dear to her, she'd loved this darling friend of her mother's. But she was … she was *his* mother. Josiah … no. No, she wouldn't be made to face all that she lacked by the expression on his face if he saw her. She could not. Her mouth fighting to inhale, her lungs frozen, her lips curved into a cry, and she turned hastily for the door. Ellison stood unsure what to do as he glanced about at this strange scene.

"Adeleine! Addy!" Lady Joanna cried out as a sob dislodged in her throat. The girl stood ramrod straight, her back to the room, her fingertips on the doorknob. She began shaking her head, then a choked sound came from her throat. She turned with desperate eyes, glancing up the stairs, down the hall, prepared to bolt. Her jaw working furiously, finally she said in a thin voice that sent a chill through them all, "I don't want to know. I don't want to see him, don't want to face whatever his life is now. It's too much. I can't bear it. Please." As her hand clutched the knob, her uncle edged through the group and turned her to face him gently. He drew out his kerchief and dabbed her frantic streaming eyes.

His hands on her shoulders, he soothed "Addy, we didn't bring you here to trap you into seeing Dr. Cairns.

Doctor Cairns?

We made this appointment with Lady Jo several weeks past because the fellow has ignored my attempts to reach him for years now. We wanted to sit with him together and help him put the past to rest. Lady Jo didn't know of our circumstances of these past two weeks, that we found you yet lived. Now that you are with us, we thought it best you came. There are stipulations in your father's will having to do with large sums of money and betrothal and property. They have to be set to rights."

"No, *no*, Uncle Ben. I can't see him. I won't! Look at me, an awkward old spinster, and he is sure to be married with children by now," she cried. "I cannot. I didn't ask you about him in weeks past, because I simply cannot bear it." The frantic grief etched onto her face was heartbreaking.

Lady Joanna was right at Benjamin's elbow and put her hand out to Adeleine. "May I?" she asked. With a deep breath and a single nod, he backed away, his eyes desperate for his niece's comfort. Lady Joanna murmured, "Ellison, would you please take my guests to the dining room? We'll join you shortly." Tenderly putting her arm around the girl's heaving shoulders, Lady Joanna steered her toward the sitting room. The fire crackled merrily in the grate, and Adeleine tried desperately to regain her composure.

"I remembered coming here before as soon as we stepped out of the carriage but thought surely I was mistaken. Do you remember bringing me here?" Adeleine said softly.

"I do," Lady Joanna quietly responded. "Last you were here, we sat in this room and packed away Christmas things, and then I showed you how to sew a ruffle while we waited for your mama and papa to come with Josiah and his father later that afternoon. You loved the ruffles I'd made for your doll's dress. I remember you saying you wanted to make something for your mama."

They both smiled tremulously at the memory. "I did, do you remember? I think Mama showed you her quilt and pillows that summer." Lady Jo sighed, tears beginning to course down her face. She nodded.

"She did, indeed. That quilt was a masterpiece, but she was so proud of those ruffles on the pillows." They both laughed through their tears. "I'm so terribly sorry, Addy. I don't know how you came to be here, but my heart is overjoyed. A part of me died when we found Christmas came and went with no news of you because smallpox had ravaged the town and your family." She stared at the fire through her tears and added, "A part of my Josiah died that day, too, Addy. He is alone."

Adeleine felt a strange sort of stillness settle over her at that news. She tentatively grinned and took Lady Jo's arm and said conspiratorially, "Good thing. That Josiah was always pulling a lady's hair." The comment lightened the moment and sent them into peals of laughter, and throwing their heads back onto the sofa, they laughed until they could barely breathe. Lady Jo pulled Adeleine close and sighed.

"Oh, Addy. How I have missed you, my little darling."

The gathering dark and a quiet door latch served to keep them unaware of a tall figure just a few feet behind them. He had entered quietly without his usual jovial bluster at his mother, knowing he was late for dinner and had come to a dead stop as he heard quiet laughter in the sitting room. Somehow, he found himself moving through the foyer, then staring into the sitting room at the back of the sofa. His mother and a woman he'd never seen sat closely there. What his mother was saying didn't make sense, the laughter before didn't make sense. He knew it;

it had knifed into him as he'd stepped into the house and squirmed through him. Had she said Addy? Impossible. He stepped closer. The woman's hair was in shadow, but as she moved in closer to his mother to take her arm, the fire glinted on a depth of color he'd only known once. He couldn't quite see and moved still closer. He heard snippets of his mother's grieved voice saying "heart overjoyed," "smallpox," "ravaged," "died," "Josiah," "alone." *Alone*. Moving closer but just out of sight in the deepening shadows of the fire, he clearly heard the woman's words. *"Always pulling a lady's hair ... "* As she said it, they both dissolved into laughter, their arms about one another tears visible on their faces, and his throat clenched. As they laughed, they threw their heads onto the back of the sofa, and a thick waterfall of waves fell from its pins and over the sofa's back. He suddenly ached to take that hair in his hands. He shook himself. The laughter was so like a bubbling brook ... He could see the creamy skin of her forehead and bridge of her nose. He didn't believe it, would not believe it. And then his mother said her name and called her *darling*, and there was no mistake. Whether in a nightmare or hallucinating, he did not know, but he could not stay another moment. Caring not if they heard, he turned on his heel and made his way to the connecting door of his study and escaped inside, leaning hard against the closed door. As he sank to the cold floor, he raked his hands through his hair and over his face. It couldn't possibly be so.

It isn't real.

It can't be, I can't...

She lives?

CHAPTER 16

$\mathcal{A}$deleine and Lady Joanna jumped and stood up as the heavy footfalls retreated from so close behind them and a door slammed. The pained and somewhat alarmed expression on Lady Joanna's face did nothing to settle the hard thump of Adeleine's heart. Lady Joanna still held her hand and brought it to her, cradling it in both of her own as Josiah so often did with her. "Addy, you knew my softhearted, laughing boy once. That would have been him just now. As children, you were nigh inseparable whenever we came together. Will you go to him? I don't know how he'll work his way through this, so perhaps if you seek him out, you can help him understand. I'll go to hear of what's come to pass with Dottie and Ben if you'd be willing to see him."

"I'll go," Adeleine said softly. Another resolute facing down of past fears couldn't hurt.

As they stepped into the hallway, Lady Joanna looked over her. The lovely thing had pins sticking from her hair, which had all but completely fallen down. "Let me settle this hair down. You ever did have thick hair that would never stay coiffed." She laughed. She worked the pins from Adeleine's hair, then worked through it with her fingers. She pulled the upper part away from her face and made a simple braid, then coiled it into a soft bun at the back of her head. She left the rest to hang, pulling it over her shoulder, then moved about the girl, straightening and smoothing her dinner dress. Standing back to look her over once more, she was overcome at the young woman Addy had become. The crimson brocade gown gloriously framed the beautiful girl, with its high split collar and fall of creamy pale gold lace at her throat. Her eyes glowed radiantly. Her zest and spark still shone, but the sadness in her was palpable. Her eyes damp, she showed Adeleine to the door down the hall that connected the two townhomes and explained Josiah's work briefly. She noted no look of horror or disgust, and her eyes smiled at the thought, the possibilities. Perhaps these two might work through the pain they'd suffered and find an abiding love. Oh, how she wished it for them both.

With a kiss on her cheek, Lady Joanna left her at the door and went to join Ben and Dottie. Standing alone in the silent hallway, Adeleine was terrified. What would she find? Who would she find? What would *he* find? Knocking softly at the door, she heard a sort of scuffle coming from the floor. The knob jerked, and the door swung open. She saw his retreating back and stepped inside. The door clicked closed behind her. She heard him say, "Ellison, hoped you'd want to come scold me for being late. Need firewood and blankets, my good fellow, for I'll not leave this study until whoever these people are have gone." She stood silently with her hands clasped, realizing she still had

Uncle Ben's kerchief. At the silence, he turned, and his jaw went slack.

He clamped his mouth shut even as his eyes widened, drinking her in like a man dying of thirst. Nothing he'd ever let himself imagine in brief moments came close to the very grown-up, very intensely lovely creature standing before him. Her eyes rounded as he strode toward her, not stopping until he towered over her just a hand's breadth away. She felt his breath on her face and his eyes boring into her, and hardly dared to breathe herself lest their bodies touch.

Her gorgeously hued hair cascaded over one shoulder. Her skin was golden in the light of the waning fire. The curve of her mouth, the dancing notes of color in her eyes, the very expression he'd seen before told him it was her. If he was dreaming, so be it; he'd never attempt to wake. A warmth unfurled in his chest, and he felt his mouth hitching into a grin. He couldn't speak or tear his eyes from her. He noticed the blaze of red matching her gown creeping up her elegant neck and found an odd satisfaction in it.

She swallowed hard and lowered her eyes. Why didn't she move? Or speak? Was she as riveted to the floor as he? Surely, at four and twenty, with that beautiful mouth and her stunning eyes, some brigand or another had kissed her? He absurdly could suddenly think of nothing else. He considered how he'd never bothered with such things, and a feeling of joy sparked in his chest to acknowledge no foolish girl could have compared to the tall winsome beauty standing frozen before him. Against his will, it came naturally as breathing to slide his hand around her waist, the other across her cheek and into her hair, and lift her chin. She would not look up at him. She was trembling, he realized. In a low soft growl, he murmured, "Addy, my girl, is it truly you?"

She gave a start and looked up at him with a sharp intake of breath. Within her eyes tumbled a thousand questions, and peering into his own, she barely whispered, "J-Joe?" Her expression began to lighten, and she gave him a small soft smile. He felt his heart twist at the sound of her voice, her smile, at the sound of the childhood name on her lips.

He could stand no more, propriety be hanged! The girl who had haunted him for years stood in his own arms a woman. A woman promised to him. He swept both hands up her back, over her hair, and came to a stop back at her shoulders. He was surely out of his mind, so he released her, but even as he did, he stepped toward her until she was against the wall and dropped his forehead gently against hers. A ripple went through her. To keep his hands from daring to touch her again, he put them against the wall on either side of her. She'd lowered her eyes again, but he was desperate for them, starving. "Look at me!" he thundered. She jumped, and her head bumped the wall behind her. She looked at him, and what he saw seared his gut. Was she ... *afraid?* Her breathing was shallow and panicked. Her eyes were wide and had misted over, and she was almost shivering. He backed away a step and brought his hands back to her silken face.

The faint freckles were still there. He couldn't fight anymore; he was drowning. She was here, his heart raged at him. He abruptly gathered her to him, one hand wrapping itself into her hair. He brought his lips down to hers and felt her body tense just briefly. Her hands were trapped between them, splayed against him. He allowed himself the merest brush across her full lips and jerked away as if burned.

Removing himself to his desk by the fire, his breathing ragged, he barked at her to come sit. He couldn't collect his wits; the reeling intensity of seeing her before him, of utterly losing his composure, was fighting against a flame of fury that had quite suddenly ignited. The thought of her laughing so lightheartedly with his mother ... while for years he'd ... he'd mourned her, pined for her ... something snapped within him. She waited several seconds, indecision screaming across her expression as if she knew his thoughts. Her eyes seemed to caress his face, and he began to soften, but the anger came throttling back. He realized she was fighting not to cry, but a million conflicting feelings were crashing into him. Why did he keep shouting at her? He never once considered it likely she felt just the same as he. Confused, tortured. Elated. He stood and began to pace in front of the fireplace, hands balled at his back. He couldn't keep his breathing even or his raging feelings at bay, and so the thoughts began to tumble out in angry waves.

"Tell me, Lady Ashton, what brings my dearly departed *betrothed* to me this night? Why show your living, breathing self to my mother and myself now and not in years past, eh? My father died a year ago. Did you see it in a paper over your morning chocolate and wish to offer your condolences?" His voice was harsh, bordering on cruel. She began shaking her head furiously, a look of shock and hurt marring her face, and she began to rise from the wingback chair she sat in. With two strides, he reached her, and with both hands, he pressed her back down and dug his fingers into her shoulders. She winced and cried out, struggling from his grasp. He would not be deterred.

As he painfully held her captive, rising so closely above her, she was helpless at his intensity, confused by what she saw playing out in his eyes. Yet she wondered at his nearness, the delicious spicy fragrant scent of him, this man she'd not dared to dream of. Lavender, citrus, rosemary, and perhaps pepper tickled her nose as she breathed deeply of him. Had he truly grieved for her? She jerked from her introspection as he angrily barked right into her face.

"I was just turned fifteen when my parents told me with tears streaming down their faces that '*my Addy*' had died, along with her whole household, and the funeral held months before. Why were we last to know?" he shouted as he released her and returned to his pacing.

She shook her head again, throwing up her hands weakly and wailing plaintively, "I don't know. I myself didn't know of it—" But he was beyond hearing. "I have spent my life wishing for one more chance to see you, to know you grown up, all the while broken over your death just weeks after we'd come home that summer. I've spent my life bitter and consumed, always trying to get away from you, yet not able to let you go, to just let you rest. And here you rise up like steam from ash to taunt me? Why was there never a letter, never a *word*?"

"I was ten years old!" she shrieked, putting her fingers to her temples and jumping up from the chair. Still he cut across her, giving her no chance to explain to him all that had happened.

"You were always smart, Adeleine! A letter addressed to my family in London would have found its way! Your uncle Benjamin and his continual attempts to settle your father's estate, did he know? Did you not care for a betrothal to me? Did you prefer the country life to my parents, to our life in London?" he sneered. "To *me*?" His breath was coming hard and heavy as he dropped into the chair at his desk.

For a moment, she stood speechless, winding her uncle's kerchief around her hands over and again. Shock and hurt from his words pressed over her like a gale. She suddenly clenched her fists tight and felt herself begin to burn with rage. She pounded on his desk, furious, her eyes flashing. She leaned forward and lay her hands flat on its surface.

"I watched my entire household die, no matter that I'd done all I could to help them, no matter that my papa prayed for mercy," she spat. "Those disgusting pox, the awful smells, I couldn't stand to be there after the day my papa finally slipped away. And so I left. I packed a few things, and I went the only direction I knew to go, to Bourton-on-the-Water. My parents spoke of it often, and I wanted to see this place they loved. I fell asleep at some point and fell from my horse. I couldn't get back onto her, and so I walked and walked, and finally an apothecary and his wife saw me and took me in. Just weeks ago, I summoned the courage to tell them my true identity, how that, in my cowardice and fear, I left those I loved to rot in the only home I'd ever known!" Slamming her fists on the wood once more, she spun away from the desk and strode toward the door, then turned back. Returning to stand before him, she looked down into his simmering eyes, not understanding what she saw there and, in desperation, started to cry, breathing in great gulps of air. She wrapped one elegant arm around herself, heaving, wishing after these weeks she'd just run out of tears.

Wrenching the words out between the cracking in her voice, she said, "Before I knew what it meant, I wanted whatever this betrothal was because it was you, Josiah Cairns. But once I realized as I was coming of age, I'd never have any London season where you may find me, and that I was going to be a spinster because no one else would ever come close to my girlish imaginings of you. I knew there was nothing left but a faded dream. How could you want me at that point? How could anyone after what I'd done? I thought neither you nor any of my family could ever forgive me running away as I did. But my uncle came for me immediately after he was contacted. He and my aunt welcomed me right back into their hearts." She paused, catching her breath. "When we arrived tonight, I didn't know we were coming here, and I all but ran from the door as she recognized me, but your mother"—Adeleine sobbed—"your mother sat with me and calmed me, and I remembered how much I'd loved her, loved all of you, as a child, and for just a fleeting moment, I thought maybe it wasn't too late. And then ... then ..." She gestured wildly about his study. "I never dreamed you could be ... you could be ... so cruel or come to hate me so." The words were strangled, tortured.

She gave him one last long, beseeching look. He sat leaning forward in his chair, hands gripping its arms. He was unable to speak, his face granite, unreadable. Another sob escaped her as she turned and ran again for the door.

Shaking himself, he stood quickly and began to follow her, crying, "Addy, Addy wait. Please wait," but it was too late. She'd let the door bang against the wall as she fled, and he heard the sudden cry of concern in his mother's voice as Adeleine entered the dining room.

In the sudden stillness, he heard her choke out to her uncle, "Please take me ... take me away from here."

As the fire guttered out, he sat in the blackness, unable to comprehend what he had done. He buried his head in his hands, and for the first time he could remember, he allowed himself to weep.

CHAPTER 17

August 1888

Adeleine removed her long white apron and cap and hung them in their place. Next were her stiff wool charcoal-gray blouse and skirt, and all the other trivial annoyances that afforded the starched, flawless form of a proper good nurse. She raised one brow glibly to think of such things. She washed slowly, relishing the shock of the cool water and the silence around her. She pulled her long butter-soft flannel gown over her head, careful not to yank her hair with the buttons. She pulled pin after pin from the prim coil at her nape and sighed as the weight of her braid fell down her back. She stretched her neck and kneaded the tight muscles, padding over to the bed. Her eleven-hour shift had gone very well, if tedious. Her studies were going wonderfully, and her classmates were good women, intent on their studies and not given to much foolishness. They were all pleasant enough. She'd gained the trust of all her patients it seemed, for they were always content in her company.

She'd seen more than she'd imagined she would since beginning some seven months ago, but not in the way one might suspect. She'd been utterly nonplussed over blood, breaks, infections. But she'd never imagined having to fight and restrain a sick patient to help them or dodge flying items thrown by furious or delirious patients in dire straits. She'd always thought nursing was perhaps more straightforward—a sick patient needed care, healing, comfort. But it had occurred less to her that healing as a nurse had to come from a place deep within the heart as well. As the idea had formed in her awareness, she began to spend just the few moments it took to ease her patients by cheering their hearts before nursing their bodies. She offered a ready smile, a warm voice. Compassion. It came naturally to her; after all, she'd spent many an hour visiting ailing folks with her papa, then with Christine and John, and then alone this past couple of years with them. And so she truly enjoyed her time here, though the studies were grueling and the shift hours long. She made sure to have no time to think on her own life, either engaged fully with her duties or falling exhausted into her bed at night. She could scarcely keep her eyes open to write letters, she thought as she yawned.

She glanced at the letter on the small desk for Christine and John and made a mental note to drop it in the bin first thing in the morning. Tomorrow was her evening off, "courting" day it was called by the giddy other nurse probationers who meddled in such things. She wanted to post her letter before evening, though, as it had already been sitting a few days waiting. She took the courting hours off each week to go visit Uncle Ben and Aunt Dottie, or

Emily or Kate's families. Everyone had cared for her with such warmth and included her in every way. Still, she held herself just a little aside, never wanting to become tiresome or seem an out-of-place imposition. The visits had a time limit; there was a rigid curfew, and so no one had been inclined to ask difficult questions or press her on sore matters. Sundays, she was allowed out of rotation only if she attended church, and so she filled in for the girls who cared to go, for she cared not a whit. Of course, Uncle Ben had encouraged her to come with them but in his gentle way. He'd not foisted the idea on her again, and she was grateful. What did she have to do with God? And what had he ever had to do with her?

Uncle Benjamin was so like Papa in the dearest ways. But he was very much a polished businessman as well. He was a much sought-after solicitor, and his dealings were extremely refined. He gave a very different, though not unpleasant, approach to business matters. With her, with his wife and daughters, he was gentle, patient, always anticipating their thoughts or desires or needs, and meeting them or helping to articulate their thoughts before they even realized the need. He was always aware, always present, yet still gave them all the space and time they needed to resolve matters themselves. Patient, never in any hurry. In business, however, decisions were made quickly after careful but brief consideration, plans put into motion with haste, like the finest clockwork, and resolved perfectly. Though it tore her heart to shreds, she'd determined not to find herself in a position of sitting with him quietly, for whether in his personal or professional way, he'd have her heart laid bare in his hands before she even thought to protect it and all its secrets. He'd pull the humiliation and pain from her that she didn't care to face, then help her in whatever way it took. Yet she did not *want* to discuss Josiah Cairns in any fashion and was determined to shed not one more tear in front of others. And any form of helping would surely mean more heartache. And so she restrained her affections for her family and stifled the urge to seek a shoulder to cry on, hard as it was.

Remembering Lady Joanna's horrified expression that night, she felt her face flame. Aunt Dottie's pained expression in the days that followed, and Uncle Ben's pensive and utterly disappointed expression as they'd immediately left Lady Joanna's table and home were still more than she could bear. She'd felt the sympathetic looks her way, the aching curiosity and confusion all around her. Still she'd remained silent and would continue to do so. She knew she was radically changed somewhere in the very fabric of her being, but she cared not. As the days went by, the walls around her rose higher and higher. All that now mattered to her was finishing school and leaving from this vile London as immediately as possible.

But in the quiet at night, alone with her own thoughts in the moments before sleep claimed her, unable to escape, she'd cried keening sobs from her very depths until her throat was raw and her eyes swollen and then cried some more. She curled up into a ball now, pulling one of Mama's crocheted blankets over her. If only Mama were here. The shame and throbbing pain swept through her afresh, without mercy. Her treacherous mind began to replay again every moment from that night. His face hung in her vision, and she squeezed her eyes tightly, but to no avail.

When he'd turned toward her, thinking she was the butler, his face had been soft, with his familiar lighthearted casual expression. As his eyes found her, however, his face hardened before her eyes into stone. For several beats, they'd simply stared at one another. While she watched, his eyes swept over her time and again, as though not trusting what he perceived. When he suddenly strode her way, her heart had lodged in her throat. She'd felt both hunted and acquired, familiar and forsaken. A feeling of dread had washed over her as he'd stopped right before her, so close, as if inspecting goods. As he'd continued to stare, his eyes roaming over her face, she felt certain he was disappointed with what he saw, and she couldn't bear to keep her eyes on his and see disdain reflected there.

When he'd said her name—just as he had years before—every defense she'd desperately started constructing fell into rubble at her feet. Oh, how her heart had leapt at his words! The way he'd suddenly touched her face, touched her hair had been almost reverent. The gentle kiss would have been her emotional undoing she'd felt sure; as it was, it had left her heart vulnerable, raw. Defenseless. But just as she'd somehow thought boldly to run her fingertips over his face, maybe into his loose curls, he'd broken the kiss and in just moments had become another person entirely.

The thought again that he must have been repulsed slashed through her. Try as she might, she still could not escape the thought of his suddenly cruel face as he pelted her with his mocking, accusing tirade of questions. She remembered how she'd let her eyes roam his face just before ... He was so changed and yet just the same. Grown into an intimidating giant of a man, he was no longer a skinny, gangly boy. His eyes were yet a glittering cinnamon brown, not flat dull brown, but a lively blending of shades and full of intelligence and passion. His hair was nearly black, carefree, windblown; it twined around his beautiful face and head like a crown, curling at his ears and collar. The same wave that had always fallen over his face was still there, waiting to be run through his fingers and put back in its place. His brows were full and dark, like the lashes that swept his cheeks. His strong straight nose and fine jaw were hallmarks of his lineage, yet the days old bristle on his face along with a stylish moustache lent him a dangerous air. His lips were full for a man, with a perfect cupid's bow, which somehow coupled with his brooding features made him all the more ridiculously handsome. Almost feral, like a prowling black jaguar. His towering height and powerful form had instantly reminded her of his father, who'd loved to laugh and tease, and could yet always be persuaded to read her a book as a girl. She hadn't even begun to have a chance to truly say how sorry she was to hear of his passing, yet she certainly was, indeed. The mockery had been all the more cruel as her heart ached over the sudden news of the loss of his father.

For the briefest moment, she pushed all the ugliness from view, holding tight to just the few sweet precious things that had passed between them … that first embrace, the too-quickly-gone smile, him holding her tightly, his forehead simply resting against hers as they both struggled. Her first kiss. She pressed her fingers to her lips. She felt the heave of a bitter sob rising on forlorn torment, and though she tried to stifle it, it broke free.

She ground her teeth, clenching her jaw so tightly it hurt to stave off the swell of bitter emotion. She had been right in thinking her betrothed would surely reject her, yet the fact rattled her. How could the boy who'd meant so much so long destroy her so mercilessly? She remembered no point in her life when he'd not been part of it, whether in person or in thought. Her dreams were tattered and worn, but she'd begun to hope, to imagine perhaps a silver lining. What a fool she'd been, and how brutal he'd been. It had all broken something integral within her, some main support, collapsing her like shattered glass. She truly would remain just another unwanted spinster for life.

Josiah was not the kind boy she'd known before, not in the least. His actions that had seemed so precious that night had been nothing but a cat toying with a battered, dying mouse. More than breaking her heart, he'd smashed her memories of the most precious years of her life, leaving them to mock her as cruelly as he had.

And for that, she could never forgive him.

CHAPTER 18

$\mathcal{T}$he job of hospital orderly suited him perfectly. Lowly enough to ensure a certain anonymity, still it allowed him to see all he wanted to see while remaining unseen. He merely showed up when assistance was required to the nurses and other hospital staff and dwelt among the shadows the remainder of his shift. The pay allowed him out of the stinking cesspit that was Whitechapel, affording him sparse yet comfortable lodgings. He was an observer, always patiently waiting. He learned quickly. He thought he may have liked to be a doctor of some kind. He was obsessed with watching the injured, curious about their accidents, their lives. He supposed he loved morbid, macabre sorts of things, but for the workings of it all. Not the ragged, broken bodies. The pulse of the beating heart, how quickly it was gone.

Looking back as he often did, he wished yet again he'd been stronger for Caroline, there for her when she'd needed him. The familiar rage swept through him, setting his face into a wicked snarl. His mother had fallen far from grace after her fancy London season and found herself increasing with him after the rake had abandoned her. She'd been forsaken and disowned. Cast out. He'd been born into stinking squalor and raised by the cruel streets. His little sister came three years later, another unwanted bastard sired by another conniving so-called gentleman. Until then his mother had tried, working her fingers to the bone and sewing until complete blackness made her stop at night. After Caroline's birth, she went to work lying on her back. He ignored it and somehow still loved her and tried to do his best as he matured into understanding. That is until the day he found his sister weeping on his cot in the shadowed corner. At fourteen years old, his mother forced her to bed with a man offering a huge sum for the girl. At first, he'd sought to soothe her, filled with the thought of running with her. But he could not, for they'd surely starve. So he held her close and told her to stay out of sight, and he'd protect her at night. Four months later, he came home to find her dead on the table, her petticoats pulled high, legs covered in blood. The floor ran crimson with it. His mind fought against what he saw before him, against what he knew to be true. He'd sat waiting for hours for his mother to come back in the dark, running his fingers through Caroline's bright hair, whispering to her that everything would be all right. His mother had coldly explained when she'd finally stumbled in half drunk and stinking that she'd attempted to give her daughter an abortion, all the while speaking of her like a tramp, even calling her a harlot. In the pure rage that engulfed him then, he'd leapt at his mother and choked her to death. Her body had fallen hard to the floor, her head coming to rest with a splatter in her daughter's own blood. He'd spent the rest of the night singing quietly to Caroline while he rocked her as he had when a lad, holding her cold body to his. Early in the morning, he'd burned his bloody clothing in the stove and found whatever money there was. He put on his only other clothes, kissed Caroline's face as he lay her gently on his cot, and set the tattered drapes ablaze. He'd gone looking for work and had found himself here.

He wheeled the dead gray cadaver woman through the halls to the nursing anatomy theatre. The probationers started their anatomy lessons coupled with dissection this day. He'd heard their excited chatter for a fortnight over the start of these lessons with the great research surgeon himself, and he was inclined to agree with their excitement. He'd made himself available years ago to collect and wheel the cadavers about after all, and thus was allowed to watch the dissections, remove the then mangled corpses, and spend a few minutes studying them before shrouding them and sending them for burial. As he approached the theatre, the doctor and matron stood talking in their aprons by the doors. They quickly held the doors open for him.

He nodded and, leaving the body in its place, slunk away, up into the raised seating coming to rest just a little off to the side behind *her*. She smelled of honeysuckle and lavender, he thought. He'd never dared get so close. He'd watched her for weeks, the loner among the students. She was ever kind and gracious, never cold or hard, as some of her inclination were prone to be. He wondered what life had settled upon her that she walked about with kindness yet cloaked from the world. She had no begging about her, not for friendship nor acceptance, nor did she flaunt herself in petty arrogance. A true lady, indeed.

He heard her sudden gasp and watched as her shoulders stiffened. The doctor had just entered the room. He was addressing the probationers and explaining what they'd be studying this day. He noted the leap of her pulse on her smooth neck and the redness climbing into her face. As the doctor gestured with his hands while he talked, his eyes came to rest on her. His talking stopped, his hands hanging in the air for several seconds. He nodded at the girl almost imperceptibly and continued on. She swallowed hard and blinked rapidly. She didn't appear sickened or overcome with nerves by the lesson. What intrigue was this?

As he continued drinking in her soft flowery scent, the doctor began to cut. The vein continued to throb in the lady's neck, and as though summoned, he felt the silky darkness unfurl through him. He felt the throbbing begin, the deep all-encompassing aching. The sweat began to rise on his brow, and his black eyes hung on every cut the doctor made. First the reflecting back of the skin exposing the rib cage, then the snapping of bone. The organs glistened dully as they saw light for the first time. His nerves seethed as more and more of the woman's dead body was opened. He took in the kidneys, liver, heart. As the doctor spoke of childbearing, he removed the uterus. The man's body thrummed with fiendish fury, and he struggled, forcing himself to focus on returning from his passions. He dabbed his brow with a slip of muslin, straightened his uniform, and silently began to find his way to the theatre's floor. He saw her turn her head toward his movement. Finding her eyes on his face, he glowered back, but she offered him a kind smile and turned back to the doctor. He froze for several seconds, then scurried to the floor. This night, he thought.

As the doctor finished up, he nodded at the man with a slight grin, then made his way to the water basin. Now that the dissection was complete, he'd ask for questions and begin discussion. As the man covered the body with a sheet, he glanced up and found the girl's eyes riveted on the doctor. What interest had she in him? He slowly began making his way from this bright room to the dark bowels of the hospital below.

Arriving there, he greedily snapped back the sheet. So like those he hated, he thought with a sneer. Older middle aged, no signs of accident or beating, he thought. Lungs did look horrible bad, though. He took in the deft cut marks, the not-quite-perfect replacement of the viscera. He carefully shifted the organs so they lay perfectly. Suddenly, fighting a sickening fury, he displaced them all worse than before. Taking pause, he lifted the sheet further to see all of her. No, no, she was no whore. He'd not treat her so. Gently, he put everything to rights, pulling her skin back tenderly over the replaced ribs. He washed the stale chemical odor from his hands and gathered the needle and thread, and a lace-up burial bag. He slowly and carefully stitched her skin back together, and when he had finished, he gently lifted her body, placing it in the burial bag. He ran his fingers through her hair, kissed her face, and laced the bag closed. Ringing the bell to alert the carter of a readied body, he scurried back toward the theatre.

She stood just outside the theatre doors, her back to him. The doctor seemed to be trying to talk to her. She stamped her foot, her hands balling into tight fists. He went to take her hand, and she pushed it away, almost slapping it. What intrigue was this, *indeed*? Suddenly, she was running toward him, her face red, her mouth turned down bitterly.

As she ran past, the scent of honeysuckle and lavender enveloped him. Instantly, he thought of the vein as it had throbbed in her neck.

This night.

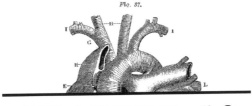

CHAPTER 19

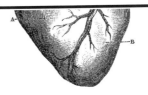

*J*osiah spent an hour pacing the empty anatomy theatre. He had to see her, to apologize, to somehow set them on better footing. Notes to her uncle's home had gone unanswered, the irony not escaping him. His mother knew things she wasn't sharing, only he assumed now he knew.

Looking into the probationer's faces and finding his eyes on hers had shocked him speechless. He'd seen the look of utter disbelief—and fury perhaps?—that wrestled across her features. He'd wanted immediately to comfort her somehow, but a slight nod was all he could offer then and there. He'd watched her long enough to see her eyes narrow and her jaw clench. He mused half-heartedly that they must be at war, for which he fully accepted the blame, and so decided to speak with her after discussion ended. He felt her eyes burning into him the entirety of the session and had hoped she'd hear him when the time came. But she had not, would not. She'd even asked why he'd humiliate her in front of her peers, which, to his chagrin, he realized were, indeed, staring. He barely kept himself from racing after her when she fled, his heart crushed in a vice watching her flight from him. So he'd paced until an idea came to him. He'd share something dear to his heart with her and take her to Whitechapel this afternoon.

His mission clinic had been a sudden thought two summers ago, when a sick child had collapsed just feet from him. He'd been preparing to leave after having been called to a particularly grisly attempted suicide. A man had jumped from a window thinking to end his life and had instead impaled himself on an iron gate, hanging upside down all night. The man had survived but suffered grievous injury as a result. As Josiah was leaving to follow the maimed man to the hospital, the boy had swayed on his feet and fallen into the muck. The workhouse had been cruel to the child, who was malnourished, dangerously exhausted, and wandering disoriented. Josiah had scooped the lad up and shouted for help. A shopkeeper offered shelter, and soon Josiah found a raging infected wound down the back of the boy's leg. Thank God it had been simple and straightforward to mend, and medicine easily given. And so Josiah had wondered if he might offer help a few times a month at no cost, so that hurting or sick children, and adults, too, if they wished, might be brought in and treated. So many died horrible, miserable deaths in the cesspit that was Whitechapel for no reason but inability to pay for help. It fulfilled a deep need of his heart to make himself available thus.

He wondered if sharing one need of his heart would bring her, the deepest need of his heart, back to him.

He didn't know exactly how, but he loved her today as though she'd never been gone from him. He'd tried in the last months to fathom how he'd so easily exchanged his fourteen-year-old love for her, all the childhood affection and shared memories, the understanding of betrothal, for the love of a smitten, heartsick pup. There was no doubt he wanted the betrothal to stand. He wanted *her*, all of her, in his life and heart. In the future he'd sought to avoid so long. Standing before him alive, vibrant, months ago, he'd been overcome by the desire to just touch her face, her titian hair. Just to know she breathed, truly. Then he'd wanted to embrace her and hold her and not let go. But in the intensity of those moments, the fury of questions had erupted and seethed through him, and he'd lashed out. Even watching her face turn to misery and finally fury, he could not stop himself. To say he regretted his cruelty and mockery would be the understatement of the century. That he could have been so cruel to one he'd suffered so long without shamed him deeply. It had left him in abject misery to have no contact and therefore no hope.

Over and over again, in pensive thought and in prayer, he'd cried out, "Lord, what have I done? Please help me. Please help her. Be with her." He'd begged God to give him a way back, a way to restore their friendship and a future together. Having no way to contact her and no response from her uncle, he'd felt so helpless. A worse helplessness than he'd ever felt believing her to be dead.

And so looking up into her dear face today had staggered him. He'd not take it for granted.

After speaking at length to the matron, who was shocked and then delighted to know of their longstanding betrothal and Adeleine's resurrection of sorts, he stood now at Adeleine's door with the lady's blessing. Ironically, it was "courting day" as the probationers called it. He felt his heart beating wildly in his chest. He paced a few times, then squared his shoulders and took a deep breath. "Lord God, be with me, my every word. Win her for me. Help me help her to heal after my cruelty to her," he uttered humbly. Finally, he resolutely returned to her door. It was time.

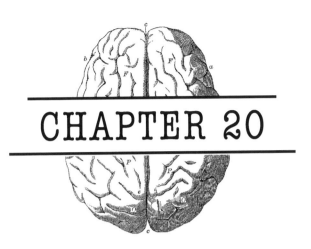

CHAPTER 20

Josiah squeezed his eyes tight, then reached to knock but found the door ever so slightly ajar. Curious, he thought. Gently easing the door open, he was startled to find Addy on her knees on the floor, staring into oblivion. Her hands were balled into tight fists, her hair escaped from its pins. Her riotous hair had always been a presence all its own. He almost chuckled and caught himself. At the same time, his heart tore a little further taking in the pitiful sight of her. Instead of knocking, he called to her gently. "Addy," he whispered. He saw her head jerk toward him and stilled himself.

"You," she hissed almost inaudibly. Suddenly, she unfolded herself from the floor and came to be toe to toe with him. "How dare you come here? Am I to have no sanctuary from your mockery? Please never address me or speak to me again, *Joe*," she growled, turning away and separating herself from him by several feet.

Her fury at his arrogance coming here was only compounded by how dashing he looked, devil take him!

He winced at the sting of her childhood name for him used this way but knew fully he deserved it. He'd injured her so carelessly in the very same fashion. Taken aback, he thought a moment. He didn't care to tower over her as he had that night in his study, like some predator about to attack. Still standing in her open doorway, he asked if the other girls had gone out already. "I suppose so. Why should I keep any apron strings on them?" she said sourly with a harsh shrug of her shoulders. Her eyes flashed contempt at him, and he felt himself begin to crumble under her blazing scorn.

"Well, then," he began softly, clearing his throat and dropping to his knees in the open doorway. "I've come to beg apology of my dear childhood friend, my Addy. Adeleine," he corrected. She turned slowly and stared at him for several seconds, mouth agape. Her eyes narrowed and her mouth snapped shut, but he saw the hard swallow torture her throat. He reached his hands to her. She came closer but did not take them.

"Don't dare mock me, trifle with me," she said down at him menacingly.

He held his hands up in surrender. "No, anything but that. I ... I am deeply ashamed of my horrid treatment of you, Addy. *Adeleine*. I was overcome in many different ways that night. But what suddenly overtook me and twisted out so ... horribly ... is that ... that ... you never sought me out, never thought to come to us in your plight. To *me*." His voice was ragged, but he'd not hide the depth of emotion spiraling through him. Not from her. Clearing his aching throat, he held out his hands to her again. She came forward tentatively, never taking her eyes from his. Pushing his hands upright as she reached him, she touched her palms to his. His blood jolted and pumped furiously through his veins at the touch of her hands to his. Clearing his throat yet again, he said just above a whisper, "I've come also to beg apology of my betrothed. I'd … I'd do anything to win her heart." The earnest, tender expression in his eyes, his face, even his bearing screamed of longing.

Sincerity.

She wanted to tell him he'd always had it, her heart. But she could not bring herself to speak it, not now. The wounds had gone too deep. All she'd carried with her of their childhood had been destroyed, and she no longer trusted in her perceptions of those many years ago. So she smiled at him as convincingly as she could, squeezed his hands, and let go. Standing, he dusted off his knees and reached again for her hand. She pretended not to notice, and he dropped it back to his side.

"I've something I'd very much like to share with you. Would you join me?"

"Well," she said uncertainly, peering into his face. "I suppose so." She rolled one shoulder in an attempt to seem nonplussed. He focused closely on her eyes a moment more. She looked exhausted, gaunt. Hollow. He could see the tracks tears had left on her face. She looked … broken. He ached for her hurting through to his core. He knew she was holding back. He knew she was willing to give nothing. Her eyes were somehow blank, empty. Nothing like they'd been that cursed night in his study, when they'd been so tender and open, accepting and hoping for acceptance. Then on fire from his cruel words. They were dull and dead, like a fire extinguished. He was well and truly cast out, and he felt it like a freezing blast.

He felt himself swallow the lump rising in his throat and felt guilt course through him yet again, so familiar now. He had no doubt the fragile flower that had come innocently to his study seeking her old friend had withered at his own ill treatment. She looked as if she'd not eaten for weeks, nor slept. Her heavy wool nurse's frock hung from her frame. He'd not seen her at any party her aunt and uncle had attended, nor her cousins. He never caught sight of her at the church they all attended, nor anywhere else for that matter. If she'd come with him today, maybe he could win her trust again and bring her bubbling spirit back to light.

Steeling himself for her refusal, he began. "We'll be outside in this peculiar chill where we're going. Change into something more comfortable and warm, but serviceable, would you please? It's a strange bit of weather out today, and I don't wish you to be uncomfortable. I'll just wait for you in the hall." He waited and watched for some sign of acceptance. She stared into his face, her eyes resting somewhere near his jaw, avoiding his gaze. Finally, she nodded. Turning into the hallway with a flash of his crooked grin, he whisked the door shut.

As soon as the door clicked closed, she sagged against it, putting her face into her hands. She'd longed for him to come to her, to seek her out. She'd dreamed, hoping against her hurt. And suddenly he was here. And now she found herself in dangerous waters. She couldn't hate him while she was there with him, not with his earnest apologies and searching looks. And to spend the afternoon with him some place … she couldn't imagine how this day would end. Somehow, she hadn't minded his gentle bossing request for her to change. Turning to the looking glass as she pushed away from the door, she almost gasped aloud at her appearance. Her face was pinched and sallow, with dark circles under her eyes, tracks left by tears crossed over her cheeks, and her hair flew all about her head. She hurried to remove the heavy wool garments, tossing them aside and rummaging through her unworn dresses. A pale green caught her eye. The style was prim but stylish, lightweight but warm, elegant but not ostentatious. Aunt Dottie and the girls had picked it out as part of her new wardrobe. The high neck had a split collar, with frogging and military buttons down the front in a slightly darker green. The sleeves were long, falling crisply at her wrists. The sleeves and skirt were embroidered and edged in a flourish, in military style. She quickly shook her hair loose and brushed it out, the wretched mess. She decided to wear it mostly down. Her head ached from the weight of it piled high most of the day. She pulled the front to the side and secured it with a jaunty peacock comb, then donned a smart green hat, simply appointed with braided trim and a peacock plume. Turning back to the basin and mirror, she splashed her face and pinched her cheeks. She dabbed on her favorite perfume and turned toward the door. Pulling on her short green kid gloves as a last thought, she took a deep breath and opened the door—and nearly slammed it shut again as he turned and went still, staring at her.

She waited several beats, then gathered her courage. Straightening stiffly to her full height and lifting her chin, she said, "You are displeased?" She yanked her door shut with a sharp crack behind her.

"No. *No,*" he croaked out. She smelled like heaven. She *looked* like heaven. Like more than his frail mind could have ever imagined. He fought for words, knowing it was not the time nor place for what he wanted to say. "Merely speechless." He chuckled, holding out his arm. He looked over her again, his mouth working but no words coming out. Suddenly, he smiled hugely at her and said joyfully, "The color green of your dress, do you remember? That day we'd arrived for summer, you were hiding and fell into the brook."

His smile was so open and familiar. His eyes alight, his gaze full of expectation. Her heart fluttered and ached in unison. While she firmly held control of her emotions as her traitorous heart leapt at his words, she considered wounding him as he'd wounded her months ago. Yet words wouldn't come. How could she tell him he'd viciously destroyed that sweet memory for her that night in his study? The memory she'd clung to so long, the memory that she knew moment by moment with startling clarity? She simply shrugged nonchalantly, looking purposely as far from his face as possible, giving no sign of the throb of emotion tumbling through her. She felt her throat tighten as she caught the fall of his face in her peripheral vision. She hated feeling so strongly and wished she could yank her heart out for the trouble it caused her ceaselessly. Forcing a smooth, serene expression, she looked up at him and changed the subject.

"Where are we going?" she asked.

"Well, first, if you don't mind, I'd like to change clothes myself. Would you welcome seeing mother?" She fought down the urge to bolt. She did love his mother dearly and treasured the kindness she'd shown her months ago.

"Of course, I'd love to see her," she replied. He smiled kindly down at her, and she felt her stomach twirl like a spinning top.

They'd somehow already passed through the hospital's corridors and out into the unseasonably cool air. She was grateful, indeed, he'd suggested she change into a warm dress. She'd have surely frozen otherwise.

As his carriage pulled up to his townhomes, her eyes were drawn to the one holding his practice of sorts. She found herself wondering what exactly it was used for and why the amount of privacy. His mother had told her some details that night before she'd entered his study, but she couldn't remember a single one in entirety. Something or other about anatomical and medical research, which, of course, explained his lesson today and those scheduled in the days and weeks to come.

Her thoughts were distracted as he stepped down from the carriage and turned back to help her down. She found herself wishing she hadn't worn gloves as his hand reached for hers. Shaking the thought from her mind, she allowed him to help her down. Finding herself suddenly too close, eye level with him as she stood on the last step, she had the incredible urge to throw her arms around him. As she fought to smash the thought, she gave a small stomp of her foot as was her habit and found herself tumbling off the step. He was suddenly holding her close, her face crushed to his chest.

As she drank in his spicy scent, she felt the muscle of his arms flex around her. In the moments before he settled her to the ground, and released her, a thought she could not refuse filled her mind. No matter how she tried to fight it, to spit it all back in his face, she could not. Something within her would not allow it. Looking up into his wide eyes gazing down at her, she felt unsettled. Restless. Somehow angry, but she knew not at what. She turned away from him with a hard glare and walked toward the door.

Shaking herself, she resolved that Dr. Josiah Cairns must simply be considered a new acquaintance, nothing more. Another means to an end. It was the only way she could survive the afternoon. He would not dissect *her* again.

CHAPTER 21

$\mathcal{A}$deleine was disappointed to find Lady Joanna to be away out visiting. Feeling shy and foolish, she, nevertheless, wondered if Lady Joanna would allow her to visit her on one of these afternoons off. Suddenly, she remembered walking hand in hand with her right here some snowy day. She remembered calling her auntie Jo, and immediately her eyes filled. She'd come back out to Josiah's fancy carriage to sit and wait for him to return from changing his clothes. A loud thump against the carriage door startled her. She felt the carriage move as the horses paced expectantly. She leaned to push open the door just in time to see Josiah lose hold on a medical bag and basket of medical supplies held in one hand as he fought to keep from dropping a leather roll of instruments and another smaller basket in the other hand. His driver came barreling around the side of the carriage just as Adeleine jumped down from the carriage to retrieve the dropped basket and supplies.

"I am so terribly sorry, my lord. Please forgive my tardiness! I must have been woolgathering to have missed you coming from the house!" the young driver offered as he scrambled to set things to rights and get them settled back into the carriage.

"I took longer than I intended, Johnson, no harm done," Josiah said kindly to the boy. She figured him to be about her age, perhaps two or three years younger, and watched him smile heartily and close the door. As the carriage began to move, Adeleine felt Josiah's eyes on her.

"Addy! You've tears on your face!" he said suddenly, his eyebrows raised in concern. She considered laughing at him, or correcting him, then realized she *did* somehow have tears on her face. Swiping at her cheeks, she gave a half-hearted chuckle and said, "I rather unexpectedly remembered walking with your mother as a girl and calling her auntie Jo, is all." She flashed a soft grin at him and quickly turned to stare from the window.

He sat back against the seat and watched her closely. He realized he'd called her Addy, and she'd not refused the affection relayed therein. She was at once fiery, cold, soft-hearted, tough as nails, and sweet. Hard to fathom yet so like she'd always been. Except that grief had taken a toll, and something else struck him. She exuded a strength and yet a feeling of melancholy hopelessness. And a certain separation, a holding back as though she felt she never truly belonged any place. With *anyone*. She had been orphaned after all ... *She belongs with me*, he thought gently, the emotion reaching through to his soul. He would have to study her carefully if he was to win her. He ached to set all the world right for her. To show her how desperately he longed for her, all the fire and ice that made her. All the laughter and joy he'd known her to possess. Indeed, he realized he was looking for a bright ten-year-old girl in a way, but, of course, that was no longer her. He realized then he'd taken for granted that loving her was more than accepting the betrothal and the keen fondness he felt. He yearned to look into her eyes and find a woman he'd come to know and understand today looking back at him. He felt his chest fill with the challenge.

Drawing close to the streets of Whitechapel, the dregs of human suffering became more and more pronounced. He watched as she drew her fingers to her lips time and again. Children in rags ran past on who-knew-what errand. Empty-faced women walked about slowly as though looking for something they couldn't remember. Men from all facets of the social spectrum came and went, babies cried, and even prostitutes began to linger in the early afternoon light.

"Joe," she breathed, staring out the window. He watched her mouth snap together. Ah, his pet name she'd not admit from her own lips, though she'd not fought hers from him. She turned and regarded him, eyes penetrating into his soul, with her face softer than he'd yet seen. She swallowed. "Josiah. What are you about? Why have we come here?" Just then the carriage came to a stop.

The queue for his help wrapped clear around the corner. There were cheers and cries of relief, grinning children, desperate faces that brightened. She looked into his face, her eyes wide, out the window, and back again to him. "What is this, Joe? Who are these people? These children?"

Talking past the tug of a grin hovering at his lips, he said, "This is my mission clinic, my way of serving the Lord and those in dire need. These children suffer a cruel life on these streets, as do their parents, their families. I'd hoped you may be willing to help me. As my nurse."

He smiled somewhat uncertainly, looking to her for approval. Adeleine felt her heart swell for this multilayered man before her, and while she tried to tamp down the wave of affection, she knew her resistance was in vain. She pulled the basket brimming with supplies into her lap and nodded, smiling tremulously at him. He caught the glimmer of a tear, and his heart skipped a beat. Standing as much as he was able, he moved past her, rapping the roof for Johnson. The carriage door opened, and Josiah stepped down to cheers and hoots. Adeleine could feel the affection of the crowd for the man, and she wondered at it even as warmth continued to spread through her. Pulling off her gloves and fancy hat, she wished for the simple attire she'd worn on calls with John and Christine back at the apothecary. Josiah had changed into the clothing of any common laborer, and here she sat like a peacock, plume and all! As she sat hurriedly braiding her loose hair, she realized Josiah was watching her from the carriage door, a soft smile on his face and twinkle in his eyes.

"I, well, I feel so awkward! I am overdressed!" she cried, looking into his face worriedly.

"You are simply lovely in every way, Addy my girl."

He realized he'd said it, and his face froze as he stood waiting for her look of reproach, but it never came. She looked into his face for a long moment and gave a small shake of her head while a grin played at her lips. He reached for her hand, and as she stood, she grasped his tightly. A look passed between them that spoke volumes. Meeting his eyes, she offered just above a whisper, "Don't pull my hair, foul ogre." His breath caught. They both felt the years fall away, and he received her words as the answer to his earlier question, feeling like the world *was* right at this very moment. She giggled and said, "Would you let me out, Doctor? These darlings need a good nurse, you know."

He chuckled, shaking his head. "My lady." He bowed deeply, winked at her, and helped her from the carriage.

He reached in to retrieve the other basket and his bag, tucking his instruments inside, and as he turned back around, he found his jaw falling open. Adeleine was weaving in and out between the children almost as though dancing with them, speaking to each one and holding their rapt attention. She spoke to mothers, bringing smiles to their worry worn faces, and teased boys who stood staring at her, surely thinking an angel had come to visit. He couldn't help but agree.

All but skipping back to him, he was shocked at the transformation he was witnessing as she bobbed in front of him. Her smile was blinding. She was practically bubbling over.

"Are you ready, *Doctor Joe*," she teased.

"They've already told you that, eh?" He grinned. "Let's get going, then, shall we?"

Taking his arm, she knew this would be a very different afternoon than she had feared. And more wonderful than she could have hoped.

CHAPTER 22

The afternoon had flown on gilded wings. Josiah felt somehow privileged, blessed to watch Addy in what was absolutely her true calling. Being with these children did something for her, touched her heart in a way he'd not counted on. And not only was she quite obviously excellent at her work; she was fast and meticulous. She had a genuine heart for people and a gift for really drawing out each one, child or adult. She doted on each one and quickly set aside all but the root of each problem. He'd dare say she'd be a better medical doctor than he himself. He felt an immense pride in his lady, his nurse Adeleine. He felt another grin spreading across his face.

They'd seen all the more severe cases early on, and now as the sun began it's descent, they finished with the lesser cases. Josiah realized he'd completely forgotten the food he'd brought. "Addy, there's food here. I've forgotten all about it," he said apologetically. She looked up at him over the head of a little boy held closely in her lap.

"I'll have a look soon as we are done here," she said brightly as she squeezed the child. She'd patiently held the child, talking to him and gaining his trust. He had a vicious-looking splinter between his thumb and index finger, and Josiah felt sure it was likely infected. She began working to remove the nasty thing. As the boy whimpered in her arms, she gently held his head to her chest as an embrace, then returned to her work. She hummed sweetly to the boy and patiently worked at the ragged splinter. Something shifted inside him watching her with the child, something he couldn't name. Her hair had completely unfurled some time ago, and lay over her shoulder, strands lifting on the breeze. A tender whisper of longing passed through his heart of seeing her this way with his own child. Their child.

Just then the deep melodic brogue of the street preacher Billy Stevenson poured into the evening air as he began his nightly sermon. Josiah's heart thrilled with the thought of souls saved, maybe this night. He uttered a prayer and listened intently as he tidied the clinic.

"Damnation! Damnation!" Stevenson bellowed. "What is damnation but this, the eternal separation of mankind from his Maker, God almighty. Eternal hellfire, blackness. No drop of water, no embrace. Sin destroys us, makes us unclean, unfit before a holy God."

Adeleine fought the intense desire to drop the child and flee. Her stomach soured, her nerves burned. She wanted no part of this foolishness. God was an imagination of hurting hearts, and she knew hurt well. But she would not believe. She would not! She breathed deeply and fought to regain her composure, intently returning to caring for the child. Still the man's Irish brogue and musical lilt drew her ears back to his earnest cries.

The preacher continued, his Bible held aloft in his burly hand. "The book of Hebrews tells us it is appointed unto man once to die, and after this *judgement*! And what is the judgement against us? Damnation! We read in Romans that the wage of sin is death. Aye, the payment of our folly and sin is *death*, eternal death of body and soul! Separation from God forever. But it goes on to say that the *gift* of God is eternal life through Jesus Christ, our Lord. It is a gift, for we can do nothing to earn it! Jesus walked this earth sinless. The very Son of God came here to us to receive us to himself. There is rescue in him alone! There is a way out of the pit of hell, eternal hell and suffering, and his name is Jesus Christ! You must only believe in him and repent of the sin that will cast you to hell. Jesus says in the book of John, 'I am the way, the truth, and the life: no man cometh unto the Father, but by me.' Earlier in the book of John, he says, 'I am the resurrection, and the life: he that believeth in me, though he were dead, yet shall he live.' Dear souls of Whitechapel, won't you receive him? Won't you repent of your sin, believe in Jesus Christ to save you? Won't you allow him to be your Savior from sin and death and the pit of hell? Come! Come to receive him now. Don't delay! The hour is nigh unto salvation. You may never have the opportunity again, dear soul. Believe and repent now before it is too late!"

The preacher stepped down from his small platform and lifted his hands high and began to pray earnestly, choking with emotion in his pleas and cries for just one soul. People who had stopped in their tracks at the sound of his preaching now continued on their way, but many stopped to speak to the preacher as he said his amens.

Adeleine continued to struggle with her emotions, realizing that she still held the little boy in her lap, though she'd finally removed the inch-long splinter. Josiah was somehow suddenly kneeling before her, pouring medicine over the child's hand to clear the infection. After he applied an ointment, he wrapped the child's hand in a bandage and ruffled his hair. The child turned to her, giving her a bashful, "Thank you," and jumped down, running toward the preacher. Stevenson caught the boy in a bear hug, lifting him high above his head. Adeleine watched as the boy showed the man his hand and pointed straight to her. She felt like she'd melt into the ground.

Standing quickly, she tried desperately to find something to do as he headed toward her. She had never heard a man speak so. He had mentioned the very scripture on her parents' grave, and she couldn't displace it from her mind. If it was all foolishness, why did so many believe it? Her own parents? Uncle Ben and Aunt Dottie, her cousins ... Lady Joanna, and even Josiah? She thought back to her years with John and Christine, their gentle mentioning of God as the Father, and Jesus his Son. Without sin, a perfect sacrifice. She'd learned to simply nod and ignore it as she grew into her teen years. But never had time been mentioned as though there were danger.

As she tried to put it all aside, she heard Josiah's boisterous welcome of the preacher. Wanting to stomp her foot and grit her teeth, she instead put on her most ladylike face and turned gracefully toward the men. The little boy surprised her by running and throwing his arms about her, smiling up at her with his glittering blue eyes. She bent down to return his embrace and asked about his hand, which he said emphatically felt much better. Squeezing him again, she stood. Josiah reached for her hand and brought her face to face with the man who'd bellowed with all certainty she was going to hell for her unwillingness to believe. Or repent. Repent of what? She'd spent all her years wanting to serve people. Where was the sin in that?

"Billy, this is my dear lifelong friend Lady Adeleine Ashton. She is in Nightingale's nursing school, where I teach." Josiah introduced her, beaming. Adeleine gave a pleasant nod of her head.

"How do you do?" she said to the man. His big blue eyes annoyed her for their sincerity. They shone bright and blue in his rugged, very Irish face. His dark hair gleamed in the late-evening sunlight, and his hearty frame spoke of strength.

He smiled warmly at her and said, "Thank you for seeing to my boy, here. He has grown a wee bit fond of his bonny angel, he has." He chuckled and grinned, looking intently from her face to Josiah's.

"Any souls tonight, Preacher?" Josiah asked.

"Only God above sees the heart and the beginnings of salvation. I pray perhaps I sowed some good seed, brother. I pray I did," Billy said humbly. Growing serious, he looked straight into Adeleine's eyes. He reached his bear paw to grasp her hand and said quietly to her with pensive eyes, "Do you believe, my lady Adeleine?" Her breath caught in her throat, and her brain went entirely blank. She felt her cheeks begin to burn as she struggled for a response to the man.

Just then a boy ran up to them, shouting, "Doctor! Doctor! Me pa has broke his leg! They have him there!"

He pointed excitedly to a cart making its way through the crowded street. Billy squeezed her hand while Josiah looked intently at her. They both then quickly turned to run to help the boys wheeling the injured man. Adeleine heaved a huge sigh and put her hand to her brow. As she scanned the street awaiting the injured man's arrival, she met the eyes of a man across the way from her. Recognition began to dawn, but just before the man disappeared into the milling street, Josiah strode through the clinic with the man in his arms. He lay him carefully on the table they'd used all day and nodded to her. She brought scissors to cut the man's pant leg away from his injury and got straight to work on it. The break was bad to be sure, as the bulge of splintered bone had nearly come through the skin. As Josiah thought to light some candles, he realized the sun had all but set and quickly drew his pocket watch out to see the time.

"Oh, Addy, your curfew! I have to send you with Johnson now, or you'll never make it in time!"

"But this man is hurt badly!" she cried. "How can I leave you now?"

His eyes lit at her words, and his heart swelled in his chest. If only she'd find it in her heart to say the same under different circumstances.

"Stevenson has seen many a break, I'd dare say, and he'll help me reset this fellow and get him settled," he said as the preacher nodded.

"If surgery is required, Doctor, my hackney can take him to hospital," Billy said.

Josiah clapped him on the shoulder and breathed "Thank you, brother, thank you." He grabbed the food basket still sitting on the table and gently took Adeleine's arm. He walked her over to the waiting carriage and gave Johnson instructions to return her to St. Thomas' where they'd picked her up earlier today. He helped her into the carriage, and before he could think about it, he turned over her hand and pressed a gentle kiss into her wrist. Her mouth fell open as he rapped the ceiling and jumped down from the carriage. He hooked his thumbs into his waistcoat pockets and grinned at her, rocking back on his heels as the carriage began to move away.

Once she could see him no more, she brought her wrist to her heart, cradling it with her other hand. She thought of his tousled raven-dark waves and the sparkle of his eyes just now. Letting her head fall back on the seat, she sighed.

She needed no saving but from Josiah, she thought.

Thinking of the preacher man, her nerves and heart began buzzing like an angry hive of hornets. She practically felt the stinging beasts tormenting her, driven by questions she could not or would not answer. She shook her head sharply. She'd think on those things later. She opened the basket of food and found it filled with salmon sandwiches, berries, cheese, and fruit tartlets. But what caught her eye was the sweet sunflower lying across it all, with a ribbon tied to it. As she let out a small cry and then a chuckle, she felt her eyes prickle. Sunflowers had grown profusely at Grayson every summer, and they'd always remained her favorite.

How could he have possibly known what this flower would mean to her? As she nibbled at the glorious contents of the picnic basket, she sighed with a happiness she'd not felt in perhaps all the years since she called Grayson home. She could scarcely fathom how one man could churn up so many conflicting feelings within her. While she looked forward hopefully to nursing alongside him again, she felt spikes of apprehension sting her at the very same thought. Even while she wondered what it would be like to be held by him again, kissed by him again, she found herself squashing the thoughts mercilessly.

She thought again of going home to Grayson as soon as nursing school came to a close. She could hardly fathom it belonged to her. How wonderful it would be to own her own life, help who she longed to help, and have control of her own fate. What was any of this but a dream, after all? She couldn't trust in love, nor friendship, nor would she.

And so she resolved that while she'd enjoyed today, perception wasn't to be believed. The tenderness of today had drawn on memories alone, nothing more. No sooner had she started to feel happiness did she balk at it and doubt it, and that was safe, she reasoned.

She was safe, so long as she didn't let him in. Resolved, she gave a firm nod of her head and bit into a strawberry tartlet.

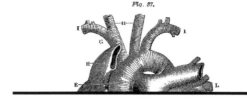

CHAPTER 23

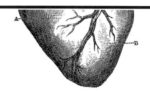

Shortly after Adeleine's departure, Josiah had to make the decision to take the injured man to the hospital. Billy had called for his hackney, and when it had arrived, the men loaded up and departed with haste. The boy had been sent home to his mother to tell her his pa would be taken care of.

The man's cries of pain nagged at Josiah's heart. He hated the distance to St. Thomas', but he had what he needed there, including the school's matron and top nurses. Every jolt of the hackney set the man's teeth to grinding, and his fingers and nails digging into Josiah's forearms. He had nothing to give him to mercifully put him out. Surgery would be necessary, but Josiah prayed he'd be able to save the man's limb. In the process of the last hour, the broken bone had begun to shear through the skin, changing the status of badly broken leg to compound fracture.

Billy glanced into Josiah's face and caught his eye. "Never becomes easy, does it?"

"No, never does," Josiah replied. "I'll need a good round or two of fisticuffs after this, after all of today, if you're willing."

"Aye, you know I'm always willing to punch you till you give up, ye wee slug!" The men grinned at one another as they'd not give in to laughter at the cheeky comment over the man in his suffering. Billy had become a dear friend to Josiah over the last year. He often had dinner on his clinic days at the man's humble home in Whitechapel where he was a self-made man, a blacksmith by trade. Sitting around the table there with Iness and Timmy, the lad, had been a balm to Josiah's raw spirit after losing his father.

Finally, reaching the hospital, Josiah called for a gurney and ether and for the matron and Adeleine to be requested to his operating theatre. The operating theatre was brightly lit as night had fallen, and the matron arrived with two hospital nurses who got to work right away. The now-open wound needed irrigation, the man's leg needed shaving, the antiseptic solutions administered. The man was given ether to knock him out and finally give rest to his suffering.

As the smells of carbolic acid, bichloride, naphthalin, and ether filled the room, Josiah washed and washed, preparing to open the leg cleanly. The boy had explained that his pa had been kicked by his cart horse, and after he had fallen unseen, the dratted horse had pulled the cart's wheels over his leg. The child had come running when he heard his papa screaming. Being loaded into a shabby hand cart by young boys, jostled and bumped down the street, then loaded into the hackney, the damage was extensive. The nurses made quick work of irrigating the angry wound, cutting away the shreds of muscle and fat, and removing the loose bits of bone. As he finished washing and was ready to operate, Josiah looked quizzically at the matron. She gave a slight shake of her head. The wound and needed surgery were fascinating, as compound fractures were not commonplace as simple breaks. Frustrated but knowing too much time had already passed, Josiah began to operate.

The kick from the horse had snapped the top of the shin just below the knee. The wheels rolling over the leg served to smash the tissues into the bone shards, further displacing the bone and damaging surrounding nerve and muscle. Josiah opened the leg carefully. Skillfully using forceps and slender, rounded instruments, he was able to untangle the soft tissues, muscle, and nerves from the ragged bone ends. He alerted the nurses that he was ready to reset the bone, and they began to pull and adjust the leg, all working together at different points of muscle attachment until the leg cooperated and the bone was settled back into its proper place. The wound was irrigated with antiseptic solution once more, and a tube was placed for drainage. Josiah meticulously stitched the wound closed, leaving the drainage site open. The nurses applied an antiseptic compress, and the surgery was complete. The man would, no doubt, have a long recovery, but Josiah was relieved the repairs had been straightforward and that healing was, indeed, possible. After the wound closed cleanly, the leg would be held by plaster cast. Until then, the leg would be held in traction. The man would be immobile for months. Josiah worried for the family's survival and determined to see how he could be of assistance.

After washing again, Josiah stood drying his hands. As the two nurses began to wheel the man's gurney to a ward, the matron came to stand beside him. "Did your time today go badly?" she asked with motherly concern. Not hiding his surprise, Josiah's eyebrows shot up, and his mouth fell open.

"Not at all. We had a grand time! Adeleine is a wonderful nurse. Truly, it's a gifted calling for her. It was incredible to have her help today. Why do you ask this?" he asked confusedly.

"'Tis simply that I knocked on her door, and she didn't answer. Knowing she'd only just returned, I knocked again. When she still didn't answer, I opened the door and peeked in. She was curled on the bed in her night rail, and as she sat up and looked at me, her face was all in tears. I asked her what on earth was the matter, and she'd not say a thing. I told her you'd come here with a man in bad shape and requested her help. She shook her head and said, 'Forgive me, I cannot.' So I thought perhaps today had gone badly."

Josiah couldn't understand. Shaking his head, he said, "When I sent my carriage driver here with Addy, she left wreathed in smiles. I just don't understand." He wrung his hands slowly, trying for all the world to make sense of Addy weeping in her bed.

"The girl seems to be carrying a great deal on her heart, has since the moment I met her. She's at the top of this class, but she has opened up to no friendship. She is not unapproachable or unkind, but she is shrouded in whatever keeps her holding back. She goes to see her family from time to time on the Thursday break, but nothing else. She's hurting, Dr. Cairns. I don't know from what, but I know she's hurt a great deal since she started here."

Josiah stood staring at the floor, his hopes ignited today dashed with ice water down his back.

"I'm afraid the fault lies squarely with me, as I shared with you this morning," he said quietly. "I'd so hoped we'd rebuilt what I'd crushed months ago today."

"Ah, Doctor. The heart is not so easily repaired as a broken bone with antiseptic and stitching and ointments. It can't be reset. Trust must be rebuilt, and that doesn't happen in an afternoon. Don't give up on her. She's a fine lady, Adeleine. Keep trying, Dr. Cairns," the matron said softly. Nodding demurely at him, she turned and left, and he was alone.

Alone.

Couldn't his trespass be forgiven? He desperately wanted a reprieve from this madness he'd put onto himself in his anger that night months ago. He chuckled bitterly to himself. Flexing his shoulders, he went to collect Billy to return to Whitechapel. He desperately needed counsel and maybe a good bout of Irish stand-down to rattle his brain.

*****

Approaching the girl's door, the matron knocked again. The hour had grown late, but she couldn't stand to see the girl hurting so, nor Dr. Cairns. He was a good, upstanding man, kind, generous. Gentle. None of this ordeal made good sense to her, but broken hearts did. If she could help, she would; she dearly wanted to. The two made a fine match, the doctor and his nurse. Adeleine opened the door, and a concerned look crossed her face. "Is everything all right, Matron?" she asked, eyes wide.

"Yes, yes, dear. I want to talk to you, is all," the matron responded kindly.

Adeleine stepped away from the door to let the matron in. She pulled out the desk chair and offered it to the matron, who seated herself. Adeleine sat nervously perched on her bed. "Well, now, Miss Ashton. We have but one quarter left of this nursing session. You've made top marks and no doubt will continue to do so. But, my dear, I've heard you cry many a night. I've watched you make not a single friend, though not for lack of good character or being disliked. And now Dr. Cairns says what a wonderfully exceptional nurse you were to him today, yet you resisted being of aid this evening. He was sorely perplexed ... I think perhaps a touch hurt that you wouldn't come."

Adeleine looked down at her hands. She couldn't form the words she needed to say. She'd heard her crying? She was embarrassed and felt the redness seeping into her face like hot molasses. She was rather amazed at the matron seeking her out this way, and couldn't fathom why. She was a nobody, after all. Wasn't she?

The matron continued, "I believe you suffer a broken heart, Miss Ashton. I want to tell you to do something about it before it leaves your life cold and lonely—and full of regrets."

Adeleine's jaw dropped open; and as she shook her head, eyes wide, the usually cool, controlled matron scooted close and gathered her hands. "My heart was broken, once," she started. "I was smitten with a dear friend all through my grand season. I thought sure he'd choose someone else, but he chose me. He asked my father for my hand, and all was wonderful. I was so in love, so full of dreams and romance. But, one day, we got into an argument, and I was deeply hurt. What hurt more deeply was that he'd long been a trusted friend, throughout our childhood years. So many memories you know. As days went by without him coming to me, I became more and more bitter, more resentful. When finally he came to me, he was full of apology. But I wouldn't give in. I felt so deeply cut I no longer saw that he valued me at all. I wouldn't believe he did. I thought, how could he hurt me so deeply and expect me ever to trust him again? What I didn't see is that I had hurt him, too, but he took those days thinking about our argument and realizing it wasn't important. He dearly wanted us restored, but I remained bitter. In humiliation to both our families, our engagement was broken off some months later after I continued refusing to forgive, or to even see him and listen. Though that's been many years past, I sit before you still heartbroken. He was every dream I ever had, and I gave it all up because I was determined not to forgive, and never to trust again.

"You are the first person I have ever shared this with, Miss Ashton. I see the same sort of situation at play here, and it breaks my heart for both of you. Please forgive him. I'm afraid you'll deeply regret it if you don't." The matron's eyes were full of unshed tears, and though she'd kept her voice clear and firm, her lips trembled. She gave Adeleine a shy smile and patted her hands.

"I just can't let go of things, Matron. I can't trust myself, nor Josiah."

"Surely you can see what manner of man he is, dear? Surely you can see he is loved and respected everywhere he goes?" asked the matron.

"Yes ... No, I keep trying, but I just can't trust him," Adeleine said in despair, her eyes filling.

"In January, just before coming here, my aunt and uncle took me to his mother's home, his home, when I first was reunited with everyone. I was horrified because I was afraid of his disappointment in me. After his mother comforted me, I thought I had the courage to speak to him, to ... to ... well, to just return to my old friend. At first, he seemed hard as stone. Then he softened, but then he became cruel. He mocked my most precious memories of us as children, belittled what he said my reaction would have been to his own father's death. He ... he stared at me, kissed me, then shoved me aside in disgust. He wouldn't listen to me when I tried to explain why I'd not contacted him in years past nor my uncle. I was a coward, Matron! I ran away leaving everyone I loved to decay in their death-beds. Then I contacted no one in my misery, because I thought no one would have me for what I'd done." Her shoulders began to shake as a sob wracked her. "I'm not beautiful like the ladies here in London. I well know I am old, and I've nothing to offer. And every time he stares at me, I know that's what he's thinking, you see." She covered her face with her hands and continued. "Today was won-derful in so many ways. Seeing him with all those desperate little ones, seeing his heart in his mission. I-I let go of some of my reservation and teased him, joked with him like when we were children, and he seemed so delighted. He even packed food for us and put a flower into the basket for me. But I ... I just can't believe in my own perception. I don't know who he is, what he's really about. I see one person, but all I can think is of who he was that night, you see? And every time I feel any happiness in him, I feel I must shut it out to keep myself safe from harm."

The matron had heard the man's own version of the debacle that had crushed the girl, but it was far different hearing it from the girl herself. What horrible pain the child had experienced in Dr. Cairn's struggling to comprehend everything taking place that night. But the one thing that stuck out most was Adeleine's inconceivable view of herself. Granted, she had no patience for young chits who flaunted themselves, paraded about thinking themselves to be beauties. But here this child *was* a beauty and couldn't see it in herself. Why, she was truly beautiful because it shone from the inside out, the kindness of her nature making the outer beauty that much more pronounced. She considered her next words carefully, wanting to build the child up with honesty and perhaps give her insight to Dr. Cairn's true feelings.

"Miss Ashton, you lost your mother and father very young, I know," the matron said gently. Adeleine nodded and sniffled into a kerchief balled in her fist. "What did you think of her? Of your father? What did they say of you? Do you remember?"

"I loved them very much, of course," Adeleine said slowly. "They were such a handsome couple. Mama was dainty and precious, with sparkling warm eyes and soft honey-brown hair down her back. Papa was tall and strong. His hair was dark but not black and had a dash of nutmeg to it, and it waved a bit. His eyes were blue as the sky and kind, always smiling." Remembering, she felt her lips trembling and pressed them together tightly.

"And what did they say of their little girl, Miss Ashton? How did they see you?"

"Well, I suppose they thought well of me. Papa called me his little jewel, his gem. I remember him joking with Mama that he'd never let me have a season in London, because he'd never get me back. Mama often told me my eyes were special, and my hair. But I don't know why, as they both are so strange." The matron sighed and chuckled softly.

"Let's go to the looking glass, shall we?" she said. Adeleine began to shake her head, but the matron would have none of it, pulling her up from the bed. Stopping her just before the glass, she lit another candle and stood it where it would cast light on Adeleine's face and hair. At first, Adeleine wouldn't look, but the matron gently lifted her chin, and Adeleine, being obedient, looked into the glass.

"Now I want you to listen to me carefully, my dear girl," she said. "This morning, after his anatomy discussion, Dr. Cairns came to speak with me. He talked at length of how you had quite suddenly come back to life and how, for years, he had tried to stop remembering you, stop hurting over your loss. He told me what he saw that night when you surprised him in his study—about how you looked so much as you did as a child, but how exquisite you'd become. He mentioned how he'd always loved the color of your hair, how he had to stop himself running his hands through it. He spoke of these freckles on your face that he was glad hadn't disappeared. He described your eyes as incredible, the color something he could drown in. And, Adeleine, he wasn't disgusted when he kissed you. He had to stop himself, you see. Out of honor, propriety." Adeleine stared at the matron in the looking glass, her mouth agape and her eyes narrowing in disbelief.

"He told you all these things?" she asked quietly.

"Yes, he certainly did. I have known him for years, watched him mature as he researched and worked hard here. We've taught this nursing program together for years, and trust each other a great deal. He did not restrain himself in explaining his treatment of you months ago. He told me how overcome he became that you'd never written or come to London. And how being so overcome with the feeling that you must not have wanted to keep your betrothal, he became horribly upset and was cruel to you. And that, in crushing you so severely, he was afraid he'd never get you back. And so being matron, I gave him permission to seek you here in the probationer's corridor. These things aren't typically allowed, you know."

Adeleine stared at the floor, not able or perhaps willing to open her heart enough to believe what she was being told. Struggling to resist as hard as she might, she fought against the crumbling of the walls she'd built. But the matron had shared her heartbreak with her when she said she'd never shared it with anyone. She'd taken the time to seek her out. Surely she'd not lie to her nor fill her head with empty vanity. These months she'd come to know matron as cool, aloof. Pristinely controlled. Never taken by surprise nor brooking any nonsense. So surely she must be speaking in truth?

"Come back and sit. I've one more thing I want to share with you, and I must wish you good night," matron said kindly. As Adeleine sat back down on her bed, the matron pushed the chair back under the desk and remained standing. "Miss Ashton, are you aware that over four hundred souls succumbed to the smallpox outbreak that took your household?" Adeleine shook her head, obviously surprised. "Yes, the epidemic was catastrophic there in Gloucestershire. And your father was a physician who would have come into contact with the disease on his visits before the pox showed itself as what it truly was and took over. It breeds and spreads before it shows, we know. Now what could you have done? The many households that succumbed were right in the area of your home where your father practiced. Your uncle spoke to me at length about all that he found out in the weeks just after your family passed when you enrolled here. Who could you have called on, child? What could you have done in aid to your household?" she asked. Adeleine shook her head, beginning to speak. The matron shushed her gently, placing her hand on the girl's shoulder. Looking deeply into her eyes, she said, "Miss Ashton, you could not have dug graves. You could not have removed their bodies from the upper level of your home. You had no way to call on anyone, as most everyone you could have gone to had died." Again, Adeleine began shaking her head, but the matron continued, conviction ringing in her tone. "No. No, Miss Ashton. You were alone, just turned ten years old, I believe. There is nothing you could have done. I fully believe, having known the conviction of your father's family, that he nor your mother would have ever expected you to stay. Your father was a doctor, Miss Ashton. He knew of what happened to the body after death. Do you truly think for a moment he would have wanted or expected his little girl to stay on? You'd have been daft to do so, and daft you are *not*. You were *brave*, child. There is no guilt that should be harbored in your heart over that tragedy. None. As for seeking out your uncle or the Cairns', again, you were but ten years old. You were brave, and you survived. There is nothing to be ashamed of, and I believe I can stand here and speak for your parents who would tell you to let this go. Please let it go, Miss Ashton. It has held you long enough."

Adeleine sat woodenly, tears pooling in her eyes, pondering these things. Never before had anyone spoken so openly to her about what her parents may have thought of the sorry circumstance. Nor of her appearance. John and Christine had ever been kind of her, complimenting her as a child and even poking fun at her about having no beau. Aunt Dottie had told her in months past how lovely she was, but she'd not believed any of it. She felt unsure but stood and hugged the matron, holding tightly. The matron embraced her in return, rubbing her hands over her back and giving one final squeeze. Adeleine gave her a shy soft smile and followed her to the door.

"Good night, my dear. You are free, child. Grasp your dreams, and don't let them go."

As the door clicked behind the matron, Adeleine felt a quaking inside she'd never felt before. Her own heart felt unfamiliar to her. She wanted so badly to do just as the matron told her. Except she didn't know what dream to grasp, for she'd let them all go.

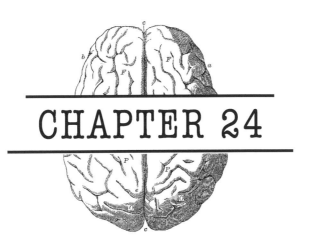

CHAPTER 24

$\mathcal{A}$rriving back in Whitechapel in front of the Stevenson home, Billy and Josiah got out of the hackney and stretched their legs. "What a day, eh?" Billy said. "Let's wrap up and swing these aching muscles loose."

Josiah chuckled and said, "Let's have at it. I need the therapy." Laughing, they walked into the house, and after spending a few minutes with Iness, they made their way to the smithy shop out back. Timmy was already abed. Billy's fires from earlier in the day had kept the shop warm. Removing bits and pieces of clothing, the men chatted amiably as they began wrapping their hands. A doctor and blacksmith had no business breaking fingers or splitting skin, after all. Billy had gotten his start bare knuckle boxing in Ireland, and Josiah in his Cambridge days. Neither man held back, but both men knew how far to go to test their limits but not their friendship. Neither man was lacking in character or humility, and so limits weren't necessarily needed, but their camaraderie had built on this stress ritual. Their best talks had come while throwing punches, their deepest admissions of failure. And so they called it therapy between them. They came toward one another and bumped fists with one another to begin.

"Who's yer bonny lass, Joey?" Billy asked.

Ducking from a swing, Josiah replied, "We were betrothed as children. Our parents were close, and we spent summers and Christmases together for years. She was dead until a few months ago."

Connecting with Billy's ribs, he failed to dodge a shot to the cheek. Rolling his neck, he returned a hard heel to the jaw to Billy. "Now how does that work, Doctor?" Billy asked incredulously as he parried another blow.

"Her whole household, mother, father, help, they all succumbed to smallpox. We didn't find out until months later. They'd been missed at Christmas, but we'd heard nothing. In his grief, her uncle didn't think at first to contact my family, though my parents were friends of his, as well. Our hearts were broken, of course."

Receiving a hard jab, he spit over his shoulder and took a deep breath. "She didn't die, as well, then? Some mistake?" Billy questioned. Dodging another jab, Josiah threw a forearm strike and followed it with a haymaker. Billy wheezed in surprise, stumbling but quickly righting himself and coming right back with two blows to Josiah's face. "Don't like my questions, there, Joey boy?" he laughed.

"Don't like what I'll have to explain, Billy."

"Spit it out, Joey. You know I can take it," Billy said, breathing hard. Josiah stood bouncing foot to foot, breathing hard himself. Approaching Billy again, he threw a hard punch that caught Billy in the chest. Spinning away, Billy came back with an uppercut. They both were starting to run with sweat and a little blood, and seeing the pain in

Josiah's eyes, Billy threw a quick jab at his side and shoved him hard. Josiah nodded as he regained his footing and bent over, hands on his legs.

"Her uncle brought her here to London when he found she was living. I've not taken in the whole story. I missed my chance those months ago. Nearly soon as they arrived, they paid a visit to my mother that was already planned beforehand." Spitting again, he straightened up, tasting blood on his lips. Billy brought over a soft scrap of toweling, and Josiah began drying himself off. "I didn't know of it, just that mother had dinner guests and expected me there. I'd ignored the uncle's letters to me for years, to my shame. He's a solicitor, and I knew I'd be forced to face my grief and whatever legalities there were. So I ignored the man. They'd planned with mother to sit and talk to me together. When I arrived home that night, I was late. I came in quietly because I knew my mother would be a tad cross. The laughter was the first thing I heard. It shot like lightning through my body. I was struck dumb with it. To think I knew it, fourteen years after I'd last heard it." He shook his head, his mouth turning down with emotion. Head tilting back, he continued, "I heard them talking, Mother and Adeleine, and I couldn't make sense of the words I was hearing. I heard my mother say Addy, and I saw part of her face in the firelight, and I bolted to my study next door. I ran scared, Billy. I couldn't fathom it all.

"A short time later, I heard a knock at my study door. I threw it open, and expecting Ellison, I'd turned my back and walked further into the room. When there was nothing said, I turned, and she stood before me just a few feet away." As his voice cracked, Billy threw an arm around

Josiah's shoulders, leading him back toward the house. A biting rain had begun to fall, but Josiah stood stock still in it, his face illuminated ironically by strikes of lightning. "I was shocked and overjoyed. My skin felt like it came alive. I felt like I was tingling with electricity. I was overcome with just wanting to touch her, with ... God forgive me, with desire. I couldn't understand that either. It seemed ridiculous. Nevertheless, I strode right up to her, hardly a breath between us, and I wrapped my arms around her like a common scoundrel. Realizing how out of order I was and seeing the look in her eyes, I let go, but then I found myself walking toward her. I fought a few moments more, and having backed her into the wall, I gave in. I kissed her. What I felt was so strong I knew I'd surely truly catch fire if I didn't get away. I went to my desk ashamed and trying to calm myself, but then the anger came." He was breathless, and Billy didn't know if all the wetness on his face was rain. Pushing him into the house, he whispered to Iness for more towels and hot coffee. He led Josiah to sit in front of the fire. Billy had never seen Josiah this way, not even over the death of his father. He was wild with it. Billy uttered a prayer for the man from his heart, begging God to help him. Gathering the towels from Iness's arms, he sat beside Josiah, throwing a towel over his shoulders.

"What made you angry, brother?" Billy said quietly.

Josiah replied, "My mind caught on the fact that maybe she didn't want the betrothal ... that maybe that's why her uncle had contacted me so many times. When all these years I'd died inside at her being gone, with wanting her with me. Then I raged over why such a smart little girl as she had been never contacted us, never came to us, to me.

To me, Billy, *to me*! Do you know she's four and twenty? About to be five and twenty next week, she is. That's seven years, not a child anymore. I couldn't let it go. I was cruel. She kept trying to answer me, but I rolled right over her. I … I even accused her of seeing news of father's death over her morning chocolate and thinking she'd pay her respects, Billy. She loved my father. I know she did." Josiah was breathless, grief rolling over him wave after wave. Billy closed his eyes at the thought of such a low blow to a girl just reunited with close family and friends.

"Tell me the rest, Joey," Billy encouraged softly.

Taking a deep steadying breath and running both hands through his damp hair, Josiah went on.

"She finally started to fight back, and it was as though she'd burst into flames. Her eyes spit fire at me while she pounded on my desk. I couldn't help but marvel at her, delight in her spirit, yet I remained silent. She said her piece, then walked away. But she returned again, her arm wrapped around her middle and told me she'd begun to hope for us, but she never dreamed I could come to hate her so." His voice choked hard on that last, and Billy's heart ached for the man. And the girl Adeleine. "She ran out before I could collect myself and begged her uncle to take her away. I tried to write to him. I tried to speak to my mother. No one would answer me where she was so I could go beg her forgiveness.

"Early this morning, as I started my first anatomy lesson at St. Thomas' with the probationers, I saw her face in the risers. I was shocked, overcome. Right after my discussion, I raced out after her, but she ran from me. I paced and paced and prayed, and thought to bring her here to

Whitechapel for the clinic today. I went and spoke to the matron and shared much of this with her, and she gave her approval. I went to Addy's room, and she was kneeling on the floor, crying, staring into space. I felt like a knife went through me seeing her that way. Once I gained her attention, I begged an apology on my knees. She agreed to come here with me today, and I ... well, I could hardly believe the change that spread over her with the children. She became a totally different person, much like the girl I once knew. Laughing and teasing, nearly skipping amongst the little ones. The affection and care she showed each one just twisted my heart in my chest. Watching her with Timmy, I ... Billy, all I could think was I wanted her to hold my child that way." A ragged sob cut him off, and he fought to regain his composure. "Tonight, when we returned to St. Thomas', I requested her specifically for the surgery, but she wouldn't come. The matron told me just before I came to collect you that Adeleine had been hurting and withdrawn the whole of her time there, that she believed her to have a broken heart. That she'd heard her crying many nights. That's *my fault*, Billy! It's my fault, and I don't know how to help her! I want a life with her. It's all I can think about. But I want her, all of her. The fulfilled woman I saw today, not the woman in such pain, the woman I hurt so badly. Why won't she forgive me? I thought she'd forgiven me today, I'd hoped ..." Billy stood and made strong coffee for the both of them. Handing Josiah a mug, he noted the defeated look on the doctor's face.

"Perhaps she still is very much the girl you knew, but she's hardened her heart to avoid further pain with what can hurt her most. With the man who can hurt her most," Billy offered gently. Josiah nodded his head gravely. Putting his hand on Josiah's shoulder, Billy tread carefully with his next words. "You saw her response to me today, Joey. She looked as though I were a lion come to eat her up. She had no answer for me, brother." Again, Josiah nodded gravely.

"I saw. Mayhap that is where my attention should be, eh, Preacher?" Josiah offered with a humble shake of his head.

"Aye, my friend. But in time I believe you can win the lass. You're only a little ugly after all," he said, lightening the mood considerably.

Billy chuckled together with Josiah over the affectionate slight. "I've thought so long I was doing pretty well at life, though loneliness has haunted me many a year in thinking her gone. And now to the one person I want to think well of me, I'm naught but a cruel monster," Josiah said with no small amount of pain in his voice.

"Ah, Joey. Don't let your heart be troubled or afraid. You know the scriptures. The Lord has brought her back to you, hasn't he? He has a design for this all. You just must be patient. Show your true self to her in every way you can, and expect nothing back. You'll win her heart sooner with patience than with another apology. She heard your apology today, or she'd not have come, eh? Take time with her. Be gentle. And let the Lord do the rest." Billy grinned kindly at Josiah, and Josiah clapped him on the arm. Billy reached to hold his shoulder again and bowed his head to pray over the matter. As he said amen, he noted the peace that seemed to settle over the doctor's face. He was a good lad, not so much younger than he, but Billy was proud of the boy, nonetheless, in a fatherly way. He'd not missed the loneliness in every kind act of the doctor. He wished him to be happy and content, and prayed it would be so.

Iness came into the room quietly bearing blankets and pillows. "Stay here with us tonight, Dr. Cairns," she said sweetly in her Irish lilt. "There's pouring rain and two dock fires, and it's downright gotten cold, it has." Nodding his head and thanking her, he accepted the blankets and pillows and stretched his frame along the couch, throwing his arm behind his head.

He heard the house settling around him, the only remaining sound the crackling fire. A short while later, he fell into a deep, exhausted sleep. His last thought was of Adeleine's face as she'd held Timmy close that afternoon.

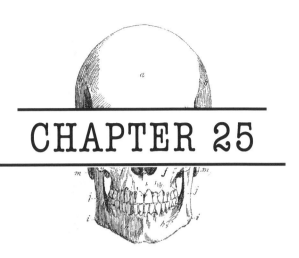

CHAPTER 25

*H*e'd watched the probationer and Dr. Cairns for some time. The connection between the two fascinated him, though he'd not been able to decipher it. The girl Adeleine had had no season in London and seemed to have no family so far as he'd seen. It was as though she had just suddenly dropped into London from the sky. The girl looked to be no older than eighteen or nineteen, but in some way, he felt she must be older. Strange thing, that. How could she be unmarried if she was, indeed, older? It made no sense, as she truly would have been so called "diamond of the first water" had she had a season. How had no man snagged her, regardless?

Of course, he'd already seen her at work nursing the sick and destitute on her shifts, the care and compassion she always gave. But seeing her with children spun into his gut like rotted fish. She rocked them, held their grubby nasty hands, sang to them. She gathered them into her arms in her fancy dress no matter the blood or filth ground into the rags they wore. His mother's face rose before him and set him into a fevered rage. He wondered about the girl's own mother, if she had one, if she'd been cared for as she'd cared for these street urchin brats these hours past. He spit at the ground and turned away with a sneer on his face.

The girl had seen him on the street, and he'd watched her face as she tried to make the connection to who he was. The doctor had lifted a man out of a shabby cart just then who appeared to be in a great deal of pain and walked through, giving him time to melt into the throng. Still he watched. The doctor had helped the girl into his carriage in a bit of a hurry, likely to be sure she met curfew at the school. The carriage door had been open to his view, and he'd smirked as the doctor kissed the girl's bare wrist. Oh, that wouldn't have done in front of the viperous ton, now would it?

The doctor himself had watched her for hours same as he. He'd spent much of the time with an idiot grin on his face as he laughed, working alongside her. It was as if … as if the doctor were in love with her! But the doctor was a titled peer of the realm, and she was … was what? She had quality about her, to be sure. He'd figure that one out, by and by! He must find the connection before the curiosity drove him mad. But the girl talked to no one, still was alone most of the time. The mood this afternoon had been quite different, indeed, from the spectacle of this morning, when the doctor had tried to speak to her before she bolted. As he'd watched the girl for months, he knew she never had taken a Thursday "courting day" before. She usually walked about the hospital, disappearing to her room, he guessed, as the Thursdays wore on. He'd never seen her hop into a carriage fancied up like the other probationers, to be sure.

After she'd left, things had taken a turn. The man the doctor had carried in had begun to scream and writhe on the table, clutching desperately at the doctor's arms until they bled from the man's nails. The fool preacher had sent a messenger to fetch his hackney, and they'd loaded the injured man and left together. Surgery likely at the closest hospital, he thought, as St. Thomas' was a longer drive. He wondered at the injury and assumed a bad break or, worse, if the doctor couldn't handle it here.

As night fell, the doctor and girl left his thoughts. The summer weather had gone quite suddenly, and he'd not dressed for the chill tonight. Hours of stinging rain tormented him, battering his face and freezing his hands. Yet he could not be cooled. The night sky blazed red from a fire not far off, and the color provoked his lust for blood. And so he waited and watched.

The prostitute Polly was deep in her cups, reeking of gin. He'd watched her in her filthy escapades for hours, and even heard her shameless remarks about having made her doss money thrice. Disgusting vermin she was! As she got closer to Buck's Row, he followed her openly. As she got into Buck's Row, he gave a low whistle.

Walking up alongside her, he fell into step with her. As they neared a stable door, he stepped in front of her. She looked at him dully, drunk with gin and stinking of the streets. "Take what you'll 'ave, chap. It's cold, ain't it, though?" she said. Glaring at her through the black slits of his eyes, he smashed his fist hard into her jaw and savored the satisfying crash of bone on flesh and the click of her yellow teeth as they bit into her nasty tongue. Before she could cry out, he wrapped his hand like an iron band around her jaw, sinking his fingers deep into the flesh. He shoved her head into the wall behind them with a thud and then wrapped both hands around her throat. As he squeezed harder and harder, he thrilled at her struggle, as she kicked and clawed desperately. Finally, he could no longer feel the thrum of blood through her veins, and so he threw her to the ground. Dropping to his knees beside her, he pulled his knife. The smoky haze enveloped him, caressing him. Calling to him. Yanking the top of her hair to lift her chin, he used his free hand to carve into her throat, but the first cut didn't fill his need. Pulling the knife away, he plunged it further down into the throat and continued the cut all the way round to the opposite ear. He relished the feel of the blade nicking into the tissues and bone, the slow draining of blood from her throat. She deserved to be punished. The hot black liquid silk spread through him, pulling him higher and higher into the throes of his dark madness. Leering with glee, he pulled her skirt all the way up, exposing her belly. She was a cleaner whore than most, he thought. He plunged the blade and dug it into the low belly, wondering if she'd had children—used them, abused them, wasted them. The thought sent him further into rampage, fueling his passion. He brought the blade roughly up through the viscera to the sternum, nearly the breast, spilling the bowels so they protruded from the gaping maw. Stabbing and cutting until he breathed hard, he rocked back onto his haunches finally as the smoke cleared and his eyes focused. Coming back down to earth after the throbbing sense of completion, he made to stand but found his legs weak with the exertion he'd spent.

Finally, he rose, pulling the muslin from his pocket, wiping the blade carefully, and letting the stained scrap flutter to the ground. He didn't bother with pulling her skirts down, for what dignity had she? He breathed in deeply the scent of blood, rain, and fire, and vanished into the night.

CHAPTER 26

$\mathcal{A}$s Adeline awoke the following morning, she felt a sense of foreboding settle about her like heavy damp wool. Trying to shake it off, she indulged in remembering the previous day in flashes. As she did, she felt sparks of joy lighting within her, and yet some things gave her pause. Considering again the matron's last words last night, she lay back and considered what dream she should fight to grasp. She was close to completing her time here, and certainly becoming a nurse had been her longest-standing dream. Or had it? Josiah seemed to have been with her all her life. A dream of forever, of restoration. A dream of a warm future where she was no longer alone. It had become tattered and worn as the years unfolded, faded. Still she'd dreamed it even as she fought to forget.

She supposed then that, in honesty, she must have come into a girlhood crush on Josiah that last summer and that, indeed, in the times she'd thought of him in the years since, she'd rather built him up as more than a boy or man. She'd built him into a fairy tale, infallible and perfect. The prince that would someday sweep her off her feet. And he certainly had at first, that is until he pulled the rug from beneath her—until he'd harangued her so viciously. And yet she faced that, in seeing his dear face, she'd rather forgotten that he was human and had feelings and perhaps dreams of his own, tattered as hers.

As the matron had shared her story last night, Adeleine had been given much to ponder. She thought just now of what she may need to be forgiven if she were to be fair, and the grief Lady Joanna had briefly described Josiah suffering came to mind. She'd been a child and frightened of rejection from both her family and the Cairns', but the right thing to do, indeed, may have been to contact them all. She thought over what changes may have occurred in her life, where she may be today. And yet she loved John and Christine and couldn't imagine her life without them. Pushing her blankets away and rising, she considered offering Josiah an apology for letting the heartache of her death rest upon him unabated. It was the least she could offer. And perhaps it would help her to heal to simply and sincerely forgive *him.* Could she?

Washing and getting into her nursing uniform, she thought back to the children she'd cared for yesterday. Perhaps she could offer the same when she returned to Grayson, there in the very village where Papa had doctored. What a joy that would be. Her mind finally came to rest on something she'd not been able to articulate in her head or heart, and that was the very fact that the dream of returning home to Grayson did not complement her fractured dream of Josiah. If she had to choose between her beloved Grayson or London and Josiah's love, she'd have once chosen him. And yet she could not say the same thing with certainty at this point. The matron's description of Josiah's thoughts toward her still seemed far-fetched, if not downright unbelievable. Still she hoped some small part of it could be true. She determined that she would approach him after discussion this morning and attempt to find words to convey her sorrow at his heartache these long years, if he would hear it after her refusal to aid him in surgery last night. Finishing her morning ablutions, she made her way to the dining hall.

The roar of noise was both strange and alarming. The probationers were talking so loudly, and many had a strange fear in their faces. "Adeleine, Adeleine!" a fellow probationer all but cried, shoving a newspaper into Adeleine's hands. "Look at the news in the Echo. It's horrible! A woman was killed in Whitechapel just hours ago, and—and ripped apart!" Sure enough there in the paper was the murder described in sickening detail. Adeleine's stomach lurched. Another probationer busted through the dining hall doors without an ounce of grace to her stride, loudly proclaiming the Pall Mall and Daily had news as well, waving both in her hand. One girl with a paper grasped in hand had begun gagging, her face gone pale and eyes glazing over. The matron arrived and immediately had the poor girl removed, calling for order and silence immediately. As the girls quieted, Adeleine noted that the matron sought her out with her eyes and gave a brief nod toward her. She nodded back. The matron began speaking, and silence took hold of the room. Once all the chittering had stopped, Adeleine noticed the pale and flushed faces, the hands gripped tightly together and tears on a few cheeks. If she was not mistaken, this was the second murder in Whitechapel in just weeks.

A strange feeling of distress came over her. *Whitechapel.* How often was Josiah there? Was he often there into the night as last night? The details of the use of his practice skipped across her mind, and she felt gooseflesh rising on her arms.

"Ladies, our bearing as nurses relies greatly on how we react to sudden trauma, to ghastly circumstances that come unexpectedly to our door. That said, this murder *is* particularly horrifying, but I ask that you keep your dignity in discussing these events. Dr. Cairns has been kept from us today, and few patients line the wards. You may have school hours off today, but do not be tardy to your shifts, or your grades will be docked. You are dismissed."

A chill passed over her again. *Dr. Cairns has been kept from us today.*

As the probationers filed out, they began quietly chattering again, and once they entered the halls, the noise was back to fever pitch. The matron clapped her hands severely and, in an icy tone, reminded the probationers that they walked a hospital, not a home for wayward girls. Adeleine felt her eyebrow twitch and nearly laughed aloud, but the matron heading straight for her silenced her. Looking up at her as she approached the table where Adeleine sat, she noticed a fevered bit of color on the matron's face. When she stood before Adeleine, Adeleine rose to her feet and dipped her head respectfully.

The matron put her hand urgently on Adeleine's forearm. "I need an errand run, and you are the only choice," she said quickly, almost stumbling over the words. "Change into the plainest frock you have. Don't bother overmuch with your hair. Leave it as it is, in fact. I need you to go to visit Lady Joanna Cairns, and don't leave until you've seen Dr. Cairns is well." At Adeleine's confused expression, the matron said, "I've not heard a word from him today. He's an hour past the time he typically arrives, and his own driver came here looking for him. The coachman Johnson awaits you outside the east entrance. Please go now, make haste, and take diligent care for your safety." Adeleine gave a loose nod of her head, figuring if this was asked of her, she would do it. The urgency and worry in the matron's tone filled her with apprehension. She hurriedly went to her room to change. Her brown wool day dress would have to do. Quickly, she changed into the dress and brown leather boots; and leaving her hair coiled at her nape, she donned her cloak and plain brown velvet Shirley. She hastily made for the east wing.

As she approached the doors, again the sense of danger jangled along her spine. Catching sight of Johnson, she waved him down and stood waiting for the carriage. As the conveyance came to a stop before her, Johnson jumped down to help her up the steps and into the carriage. "To Dr. Cairns'?" he asked. She nodded, and noting the strange expression on his face, concern, perhaps a little fear besides, she gave a shiver.

What strange tidings today, she thought.

And, suddenly, the twisting, sickening thought crossed her mind in full context. Josiah and dissections, his very private practice, his unknown whereabouts … his vicious temper months ago … could he be the murderer? Chills spread over her body, and gooseflesh rose on her arms again. What did she know of him after all? Fourteen-year-old memories were all she had to go on. What if his doctoring was an elegant cover? A farce? Or a perverse hobby of sorts? She felt her blood curdling in her veins and fought to keep herself dignified as the matron had admonished. Nevertheless, the overwhelming sensation of doubt in the man and pure terror gripped her with cruel force.

As Johnson helped her down when they arrived, Adeleine thought to ask if he knew the Cairns' to take the paper. "Yes, Lady Ashton. It should be round shortly, Miss," he said. It was barely eight o'clock in the morning, and much of the street was still and quiet. As she approached the door, Ellison opened it wide and greeted her warmly. "No sign of him at the hospital, then?" he asked imploringly. Shaking her head, she told him the matron had sent her to inquire about him here. "We've not seen him yet. Strange, indeed, for Lord Cairns," Ellison said, shaking his head slightly. "He works late off and on, and a few weeks back didn't arrive until the wee hours. But never has he not returned at all." At his words, she thought surely she'd swoon thinking of the other murder a few weeks past … It couldn't be! Could it? She tried to swallow the lump in her throat but couldn't dislodge it.

Could he have killed her *there in Whitechapel?!* She fought desperately to quiet her nerves. Following Ellison down the hall, Adeleine situated herself at the dining table to wait for Lady Joanna to come down to breakfast.

When a short time later Lady Joanna made her way down the stairs, Adeleine rose from the dining table, reaching to grasp her hands as she came close. "My darling, what brings you here this morning? Is everything all right? Does Josiah know you're here?" Lady Joanna asked, eyebrows raised high on her lovely face. As Adeleine tried to determine what to say, the front door swung wide, and Josiah's jovial voice boomed down the hallway.

"What's for breakfast? Mother dear, I'm so sorry I failed to reach you last eve—" His voice cut off abruptly as he turned into the room and saw his mother's hands clasped with Adeleine's before him. How irresistible she looked even in brown tweed, her jaunty hat setting off her darling features. The curves of her beautiful shape in her stylish dress struck him dumb. He shook his head to clear it.

"Did you never return home last night, son?" Lady Joanna asked quizzically, her mouth agape. He appeared to think over his response, and the corners of his mouth seemed to fight the tug of a grin.

"I did not, Mother mine. I traipsed about town all night, getting myself into horrendous mischief."

"Why, you trifling curmudgeon! Whatever shall I do with you," She laughed. "Now. Quit your teasing. I believe Adeleine was sent here due to some distress at the hospital this morning," his mother responded, a grin lighting her face, nonetheless.

"I was due there certainly, and I really must get a message relayed to the matron immediately," he said in a serious tone. Just then there was a knock at the door, and the driver, Johnson, was received by Ellison. Ducking his head in greeting to the strange crowd before him, he handed Adeleine the morning paper that had just come. "This is what you were speaking of, I believe, my lady," he said, releasing a nervous pent-up breath and handing Adeleine the paper. Seeing the horrid story again there in black and white on another paper, she swallowed again at the lump of fear in her throat.

Handing the paper to Josiah, she said quietly, "What do you know of this, *Doctor*? Where have you been?"

There was a pall hanging in the air, Josiah thought. Seeing the color in Adeleine's cheeks and her fevered expression, he wondered what she'd so boldly just referred to in questioning his whereabouts.

Taking the paper in both hands, the expression on his face darkened as he read the story of the ghastly murder in Whitechapel. She watched his face harden, the muscles of his jaw tightening into a fierce grimace. He gave her an incredulous look that brimmed with something akin to ferocity. Turning the page back and forth as he came to the end of the story, he walked the three or four steps to the table and slammed the pages onto the wood surface, leaving his hand on top of them for a few moments. When he turned back to them, his voice was icy, and he was quite obviously fighting for control. His eyes blazed hotly at Adeleine, but in turning to his mother, he softly explained, "Yesterday evening, I realized the hour was approaching for Adeleine's curfew at the hospital. I brought her with me to the clinic there in Whitechapel. She seemed to have a wonderful time helping me to doctor the little ones." He paused there, looking at Adeleine in such a way that her veins ran cold. Meanwhile, his mother smiled helplessly between them, no fool, but not realizing what veiled accusation Adeleine had just made.

"Right as she was about to leave, a man was carted in by his son and other boys with a badly broken leg. As my carriage left bearing her alone, I realized I'd need to take the man to St. Thomas' because he required surgery. Billy Stevenson offered to take us in his hackney, and so we left no more than twenty minutes after she did. When we arrived, I'd hoped Adeleine would assist, but she could not." He looked at her pointedly before he continued. "Once the surgery was finished, I'd missed Johnson at the hospital as he'd no doubt left to return to Whitechapel. I returned with Billy to his home there, and I imagine Johnson had left again by then, thinking to return here as the clinic was closed up before we left.

"Johnson, is that about right?" he asked the man.

"Yes, m'lord, exactly right. I came back here last night and left early this morning to reach the hospital hoping to catch you to plan for the day as you arrived at your usual time, but didn't see you. I went in and spoke to the matron, asking if she'd heard from you, but she had not. She was worried, so she asked me to bring Lady Ashton here to see if we could find out your whereabouts and see that you were safe."

Josiah ran his hand back through the mess of waves that had fallen over his brow. "Well, it appears I've worried everyone unnecessarily. Johnson, I appreciate your thoroughness. I do apologize. Please do have a bite to eat, and convey a message to the matron quickly and return with haste to return us there again to the hospital.

"Mother, I spent a while sparring with Billy last night after I'd finished with that patient, and afterward, we talked late into the night. With the shift in the weather, the rain, and dock fires burning, Iness invited me to spend the night there instead of going out into the mess. And I simply slept late, foolish as it sounds. I just arrived in Billy's hackney and sent the driver back home. As soon as I eat something, I'll clean up and head to the hospital. I'll return Adeleine there, as well, of course." Looking at her, he went to stand by his mother and bent to kiss her forehead and whisper in her ear. She gave him a soft smile and nodded. Clearing his throat, Josiah pulled a chair for his mother, then for Adeleine. "Sit," he growled at her shoulder almost imperceptibly. Johnson made his way to the kitchen to grab a bite before leaving, and Ellison brought several trays to the table where Josiah had just been seated. Adeleine removed her hat slowly, considering Josiah's true whereabouts. If they, in fact, were true … he'd not lie to his mother, would he? Gathering his mother's hand, he offered a short but sincere prayer of thanks. Adeleine watched him, her stomach in knots. Surely, he'd have come to have blood about his clothing, wouldn't he? He yet wore his clothing from yesterday. It vexed her in the extreme that her heart dared realize he hadn't taken *her* hand.

As he said amen, he and Lady Joanna gathered sausages and toast, jam, and boiled eggs. She reached for a sweet roll. Eating nervously, she wondered at the convivial banter between Josiah and his mother. How dear it seemed between them. Fighting to swallow past the burgeoning tightness in her throat, she reached for the teacup Ellison had placed before her. Tasting the deep delicious flavor and realizing what it was, she nearly choked, torment crossing her features as the irony gripped her. Chocolate! Josiah looked at her through narrowed eyes, and seeming to realize what it was that bothered her, he felt his eyebrows rise. He hurried to finish his food and, with his mouth full, admonished Lady Joanna to stay home today. "A murderer's afoot," he drawled, all the while piercing Adeleine with a fathomless look.

Lady Joanna squeezed his hand while shaking her head, her smile bright with affection for her son.

CHAPTER 27

Coming to stand before Adeleine after their meal, Josiah said, "I'd have a word." Not waiting for a response, he grasped her arm softly. Unsettled from her chair, she allowed him to steer her to his study door. Ellison had reached it just before they did and unlocked it quickly.

"A fire?" Ellison asked.

Josiah shook his head and said, "No, thank you. We won't be here long enough for your trouble, Ellison. Leave the door open please."

Still grasping her arm, he left her at the chair she'd used once before and went to sit at his desk. "Won't you sit?" he asked in a markedly chilly tone. The sense of foreboding covered her like a wet blanket again, but she found her traitorous self lowering into the chair. She perched there uncomfortably, ready to bolt. She'd walk back to St. Thomas' if she must! Placing his elbows on the desk, he steepled his fingers together. He seemed to be considering what to say carefully as he stared into her face. The skin over one cheekbone was split and bruised. Where his shirtsleeves were rolled up, his skin was nearly shredded with scrapes and scratches, and bruised besides. He said he'd slept late, but he looked exhausted. The overwhelming sense of unease lingered in the forefront of her mind.

"Why wouldn't you come to assist me in surgery last night?" he asked softly. Staying silent, he watched her and waited for her response. She stood nervously and began to pace in front of his desk, building her courage as she fought to speak without fear. She was tired of hiding and of running from whatever she lacked by his estimation.

"Because I didn't care to. Because I ... because I don't know what to think of you and what to believe of you. I don't know who you really are, and I don't wish to fall prey to you again!" There, she'd said it. The disbelieving glint in his eyes was one thing, the wounded look quite another. He stared silently a few torturous moments more at her before speaking again.

"As to your earlier comments in presence of my mother and staff, do you wish me to believe that you suspect me of the heinous crime within that newspaper? Is that how low I am in your esteem?" he asked quietly. His voice was like a scalpel, cold and thin and razor-sharp. He ran both hands through his hair slowly as though trying to calm himself.

Adeleine lifted her chin in challenge. "You flayed me alive in this very room months ago. And then you came yesterday to apologize so sweetly, a different man altogether. You invite me to help with your clinic, something obviously important to you. You stand grandly before me a hero to your throng of patients. So charming, asking me about bygone memories, making a picnic basket with my favorite flower. And yet today the matron comes to me obviously distressed because you didn't come in. Your driver doesn't know where you are. When you finally come around, your face is battered and bruised. Your forearms are scratched deeply as though by someone struggling and frenzied. You are clearly exhausted with dark circles below your eyes, and yet you talk of sleeping late. You've acted completely out of character to all who know you. Your driver, your mother, the matron. You cut people up for what is it, *research*? You cut people up in our anatomy class. And now this morning a woman is killed, cut up, while you're unaccounted for. What am I to think? How do I know I wasn't your intended victim? Are you the man everyone else knows, or the monster I've met?" she argued breathlessly, she herself shocked at her accusation. She stood staring at him, her eyes wide and cheeks flushed.

Josiah had held his head in his hands during her diatribe, and now no matter how hard he fought to avoid it, he felt himself coming unhinged. The *nerve* of the woman! He stood slowly, turning to stare into the cold fireplace, wanting badly not to repeat his grievous prior mistakes. He'd never been given to temper, nor raising his voice. Never had impassioned vitriol clawed to spew from him except in presence of *her.* Turning back to her, he splayed both hands onto his desk, leaning toward her. It was a struggle to form words. Standing before him so achingly beautiful, her eyes throwing sparks and hair waving about her face, he wanted to just grab her and kiss her. Curse it all! Still he felt his body trembling with fury. Gritting his teeth, he glared into her face several moments, and suddenly he shouted, "How *dare* you?" She jumped but glared back into his face and stood her ground.

"I look to save people, to better their treatments!" he spat. "I pay to bury every cadaver I use for my research, never mind that they'd have been thrown into little more than ditches if not for my care. I give them a way to speak after death, even after suicide, to help others with the information they give to me." He took several rapid breaths, indignation flashing in his eyes. "Yes, I dissect cadavers for you probationers to learn and to discuss details you'd not know otherwise. There are enough charlatan doctors out there, enough nurses who know little of nothing. I am committed to giving tools to nurses so that they are as aware as doctors of their patients. And you'd *mock* me?" he exclaimed. "You'd *belittle* what I do? You'd consider for one moment that I could *kill*? That I would share my heart, my clinic with you, as a diversion to *murder* you? Adeleine, take a hard look in the glass. Perhaps *you* are not what I thought you to be!" he ground out, slapping his desk furiously. Turning away from her, he struggled to control his breathing, to control the burning anger crashing over him. How *could* she?

Adeleine stomped her foot and released a shriek from deep in her throat of frustration. "Yes, and what is *that*, Josiah? What is it that you *thought* me to be? Please do tell me, because I don't think you were entirely clear before about my failings and shortcomings with you," she sneered behind him.

He barked out a bitter laugh. "Ah, what do I think you to be, Adeleine? Good question, indeed, and I'll tell you. I'll tell you exactly what I *thought* you to be!" he shouted again. She swallowed hard, wondering what on earth she'd invited in challenging him.

Laughing again, not so much bitter as pained, he started thickly, running his hand over his face and through his hair. "From the time I was a child, I adored you. The tone of your hair, the color of your eyes. I thought you so unique, wonderful for your differences to other vapid, shallow girls. So incredibly smart, with such heart to match. The way you made me laugh and think about life, though I was some four years older, amazed me. The way you trusted me, shared things with me. That last summer, I didn't quite understand the betrothal, didn't entirely understand what it all meant. But as we left to come back here to London, I realized I wanted it very much. I couldn't imagine any girl but you in my life as my wife one day. I imagined us like my parents or yours, doting on one another. Loving one another." He shook his head bitterly.

"Then, suddenly, I had to accept that you were dead and gone from me forever, and from a disease that on and off had been conquered. It made me reel with frustration and confusion, the unfairness of it all. And so I got into medicine, wanting to be a doctor like your papa but, more so, a researcher. An innovator, someone who could move the science of healing along. But still none of it could bring you back. All that I am today I became in my heartache over *you*, Adeleine. Over you. And still none of it could ever bring you back to me, nor heal my broken heart. It didn't matter. You were gone." He dropped exhausted into his chair, the fire gone out of him.

Letting his head fall back, he rubbed his eyes with agitation and choked out another sorrowful laugh, throwing his arms wide. "Then, suddenly, I come home one night, and my mother is arm in arm with someone I can't place.

But your laughter, it rolls over me like a wave. I can't comprehend it. And then I hear mother say your name, and you both laugh, and your heads fall back onto the sofa, and I recognize the color of your hair, and I'm struck senseless. I run away here to my study, but, suddenly, you're here. Standing right in front of me, alive, and so beautiful. So precious, *breathing, alive!* And all those stored-up feelings, all those aching memories, they're all buzzing about me, and I can't reason or think. I have to hold you. I have to be sure you're *real.* I was struck by your expression, by your calling me Joe. I lost my wits. I kissed you. I wanted more, more than I had any right to ask, so I forced myself away, ashamed of my actions.

"Suddenly, I thought again of your bubbling laughter and how joyous it sounded, has always sounded to me. And then ruthless anger hit me. Anger that you allowed me to suffer all those years, that you'd been that cruel to me, to all of us. While somewhere you'd lived and laughed. Perhaps loved another."

Putting his head into his hands, he let out a long ragged sigh. "Since then I've realized how hard it must have been for you and thought you so brave to have fought to survive, and I understood why you'd feel as if you'd never belong again with any of us. Why you'd feared that we'd reject you. I tried so hard to reach you after that night. I knew I'd hurt you so deeply. I thought that somehow surely I could reach my Addy, the girl I've loved forever. If only she could forgive me."

Her mind and heart caught and hung on those words, her emotions swirling within her. *The girl I've loved forever.*

He continued, his tone breaking. "But that girl I once knew and held so dear is no longer there when it comes to me. I watch you nursing others with such care, with such understanding and compassion. I hear your laughter and see your bright spirit as you lift up others. And I long for that toward myself. I long simply for your forgiveness. I long to be trusted for who I was to you before. I think you are gifted with others, with the art of healing. Yet you'll allow no healing for me. You'll give me no reprieve from my awful fit of anger. I've tried to tell you how sorry I am, to freely admit my awful error. I thought perhaps you'd forgiven me yesterday as we laughed and worked together. Yet today you accuse me of murder. Murder! You ask what I think of you, who I think you to be, Adeleine? I think the truth is, you have broken my heart more alive than you ever did dead."

He rose and walked to the window overlooking the now bustling streets, clasping his hands behind his head. He could feel his eyes welling. He couldn't bring himself to look upon her. He felt so much drain from him, from the last several months, years. Hearing a small cry, he turned to her.

She raised her chin and looked him squarely in the eyes, her own glistening. Gesturing with her own arms held wide in consternation, she cried, "You're right, Josiah. I have realized that my actions were not necessarily the best in years past. I *did* finally learn to laugh again, and to love. But as I grew older and still longed for everyone here, I felt, even if I gathered the courage to reach out, it was too late." She came to stand before him at the window. "Do you think I didn't dream of you, too, Josiah? Do you think I didn't pine for years, consider for years coming to you?

Do you think that I didn't still have the devotion of a silly little girl when I came here months ago, when I stepped into this study of yours? You stared and stared at me, and it was as though I was so much damaged goods. When you kissed me, it was so brief, so wonderful, but I felt rejected and shoved aside when you broke it off. I understand now that you did it to be honorable, but I couldn't see that until just last night. You butchered me, Josiah. You ripped my heart from my chest that night, and you say *your* heart is broken …? You mocked our memories. You … you made that disgusting reference to my supposed response to your own father's death—"

He grasped her shoulders then and cried, "Please forgive me for every word, Adeleine. It sickens me that I said such things. And I know you loved father dearly—"

She put her hands up to stop him. "I realized something yesterday while returning to the hospital. I realized that all the tenderness between us is based in the past. I don't know you, and you don't know me today any better than the strangers out there in the streets." She nodded her head toward the window. He gazed at her, feeling a new thread of mutual understanding winding through him suddenly at her words. "If there is to be anything else after today, I must feel I know you, Josiah. The person you've become. I've seen glimpses, but I want to know the man you are without doubt, without hurt feelings. All that you are, all that I am, has been built of our scars, in our years away from each other. Don't you see? We are not the children we remember. Those parts of us are still there, but we are not those children any longer." She swayed, stepping between one foot and the other, and withdrew her eyes from his face.

"I am sorry I wasted those years. I am so truly sorry for the pain I caused you." She plucked at her dress nervously, and bringing her hand to her face, she pressed her fingers to her lips. "I have never bothered to love any other, Josiah. Your kiss was my first." His heart pounded at her words even as he watched her face flush crimson with fascination. "And I am ashamed ... I ... I'm sorry my mind immediately coupled you with the awful death meted out to that poor woman ... I should never have insinuated such a thing against you. Please forgive me," she said plaintively. She forced herself to look up into his eyes, feeling the tiniest ray of hope that there was a chance for them if they started anew with forgiveness. The intensity she found there was unnerving.

"Seems we've been stuck at an impasse, doesn't it? Both thinking we are nothing to the other when, in fact, that couldn't be further from the truth," Josiah said huskily. He ran his fingertips delicately down the curve of her cheek, tucking an errant strand of hair behind her ear.

"I want all that you are, past and present, Adeleine. And I beg your forgiveness for my cruelty. And beg you for the chance to show you I am not that angry, insensitive, raging fool. Just yesterday it also occurred to me that I wanted to look into your eyes and know the woman looking back at me as she is today," he said, not hiding his emotion. A single tear rolled down her face as she gazed up at him, and for once, she didn't try to push the proof of her emotions away.

He took her hand and brought her fingertips to his lips, kissing them gently. At her soft gasp, he looked intently into her eyes. Holding his hands up before her, he waited for her to press her hands to his. As she did, he intertwined their fingers and gently brought his forehead down against hers. Feeling her breath fanning his face, he smiled and said, "You are no damaged goods to me, Addy. I think you are the most exquisite woman, and nurse, in all of London and beyond. It would bring me such joy to know my Addy again." As he pulled back, they stared into each other's faces, emotions raw, not hiding tears or intensity from one another. He finally drew her close and held her warmly.

She encircled his waist with her arms, and feeling safe and warm with his strength surrounding her, she allowed her long caged emotions to tumble out. "Oh, Josiah," she cried. "I'm so sorry you've grieved so deeply these years past. And I'd ever forgive you anything. Anything … But I cannot seem to forgive myself, not for your pain nor my family's … *nor for leaving everyone there at Grayson alone*," she barely choked out.

"Addy," he whispered, pulling her closer into a tight embrace. "There's naught to forgive. You were brave, and strong, and you've used all you suffered to love and bring healing to others," Josiah murmured into her hair. She allowed herself to break then. Her shoulders shook as she let the sobs roll from her, for wasted years, for his heartbreak and hers, her sorrow for her long-lost loved ones. All the pain she'd guarded against for years, that she'd cheated herself healing from in her struggle to be strong, she let it escape from her. And through all of it, he held her while he rocked her gently. His lingering cologne and warm masculine scent comforted her and somehow made her feel as though she'd returned home. As she calmed, she took a deep shuddering breath. He pulled a clean kerchief from his waistcoat pocket and dabbed her face gently.

Looking up at him, wondering at his nearness and the golden-brown warmth of his gaze, she found herself tracing the curve of his lips with her eyes. "Oh, Addy," he whispered. She felt her face begin to flush realizing what she'd done and started to pull away from him. A ripple passed through her as he tightened his arm about her waist and ran his fingers along her jaw. He bent to brush his cheek against hers and brought his hand to cradle the back of her neck. She sighed softly at the feel of his touch. Gently swaying them side to side, he murmured gently into her ear, "I could never reject or refuse you, my beautiful Adeleine. Rather I feel too much and would not dishonor you." She nodded her head briefly in understanding, and he began to release her.

"Josiah?" she said in a soft small whisper, tightening her arms about him.

"Hhhhmmm?" he said.

"The old memories are still precious to me," she said as she gazed at him, eyes alight. A tremor ran through her voice. He grinned as he returned his cheek to hers, his heart skipping a beat.

"Ah, yes. That they are. But you've surely been the ogre today, Addy." He laughed, swinging her in a circle and setting her down after softly kissing her cheek.

Swatting him and moving away, holding her nose, she said, "Get cleaned up, Doctor. You smell."

His baritone laughter followed her into the dining room, where she collected her hat and started to sit to await returning to St. Thomas'. She realized she was shaking, new emotions crashing over her, and considered the new beginnings that had come to pass this morning. She felt free, and she felt her heart was somehow hers as though all these years it had not been.

Lady Joanna called to her from the sitting room. "Come sit with me by this fire while my trifling rake of a son makes himself presentable," she said. Just then Adeleine realized surely their whole exchange had been heard by Josiah's dear mother. Feeling her face burn, Adeleine made her way to the sofa where Lady Joanna collected her to her side. Smiling widely, her eyes beaming, she placed her hand over Adeleine's warm cheek. She whispered, "You *were* brave as a girl, brave and beautiful as you are now. I know your mama and papa would be so very proud of you—both then and now. There is nothing to be forgiven, my darling. *You survived.* Oh, but I am so grateful the Lord has brought you back to us. I love you so, my dear Addy."

And for the first time she could remember, she believed the words and let them settle into her heart without a single doubt.

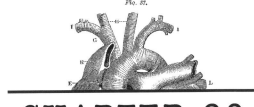

CHAPTER 28

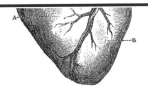

$\mathcal{S}$eptember had passed in a haze of Thursday afternoons and evenings. Picking Adeleine up shortly after classes had ended each Thursday had become the highlight of his week, and after their emotional exchange that Friday morning, he felt they'd truly forged a new bond. There was a certain harmony to their time together; an awareness, a sweetness. October had just blown in, and he excitedly, albeit nervously, anticipated asking her to accompany him to the masquerade charity ball just weeks away. He hated dressing up like a popinjay and having to tolerate the wagging tongues of the vain ton, and hadn't attended in years. But something about anticipating being arm and arm with her, or sweeping her into a waltz, caused shivers of delight to race through him. He shook his head and clucked his tongue at his ridiculous schoolboy antics. Grinning, nonetheless, he watched for her arrival at the doors of the hospital.

He was so pleased to surprise her again today as he had for her birthday, with her family over for dinner. The gruesome Whitechapel murder had fallen a week prior to her birthday, and another had taken place right after. Another two had come at the first of the month, more horrible for being two victims, seemingly within an hour of each other. The cruel and vicious killings had left the probationers rather chilled, and anatomy class and discussion had been strained. And so after even the first awful murder, he'd wanted Adeleine to feel treasured and cared for—anything but alone—on her special day. He'd wondered how birthdays had been for her in the years after her parents' deaths, and his heart ached for her.

Her birthday had started as soon as she stepped from her room, for he had left a bouquet of wildflowers at her door. A box of chocolates sat at her place at breakfast, and a beautiful lady's pocket watch sat wrapped in her usual place in the anatomy theatre. After discussion, he'd simply winked at her and disappeared. When she'd stepped into the carriage assisted by Johnson to visit the clinic, he'd surprised her again, already sitting there waiting for her. He gifted her then with her own set of nursing instruments, the leather chatelaine that contained them emblazoned with an *A*. His purpose behind the gifts was to spoil her but to also give her gifts that showed he cared deeply for her passion to nurse. Her thrill and excitement were bubbling with effervescence, and yet she seemed deeply touched and serious all the while. When they'd arrived in Whitechapel, he'd arranged for Timmy to grandly give her an invitation to a party later that day at Josiah's address. Her eyes had met Josiah's with a twinkle of affection. She had blushed furiously and finally wept as the children gave her hand-drawn notes and things they'd made for her, and before they'd left, she'd kissed each one. As they'd arrived at his townhome, she'd stepped from the carriage and brought her hand to her mouth in surprise. Her uncle and aunt, cousins and their families, the matron, and the Stevensons all stood at the steps to welcome her and wish her glad birthday tidings. They'd all stayed for dinner and games, and the time had been precious. Seeing her feel a part of something, as a special part of so many hearts, had been a joy to his very soul. Of course, tears had shone on her cheeks, and there was no small amount of love or laughter that sweet afternoon and evening.

He'd visited the clinic yesterday in preparation to miss today, as he wanted her to have a time of respite and time with her family. He knew she'd be disappointed, and yet he wanted to care for her tonight. To be to her what she was to others. The nursing session was ending soon, and her hours were long and arduous. He could feel the exhaustion in her, and something else too. A restlessness. A hunger? He tried to consider the aspects of mental and physical toil on her, and yet his heart thrummed with the knowledge that what she needed was so much more than any evening off he could plan for her.

She needed the strength only the Savior could give, and to find true peace and rest in him. He prayed as he often did for her then. He asked for the words that could help lead her to an understanding of a larger picture of her life, indeed, an understanding of a God who had designed her for his own wonderful purpose—and freely offered her his grace and love beyond all measure. Lost in his thoughts sitting on his carriage steps, he entirely missed her stepping through the doors of the hospital.

She stood still several moments watching him before coming to stand before him. He was deep in his thoughts, and she thought him so darling as he sat there, his arms casually settled on his knees. He looked somehow so boyish for what a striking man he was. His elegant but strong hands were loosely clasped, his waving hank of hair falling over his brow. Her hands fairly ached to brush it back by running her fingers through it as he so often did. Or to cup his jaw while she drank in his sparkling cinnamon eyes that were so dear to her. As she walked to him slowly, she caught just the moment he felt her presence and nearly giggled at his loss of composure, but his intense gaze drew her up short as he stood and intently looked down into her eyes. "Josiah? Are you quite all right?" she asked in a tone ever so slightly imbued with teasing.

"That I am, Adeleine, now you're here."

He grinned widely at her and reached for her hand. As she stepped into the carriage, he heard her delighted cry and chuckled. She'd found the lap robe he'd purchased for her just yesterday. "Oh, Joe! This is beautiful and feels so divine!" she said as she laid it about her. It looked as though it were made just for her in tones of green, gold, rust, and wine. Her eyes glittered as she squeezed the plush blanket in her hands.

"I can't have you cold on our days together, now, can I?" he asked, eyebrows waggling.

She laughed softly and shook her head. Looking down at the floor then back at him, she asked in a low voice, "Why are you so good to me, Josiah?"

"Don't you know?" he said just above a whisper. Giving a small shake of her head, she looked at him soberly, her teeth gently biting into her lip. "Well. I'll just have to tell you all about it later, won't I?" he murmured warmly.

Shaking off the charged air that was building, he thought it time to make his invitation. "Now, Addy, I've something to ask you. Beg of you really because I can't stay away another year, and if I go alone, well, you know how the tales and wagging tongues get going." He watched as she raised her eyebrow and nodded.

"Go on," she said.

"My lady Adeleine," he began in his most regal tone. "Would you honor and delight me, and protect me from viperous harm, by accompanying me to the medical charity masquerade ball end of this month? Of course, I shall protect you from every ardent suitor sure to seek to woo you," he teased lightheartedly. "Besides myself," he added, looking deeply into her eyes.

Her breath caught in her throat at his teasing. Was he flirting just then? But her stomach rolled within her at his request. "Josiah, I don't know. I've kept away from society at all cost … I just haven't the heart or courage for such things, you see?"

"Have you the heart for me, dear Adeleine? I've courage for us both," Josiah said softly, his eyes never leaving hers. He cleared his throat, realizing he'd said the words aloud. "Besides, it's a costume charity event, not a typical stuffy, uppity ball. Well, they're all utterly ridiculous, but at least we can laugh together at it all. What do you say? Please rescue me, Addy?" His eyes were soft, his face pleading.

"Allow me to think on it?" she asked him quietly just as they rolled up to the town house.

He nodded and smiled at her, moving past her. "Mother is expecting you, so do come in," he said with a gleam in his eye.

Sure enough, Lady Joanna stood at the window, waiting. As Adeleine stepped into the doorway, she immediately made out the sound of voices and laughter, and the scampering feet of her young second cousins. Looking from Lady Joanna to Josiah as he stepped into the doorway himself, she laughed and said, "Whatever are you two about? Such rascals you both are!" Stepping into the sitting room, she was greeted by her cousins and her aunt, as well as Iness and the little ones, who all ran to hug her and be picked up. She spun them around one by one, then went to join Dottie and the rest of the ladies. He said his hellos and ventured further toward the dining room, seeking Billy and her uncle Ben.

"Ah, come in, Doctor. Come in! We were just talking about you, you cur!" Billy said with amusement.

Meeting Benjamin's eyes, Josiah said, "I'm sure I deserved whatever you were bandying on about." Benjamin gave him what could almost be considered a shy smile and chuckled. "What say you gentlemen we move to my study and have a cigar, and leave the ladies to their amusement?" Josiah offered amiably. As the men nodded and stood up, Ellison led the way to his study. Going to speak to his mother, he came upon a pretty scene, the likes of which nearly squeezed his heart from his chest. In front of the hearth sat his mother and Adeleine, a child clasped in each lap, while Dottie read a story beautifully from the sofa. As his mother's eyes came to rest on his face, he motioned to his study, and she nodded. Looking to Adeleine, he felt his chest tighten as she held the tiny youngest of the cousins in her arms, rocking the babe and looking into her angelic face. The feelings it poured over him were almost too much to bear, and so he walked back to his study in a somber state of mind.

Moving into the study and making his way to his desk, he opened the fine box of cigars his father had given him just shortly before his death. Drinking in the fragrance, his throat tightened, and he felt his eyes prickle. The brand had been their favorite to enjoy together, and, indeed, he couldn't think of anyone he'd rather share them with now. Clearing his throat, he offered one to each fellow and took a seat.

"Say, Lord Ashton," Josiah started. "Might I speak a bit of personal business while Billy is here with us?"

"Certainly," Benjamin responded. Letting his head fall onto the back of his chair, he considered what to say a few moments and finally just said the bare honest truth.

"I want to marry her, if she'd have me," Josiah said, his voice rich with emotion.

"You know the betrothal yet stands, Josiah. In a way, you wouldn't have to wait for her to 'have you' as you say, but I think we all have seen how you adore her—how you love her, young man. So you'd prefer to ask her, I assume?" Benjamin said.

"That I would. And I am prepared to hold to all of her father's wishes. I know I have been difficult, and I hope you will accept my sincere and humble apology, sir."

Josiah let out a deep breath and looked into the man's face. He saw kindness there, and patience. Perhaps even the acceptance he longed for after having ignored the man so long and setting them at odds. He remembered the summers shared at Grayson and enjoying the man and his brother then, the fishing and horseback riding, laughing together, and running about the grounds. Adeleine's precious uncle and papa had been so dear to him too. "I suppose what I'm trying to say, sir, is from your perspective as her guardian, do you accept my suit of her? Would you give me her hand in her papa's place?"

He felt his skin warm with color and felt like a lad of sixteen or thereabouts for the foolishness and near embarrassment he felt, and yet it must be said. He wanted nothing less than to feel as family with the Ashtons. Benjamin took out his kerchief and blotted his eyes. "The fire's gotten to me, lads," he chuckled. Looking into Josiah's face, Benjamin cleared his throat and said "Josiah, it would be a pleasure and a privilege to do just that. I know your heart was broken just as all of ours were, and so I understand why you never would respond. This whole circumstance has been both remarkable and formidable. Months ago, I thought all was lost, and yet now I see our Addy coming to full bloom in your pursuit. And so I imagine once her studies are done, you could certainly seek her hand. One thing alone does concern me," Benjamin said gently. At Josiah's nod, he continued, "The matter of Grayson, and her love for the couple that raised her, John and Christine. Your business is here in London, and, of course, we are here. But I suspect the girl's heart is rather much there in Gloucestershire."

Josiah leaned forward, putting his elbows to his knees, his cigar long forgotten and grown cold. "I'd never deny her that," he spoke softly. "Many still have a country home after all outside of London. It's a few day's journey to get there, and so, of course, I wouldn't want her alone. But certainly it could all be worked out. I'd never ask her to give it up, nor would I want to give it up. I'm rather fond of Grayson myself." Josiah smiled, and relighting his cigar, he told the men then that he'd invited Adeleine to accompany him to the charity masquerade ball. They both whooped and chortled, and Benjamin slapped his knee with gaiety.

"You know, young man," he said, "the girl likely hasn't waltzed or anything of the sort since she was light on her papa's toes. Mayhap we should go gather our ladies and make sure she knows her steps." The man's face broke into laughter as he stood and patted Josiah's arm. Putting their cigars out, they made to leave the study.

Watching the two through their discussion that he knew must have been difficult for Josiah, perhaps difficult for both men, Billy thanked the Lord. He felt a lightness in his step and joy in his heart for both fellows. Ever the one to banter, Billy spoke up, "You've not said if the lassie answered you, Joey boy!" At Josiah's slack-jawed look, Billy smiled a hearty smile at Benjamin and slapped the boy's back. "You'll have to get her to say yes before we'll get her to dance!" Laughing, Billy made his way out, leaving Benjamin and Josiah standing alone.

The men faced each other, their eyes meeting with a look of compassion and grace, togetherness and shared memories. Benjamin extended his hand to brace Josiah's shoulder. "I am truly proud of the young man you've become, Josiah. Daniel spoke to me at length of your family and you yourself before the idea of betrothal was shared with your parents. As solicitor to Daniel, I drew up the papers and shared in much prayer with both our families before the ink ever dried. It's been a hard road laden with grief, but I can't help but feel an immense joy and satisfaction all these years later that things have finally come together. You're a good man, personally and professionally, and I'd be overjoyed to finally have you as family." Josiah's eyes glimmered even as the man's own eyes filled. As they both reached for their kerchiefs, chuckling together, Benjamin spoke up once more. "And Josiah? Let's dispense with these ridiculous niceties, shall we? Neither of us care a whit for titles or stuffiness. Call me Uncle Ben as Addy does, boy." He grinned at Josiah as Josiah smiled in agreeance.

"Yes sir, Uncle Ben," he laughed.

Coming down the hall together, they shared a speaking look hearing the boisterous Irishman's voice. "Come in, chaps," Billy boomed. "I was just telling these bonny lasses that Iness and I are going to the charity ball three weeks hence, and don't you know, it seems all of us are going but you, Joey boy! You must right this foolish blunder, lad. It won't do. It just won't *do* for a fine young doctor not to attend his own charity ball!"

Among the peals of laughter at his expense, he gazed as though utterly dejected at Adeleine. Coming over to stand beside him, she looked up into his eyes, her cheeks beginning to blush madly, and said sweetly, "Josiah, would you take me to the ball? I'd love ever so much to go."

At everyone's hoots and encouragement, he swept her off the floor, turning in a grand circle and setting her back down. Taking her hand and bending low over it, he kissed it and said, "Lady Ashton, I would be honored." Bending to her ear, he grumbled, "Imp."

She threw her head back and laughed, the sound running over him like sparkling water on a hot summer day. Turning to her loved ones, she sang out, "He asked me first, lest anyone find me too forward!" She looked up into his eyes again and nodded, making him feel for all the world like a king.

The afternoon passed with dinner and then much gaiety as everyone took turns reminding Adeleine of dance steps lost to her youth. The children sat on shoulders or stood on feet to learn to dance as well, for they'd not be left out of the fun.

As Josiah stood ready to return Adeleine to the hospital, he soaked in the happiness on her face and wished for all the world she'd come to love him as he loved her.

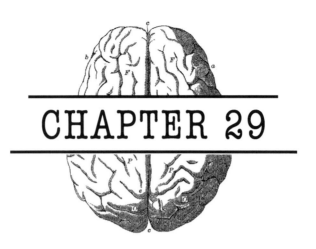

CHAPTER 29

$\mathcal{A}$deleine's room seemed strangely cold and sterile after the merriment of the evening. She sighed with happiness to think of her family. Lady Joanna's home had become a home to her of sorts these few weeks, and she didn't disparage it. It rather meant so much to her that she could hardly dare contemplate it. Learning the steps of the waltz tonight in her uncle Ben's arms had filled her with an incomprehensible feeling of elation.

Memories of summers and Christmases, and of being swept around the apothecary from time to time as she laughed with John and Christine, had coiled through her; she thought she'd burst into tears for several moments. Yet the thrill of the evening had somehow held her steady and kept her tears at bay. Aunt Dottie had made plans with her to pick her up the following Thursday to go to the modiste to complete plans for her costume for the ball and then to return to Lady Joanna's for dinner and more dance lessons. She giggled quietly into the silent room. Something seemed to have come back to her, for she took to the steps well, and both aunt Dottie and Lady Joanna had complimented her graciously. She shrugged a shoulder casually, feeling confident that the dancing would go all right. Being presented as it were to society is what kept her stomach atwirl.

She sighed, plunking down on her bed and uncoiling her braid. She eased it down, plucking pins as she went. Wondering at how long the braid had reached, she thought to ask Molly what could be done with it. Her headache was constant, the strain in her neck a daily discomfort. She only remembered it being cut once, and Mama had done it then. She both loved and hated her wayward tresses, but the time had surely come at five and twenty for something new. Loosening the braid, she brought her knees up and wrapped her arms about her legs.

Her thoughts skipped to the preacher Billy and his affection this evening. "I hear the cad has asked you to the ball, lassie. I fear his very heart will surely break if you don't ignore his ugly looks and go. He'll wear a mask after all," he'd said sweetly.

She'd let out a very unladylike snort of laughter, and that had brought everyone else in on the fun. Josiah's father had implemented the ball years and years ago, and yet Josiah had never cared for balls, she'd found out tonight. Finding out her loved ones would all be in attendance had given her ease to accept his invitation. Aunt Dottie and the girls had swept her up along with Lady Joanna and asked her what she'd like her costume to be. Upon her not having much to say on the matter, Aunt Dottie had brought her hands together with a bright smile. "Why, darling, you could be a woodland sprite, a shimmering autumn fairy!"

At this, all the ladies had burst into ideas for such a costume, complete with different colors of tulle and trailing leaves, and a mask of fern leaves, flowers, and butterflies. And by extension, Josiah would be given no detail but to incorporate leaves and the color deep green into his costume. It had sounded wonderful, and so Aunt Dottie would take the details to her modiste on the morrow to get the costume gowns started.

She returned to thoughts of the preacher Billy, and her mind flew a thousand directions and came to rest on the one thing she didn't care to consider: *"her eternal soul"* as he called it. Her sin that he said separated her from God for eternity if she didn't believe, didn't repent ... if she didn't believe God's Son, the sinless man Jesus, had died for her on a cruel cross to pay for her sin ... if she didn't receive him into her heart and life. Her mind raced on to the scripture he'd bellowed week to week, the kind way he'd asked her if she believed that first day in Whitechapel. She'd not had an answer, and so she knew he considered her an unbeliever, a lost soul. And yet his kindness remained. His wife, Iness, had befriended her, and, indeed, she looked forward to seeing Iness on every trip to the clinic. Sitting together with the sweet woman in her homey kitchen, she couldn't refuse her heart revisiting memories of sitting in her own mother's kitchen with dear Clara in years long gone. Iness's musical Irish lilt reminded her so of dear Helen's voice as she'd cooked together with mama, their laughter contagious and their devoted friendship always apparent to their girls.

Her uncle Ben came to mind then, as she remembered the cold day he returned her to Grayson and explained the reason for the scripture on her parents' grave. Suddenly, she remembered the small Bible given to her years before for a birthday or other occasion. She remembered sitting on Mama's lap tracing her finger under words as Mama read them to her. She'd brought it, not caring that she had it but feeling a connection to her parents because of it. She climbed from her bed and padded to the small armoire, and digging in the bottom drawer, she found it buried in the furthest corner.

As she climbed back onto the bed, the cover fell open. Holding tightly to it to keep from dropping it entirely, she pulled it into her lap. It was open to the book of Romans 5, and as her eyes skimmed the page, a portion of the scriptures stood out to her in stark relief.

> For when we were yet without strength, in due time Christ died for the ungodly. For scarcely for a righteous man will one die: yet peradventure for a good man some would even dare to die. *But God commendeth his love toward us, in that, while we were yet sinners, Christ died for us.*

Adeleine swallowed hard, somehow tasting tears. She lay back and stared at the ceiling, the light dim. She lay the Bible on her tiny nightstand and blew out the lamp. Wrapping in her blankets, she rolled onto her back to again stare at the ceiling. Thoughts of sin spiraled through her mind. What were hers? For years, she'd carried the weight of guilt and grief for having left Grayson, for leaving her loved ones lying in their deathbeds, alone and not laid to rest. But Josiah and Matron, Lady Joanna, and John and uncle Ben had almost convinced her she'd done no wrong in seeking to survive. She'd worked hard and with a loving heart to help John and Christine, and now Josiah. She tried to find faults in her life but could not, then thought that might itself be considered pride, but shook off the feeling, for she put no value to herself.

In a tiny voice, she whispered into the darkness, "God, you took my loved ones and left me to suffer. What sin am I guilty of? I've had naught but grief and turmoil in my life, yet I must repent to be near you. But it was you who forsook me." She burrowed deeper into her blankets, and she thought, *Show me whatever I have done makes me guilty before you.*

As her eyes began to drift closed, fear unfurled like smoke over her. A feeling of danger crouched within her, and her last thought was that surely she'd smother with the overwhelming sensation of it.

Waking the next morning, Adeleine felt as if she'd rested not at all. The nursing session about to come to a close was all running together in a big cacophony of classes, mealtimes, cleaning chores, prayer times, and nursing shifts. She admitted to herself then that she was bone tired. She wondered if she might send a note to Uncle Ben today and perhaps Josiah, too, to see if she may ask for conveyance to church and perhaps dinner Sunday. Writing the notes before she could change her mind, she signed and sealed them, hurried through washing and dressing, and headed to the dining room for breakfast. Dropping her notes into the mail, she had a moment of indecision where she considered digging them back out of the receptacle. Setting her shoulders, she forced herself away to breakfast.

Saturday morning, she received a note back from both gentlemen. Josiah would pick her up for church with Lady Joanna, and they would retire to the Ashtons' for Sunday dinner. She smiled in nervous delight, considering all that was coming to pass and finding her heart full.

Sunday arrived dark and gray, with thunder and rain. Still Josiah and his mother collected her full of gaiety. Josiah near took her breath in his Sunday suit, smelling wonderfully of his spicy cologne, and freshly shaved for once. His hair gleamed and stayed in place, framing his gorgeous face. She realized then she'd only seen him as a doctor or in common laborer clothes in Whitechapel. Catching her eyes on him, Josiah gave a low whistle and shook his head slowly at her. "I'm a beauty, am I not?" he cajoled. His mother swatted him.

"You are a brute! *She* is a beauty, you fool," Lady Joanna scolded. Collecting her hand in his and kissing it, he batted his eyes and said sweetly to her, "Ah, Mother mine, but you are the most beautiful of all." As they all burst into laughter, he caught Adeleine's eyes and smiled warmly at her, inclining his head toward her. She felt herself blush and turned to look from the window. Feeling his eyes on her, she glanced at him just long enough to catch him in a silly wink at her. Returning her eyes to the carriage window, she couldn't help a ridiculous smile from spreading across her face.

Church passed pleasantly all in all. She enjoyed the singing and meeting friends of the Cairns' and those of her aunt and uncle and her cousins. As she began to feel overwhelmed, Josiah led her to a pew while they waited for the Ashtons to be ready to leave. Taking a deep breath, she forced the courage to ask the question burdening her most. "Josiah? Constantly, these preachers fuss about how sinful we are. But …," she swallowed and whispered, "I'm not certain what mine are, what makes me so vile." He took a long pause, asking the Lord for help in his heart.

"Oh, Addy. That's a hard one to comprehend, is it not? Sin is any act against God's laws of morality. Dishonesty, cheating, stealing. Hatred and cruelty, surely. And yet we don't have to be committing constant sin ourselves to be sinners, though it's impossible as humans to be sinless day to day. The Bible says sin entered into the world by one man, by way of the disobedience to God of Adam. And so we don't just ourselves sin. We are born as though infected with it. And only by Jesus' blood can we be set free of its harm. The greatest sin of all, though, is to feel God's conviction in your heart and to resist it. He says he won't always strive with us." Josiah felt like he could be knocked over by a feather as Adeleine stared at him intently, praying to God to open her heart. Uncle Ben waved at them just then, and they rose from the pew.

"My mama and papa believed themselves to be sinners, then?" she asked in a broken voice.

"Yes, but they believed also that their repentance and belief in the Lord Jesus Christ saved them. And I've no doubt they rest in heaven above, alongside my father even now." Wiping away the tears of grief and frustration that overset her suddenly, she smiled brightly as she approached her uncle.

"To dinner?" she asked, nodding at him then passing by him and joining arms with Kate.

At Uncle Ben's inquisitive look, Josiah said softly "Praise God, she's searching. I think Billy's preaching has rattled her in Whitechapel, and the minister today seems to have done the same. She asked what made her a sinner, Uncle Ben." His voice was low with a sense of reverence. Benjamin's breath caught, and he smiled with such hope in his eyes Josiah's own heart squeezed. "Praise the Lord above, my boy." "Let's be off to dinner so we don't have to corral all these ladies and children again, what do you say?" Waving to Kate and Emily's husbands just ahead, they walked from the church with a spring in their steps.

CHAPTER 30

$\mathcal{E}$nfolded in shadow, he'd continued to watch her every step for weeks, following her without being seen. He noted her exhaustion and hard toil, and yet the difference in her. She'd gone with the doctor to Whitechapel several weeks now, yet they'd not come yesterday as he watched from his usual dirty corner.

The last three filthy whores he'd exacted his revenge upon weeks ago and just a few days ago had all been disappointing. He'd taken souvenirs to try to savor his acts longer, but no satisfaction came. The fatter whore had reeked of rum and sickness. It seemed a mercy to put the wench out of her misery, but he'd been distracted. She'd fought back, not drunk or sick as he'd thought. Days ago, he'd been interrupted twice by the blasted bobbies on their pathetic rounds. He'd had little release somehow, which left him longing for the unfurling darkness, the black waves of fulfilment. The distractions had become too much, his mind not engaged in the swells of passion. He longed for the silk of release, the intoxicating sensation of it. It wouldn't happen again, he'd sworn. Next time he'd be smarter, plan better, clear his mind. Hearing the probationers whisper and guess at the identity of the Whitechapel ripper was oddly thrilling, and yet he must be careful. He'd surely be caught if he didn't maintain his focus.

The black obsessions, the passionate bloodlust rose and swelled continuously within him now thinking of *her*, and her alone. The girl Adeleine continued to make him fester with unanswered questions, yet he'd heard there was, indeed, a connection between she and Dr. Cairns. Others had noticed their behavior, too, and though they said nothing unkind, they did titter on about it. He knew not what overall lay between them, but it was clear the two were in some way devoted to one another. He'd not missed the nauseating display of gifts on what surely must have been her birthday, nor the way, of course, Dr. Cairns collected her on courting day and took her to his clinic each week.

He could find no fault in her, and yet the darkness inside had begun to call for her. He'd begun to desire the spill of her blood from her beautiful throat, and more. He closed his eyes tightly and gritted his teeth.

No, no, he fought against the heating fury in his veins. She was good and blameless. She didn't deserve his passion of hatred. As that thought prevailed, he, nevertheless, considered that he'd begun to enter her room. He'd begun to watch her depart from it every morning and had come to spend a few moments inside day to day, this morning, in fact.

He'd breathed her in and stroked his hand across her pillow, his craving pounding through his joints and marrow. "Adeleine," he'd whispered softly into the quiet, tidy space.

The wildflowers the doctor had left on her birthday hung suspended by ribbon, drying over the window sash. He had carefully pulled one flower from the bunch this morning and spun it carefully between his fingers within his apron now.

"*Adeleine.*"

CHAPTER 31

The matron had given any probationer going to the ball the whole of Saturday into Sunday afternoon off, provided their families gave approval. And so Adeleine watched for her uncle Ben to arrive to collect her the morning of the ball. Once he'd arrived and they were seated side by side, he gave her a squeeze. She was simultaneously excited and terrified, and clung to her uncle's arm like a little girl. He tucked her hand into his, smiling sweetly at her. Teasing, he winked and said, "Your handsome doctor will surely see that you have a most wonderful time. And if not, you can fill your dance card with myself, and perhaps Billy."

"Oh, Uncle Ben!" She laughed. "I do hope to dance with you a time or two," she said, grinning at him. Their lessons had been full of teasing, but she'd learned a great deal. Lady Joanna had gushed over her grace and bearing, and said she could hardly wait to see her in the ballroom.

Growing serious, she said, "I worry about what people will say of me, though, and how like a silly giraffe I'll look."

"Adeleine, my dear girl. You are no giraffe, and I daresay all people will have to talk about is how stunning you are and how jealous they are of your Dr. Cairns." At that, she blushed, and Uncle Ben chuckled merrily.

"Addy, I wasn't sure if I should tell you this, but the doctor has asked for your hand," Uncle Ben said carefully.

Her eyes rounded, and she fought for words. "You … you mean even with the betrothal he came to you?" Uncle Ben nodded. "What did you tell him?" she asked, gripping his arm. "I told him how proud I am of the young man he's become and that I would be delighted." Turning toward her, he looked over her with affection and said earnestly, "My dear girl, the man loves you. You've nothing to fear from him, and much to gain. Now I want you to be happy over all else, but I'd love to see you trust that his feelings are true, Addy. Won't you open your heart to him fully? Will you try?"

Adeleine swallowed hard. How did the man see right through her? Things had been simply wonderful with Josiah, and he'd surely give her the moon if she hoped for it. His bold flirting of late made her blush and made her heart thrill. But still something held her back that she couldn't understand or articulate. Her heart swirled in her chest at Uncle Ben's sharing that Josiah had asked for her. The fact was his legal right was, indeed, to marry her when he saw fit to do so. Yet still he'd come to Uncle Ben to ask for her, and that filled her with a sense of wonderment. And she knew not what to do with it.

"Take your time, Addy. You needn't worry over it now. I want you to have a wonderful time tonight. Won't it be fun to see how long it takes for Josiah to find you in the crowd?" He chuckled again. Leaning over to kiss her cheek he gave her a loving and fatherly gaze that settled her heart, even if her nerves were still jangling. To think again that Josiah truly wanted her enough to ask for her, even though she was promised to him, filled her with a delight she couldn't deny. She shook her head in trying to clear her thoughts and leaned into Uncle Ben's shoulder.

"We'll have an unforgettable night, you'll see," he said.

As they arrived, the girls couldn't collect her fast enough. She'd grown used to the way they whisked her about when she visited and, had come to rather enjoy it. She giggled and spun about with them as though they were children again, and Aunt Dottie couldn't help but become tickled at their antics. Her shoulders shook with mirth until she harrumphed and shouted, "Girls, girls! Cease your foolishness this instant!" Yet laughing, she turned and said, "Adeleine, go with Molly, and I'll have a bath drawn for you within the quarter hour."

Adeleine smiled at Molly, and as they left the parlor, she shyly asked if Molly knew what to do about her hair for the pain it caused her. "Oh, Miss, that I do! If you'll just go up to your dressing room by the upstairs bath, I'll be there momentarily! Oh, but this will be fun!" she exclaimed. As she'd promised, Molly came into the dressing room just moments behind Adeleine. As she helped remove her blouse and skirt and began pulling the pins from Adeleine's hair, Molly began to excitedly chatter about how cutting just a few inches of her hair and then trimming layers into it would take a good deal of weight away. Adeleine nodded a little nervously and agreed Molly should begin. Her unbraided hair hung nearly to her hip, and though it was an annoyance and burden, she did love how long it was. Molly seemed to sense her bout of misgiving, for she gently assured her. "It will still be down your back, you'll see. It just won't hurt you so much and, for that matter, will be easier to style." Adeleine nodded again, her eyes on the vanity glass before her as Molly cut away several inches of her hair. It did feel lighter, the beginnings of relief nearly immediate. Molly continued snipping efficiently, ending with two pieces framing Adeleine's face. She left the pieces to her shoulders, and when she'd finished, she beamed at Adeleine. "I think I hear your bath running! I cannot wait to style your hair to go with your mask! Let's hurry to your bath. Time is flying, and you've a ball to get to!"

Sinking into the delightfully warm copper tub, Adeleine felt her muscles and nerves unwind. The delicious fragrance of lavender oil and honeysuckle filled the room, and lemon besides from a new cake of soap Aunt Dottie had left for her. Molly began washing her hair, and it was all Adeleine could do to keep her eyes from closing. Molly laughed softly, and Adeleine gave her a playful grin. "Wait till you see your gown, Miss! No one in all of London will be a match to you, m'lady."

"No one? I daresay I could think of one," Adeleine said softly, conspiratorially, turning a blazing pink and sinking further into the water. Molly laughed happily and responded "And mark my words, Miss, his eyes won't leave you for a moment!"

As they entered the dressing room after Molly had brushed Adeleine's hair and nearly dried it, Aunt Dottie and the girls were chattering excitedly. A gown hung from the wall that could only be someone else's, Adeleine thought. As she looked around her, everyone was gazing at her expectantly. Kate had arms full of beautiful

220

sable, chocolate, and misty-green petticoats. Emily had stockings that seemed to sparkle in a paler silver green, and Aunt Dottie had everything else. Molly stood ready to help and to dress her hair. Eyebrow arched, Adeleine gently rolled a shoulder and said, "Oh, all right. Have a go at me!" Peals of laughter echoed around the room, and Adeleine smiled, basking in the sensation of being cared for. Of belonging.

Adeleine was mesmerized by her skirts as she stepped into the flowing layers of silk and tulle. Alternating shades of deep-forest green, emerald green, and finally kelly green rose to her waist in an elegant spiral of color, until they met at the left of her waist in a final layer of ruched watered silk. The lowest layers and the layer that came to her waist were shot through with glittering copper thread. The effect was such that it made her appear to rise from shimmering, unfurling tender leaves. The bodice of the gown was emerald green watered silk, embroidered with autumn leaves in shades of copper, gold, and silver. Over the shoulders on each side were gathers of tulle, dotted with various-sized silk and tulle leaves that fluttered with any movement. From the backs of her shoulders trailed a shimmering, diaphanous cape also bedecked on its edges with tiny delicate leaves. It draped just above the small of her back between her shoulders, and its length fell to the floor to meet the pooling layers of silk and tulle that gathered about her. Adeleine could hear the gentle whisper of petticoats and rustling of silk, and felt truly as though she'd stepped directly from a forest of make-believe. As she made to go to the long mirror, her cousins grasped either arm and chorused, "Not yet!"

Gently helping her be seated, they went to step into their own creations for the ball as Molly began on her hair. Molly brushed and brushed Adeleine's hair to a gossamer sheen and then pulled just a small portion of the front over to the side, braiding and twisting, pinning as she went, until she was satisfied. Aunt Dottie handed Molly the mask, and she placed it carefully onto Adeleine's face, arranging its cords under locks of hair and pinning it expertly. Finally, she worked Adeleine's flowing tresses into several fine braids that appeared to wrap around and in and out of the length of a wide, more loose braid that seemed to pour over one alabaster shoulder. Small silk leaves of green and coppery gold were pinned in every few inches to finish the effect. Waving tendrils were freed about her other shoulder. Molly then took a pot of delicate pink lip rouge and carefully applied it. Stepping back to study her work, she clasped her hands and trilled, "Oh, I told you, m'lady! No one will compare to you this night!"

As they helped her to stand, Emily and Kate looked as though they may shed tears, and Aunt Dottie already had. "Oh! Mama, we forgot!" came Kate's excited cry. Rushing over to the corner of the dressing room, she produced something that shimmered orange and black and several shades in between. Gently turning Adeleine around, the sisters brought something over both shoulders and tucked it about, fussing with the delicate cape until it was just so. Emily shrieked rudely in delight, which brought laughter tumbling from Adeleine and then the others.

"May I see what you sillies have done to me now?" Adeline asked nervously, her lips twitching.

Before the looking glass, Adeleine became speechless with wonder. She'd marveled at the beautiful skirts and bodice, and thought how lovely the cape was as it was placed at her shoulders. And yet as she beheld herself in the long glass, she could scarcely believe the woman standing before her was truly she herself. Her form was slender and statuesque, her skirts full and beautiful, and yet they gently caressed her shape. She spun in a circle and gasped as she delighted in the combination of whirling colors that came together to accent her costume. The fluttering at her shoulders of leaves and on the cape were a wonder, as was the delicate trailing in the air of her cape as she turned. Stepping closer to take in her mask, she sighed in wonder again. It sparkled in a blend of gold and green, with copper and gold leaves dotting it gorgeously. From one side, a large fern leaf reached across and below the mask to caress her cheek and jaw, coming to rest nearly at the corner of her lips, with tiny butterflies alight on it. And from the opposite side, beautiful quail feathers of differing sizes reached above a spray of autumn leaves in a riot of speckles and stripes in cream, orange, and deep brown, curving over her head to lend a playful air. But perhaps the most dramatic detail of all was what lay across her back, for, it seemed as though a delicate monarch butterfly had lit upon her in the sun. She was overcome, and yet she would not let a single tear fall. She truly felt, for perhaps the first time in her life, as though she were beautiful. Smiling tremulously at the women gazing upon her, she merely shook her head and held out her hands, as no words would convey her gratitude nor how she felt. They came to grasp her hands and sigh over the costume together and then took her to show Uncle Ben.

They arrived at the masquerade just as dark had fallen. Uncle Ben helped her and Aunt Dottie from the carriage and led them to the doors. Inside, the mantles and fireplaces and any other bare surface shimmered with blazing candles. The huge ballroom was festooned with ribbons and streamers, and enormous candelabra flamed in every corner. The grand staircase held huge brass pots filled with topiaries of autumn mums. Standing nervously with Uncle Ben to be announced by their costumes, as they were free from names this night, Adeleine felt sparks radiating along every nerve of her being. When, finally, it was time, they began descending the staircase. Upon reaching the middle landing, Uncle Ben kissed her cheek and said he'd return now to escort Aunt Dottie. As he retreated, Adeleine felt as though she'd surely humiliate herself losing her stomach on the stairs before she reached the bottom. Still, she forced herself to face the crowd as they'd turned to face her. She heard the crowd begin to buzz and felt the stares as though through to her bones. She descended carefully, watchful, lest she miss a single step, head held high. Her throat ached from the strain. And then her eyes came to rest on him, for the tall man with the powerful form and curling dark hair could be no other.

Josiah stood speaking to a group of his Cambridge fellows, catching up and laughing at the old tales of school days. When a hush descended on the room and then a buzz of excitement rippled through the crowd, he turned to see who had arrived. His chest tightened, and his pulse leapt. Just there, his Adeleine descended the stairs before him gracefully as a doe, her costume shimmering and floating in the breeze about her. She looked like a child's imagination come to life, as though born of a fairy tale. Her costume embraced her with silken leaves, while flora danced about her. A gilded monarch rested gently on her back, its wings framing her beautiful shape, dancing as her cape caught her every movement with its own dancing leaves. He'd not realized he was moving toward her until he saw his hand reaching to grasp the shimmering green of her glove. As his eyes met hers, her lips parted into a soft shy smile. The fern on her mask taunted him, resting just at the corner of her tender lips. He noticed then that tendrils of her waving hair hung loose about her creamy shoulder, and a majestic braid lay over the other. He found himself wondering if anyone had considered how desperately everyone would fall in love with her tonight. He felt tongue tied and weak kneed, like a proper fool. But he cared not, for she was the most beautiful vision he'd ever beheld.

As she stepped onto the floor, he could barely form words to convey how stunning he found her to be. Gorgeous, glowing. A dream, his dream. Realizing he was mutely staring at her and had taken both her hands in his, he looked about and noted the crowd staring at the scene they made. He shook his head and chuckled, smiling into her bright eyes. Just then her uncle Ben slapped his back. He and Aunt Dottie had reached the bottom step and now stood beside them. Josiah kissed Dottie's gloved hand, telling her how well she looked, and shook Ben's hand. "Young man," Ben said with a grin, "I fear you've set the whole of London on its ear just now with your gaping. Tell my niece how extraordinarily beautiful she is, and let's be off to get some punch while these ladies find your mother."

Unable to hold back a hoot of laughter at the man's razor wit, Josiah nodded sheepishly and said, "Indeed, Uncle Ben." Grasping Adeleine's hand, he kissed it gently and held it warmly a few moments more. Gazing at her intently, he said softly at her ear, "I'll be back with haste as the dancing is about to begin. Mother is just there." He pointed behind him and kissed her hand again, then strode from her alongside Uncle Ben.

Aunt Dottie linked arms with her, and she awoke from the glittering haze about her as the musicians began warming their instruments. How fine Josiah looked in his costume and mask. She realized then with a start that his costume, indeed, complimented her own. Was that how he'd known her so immediately? She walked along with Aunt Dottie fighting how entranced she felt, for surely she'd make a fool of herself yet. In a hushed whisper, Aunt Dottie suddenly said into her ear, "My darling, this may come as a shock, so forgive me. I didn't think to see this tonight."

At Adeleine's wide-eyed nod, she continued. "Your dear mother's parents—your grandparents—are here not ten paces from us." Inclining her head ever so slightly just beyond where Lady Joanna was rising to meet them, a beautifully appointed elderly man and woman stood talking to one another. Being masked, she couldn't see their faces, but the chill that raced down her back was like ice water.

"Oh, Aunt Dottie, must we say anything at all? Mama always seemed so upset after seeing them."

"No, child, at least not now. But when the time comes for unmasking, if they are still here, I couldn't deny them."

Taking a deep breath, Adeleine nodded. Then thought better of it and asked, "But how would they know me?"

"They loved you very much, same as we. And though you were but a wee girl the last time they saw you, you are much the same. I've been in turmoil over Benjamin writing to them, and to our shame, he has not as of yet. But if we continue that way, you see, and it comes to light that you and Josiah are … well, that your betrothal comes to marriage, it will be as though our whole family has given them the cut direct. And … well, Adeleine, you are the image of your mother. Taller, yes, those green eyes instead of her sweet sable and that burnished red in your hair instead of her golden brown. But to any of us that knew and loved her, you are identical in every other way." Adeleine swallowed back the sweep of emotion that overcame her at the words.

As they came to greet Lady Joanna, she noted the tightness in Adeleine's shoulders and lips, and asked what was amiss. Thankfully, Aunt Dottie shared the situation with her, and in her typical fashion, Lady Joanna simply acknowledged the difficulty and moved to casually comfort Adeleine with just a touch of her hand. Just then Josiah came back into her view, and all was forgotten. Standing so tall, he made a grand appearance even in his humblest attire. But as he was now, he took her breath away. His trousers were the darkest charcoal gray and pinstriped, while his waistcoat and cravat appeared to be the same emerald watered silk as was her gown. His crisp white shirt with its notched collar made his chiseled jaw and dark hair that much more beautifully stark, and his black velvet jacket bore elegant tails and cut away from his waistcoat handsomely. His mask was deepest black with glittering silver and copper detailing, with an elegantly embossed single golden-red autumn leaf over one side. He'd grown out a jaunty goatee that made him more darkly dashing than she could take in. As his hand reached for her, she heard nothing but the humming in her ears and the beginning strains of some dance or another.

Leading her onto the floor, she realized he was in just as much a haze as she, and, suddenly, Molly's words of this afternoon danced over her. Beginning to giggle like a schoolgirl, she forgot to feel awkward and melted into Josiah's arms, fighting to get hold of herself. Flashing his dear crooked grin at her, he waggled his brows questioningly. "It's just that-" She gasped for breath as another wave of laughter assaulted her "Well it's just that Aunt Dottie's lady's maid, dear Molly, she said this afternoon you'd not be able to take your eyes from me. And it appears that I ..."—she paused and glanced up at him rather shyly—"it appears that it is I who cannot take my eyes from you."

Josiah smiled endearingly at her while he gave a short nod of his head to receive her compliments and replied, "She was surely right, because, Addy, I, indeed, cannot take my eyes from you. I wish I could call to mind some sonnet or word of poetry, but none would be beautiful as you." He gazed so intently into her eyes that her giggling died in her throat, and, instead, she felt a heat enfold her she didn't care to be free of. Breathing in deeply, he said, "And you smell divine. I confess I can't stop breathing you in." Her lips curved shyly at him as she considered the man. Looking up into his shimmering eyes, she again wondered at his asking for her hand. She felt something break loose inside her, and as her eyes welled, Josiah's face grew concerned. "Are you all right, Adeleine?"

She nodded quickly and felt as though if she didn't gain her composure she'd become a silly watering pot. The whole afternoon, the way she felt in her gown, the way he'd gazed at her in something akin to awe as she made her way down the staircase, it all bubbled within her, and she found she couldn't contain it. Looking into his eyes, she softly shook her head and said, "I don't know if I am all right, for I hardly know myself this evening."

Raising an eyebrow, Josiah grinned at her and murmured, "I know you, and know you are certainly setting my heart afire, Addy."

Feeling as though she were jumping from a great height, Adeleine asked the question that had tumbled about her heart for weeks. "Do you remember that day in your carriage that I asked you why you are so good to me? Would you tell me now? And … well, how did you recognize me so quickly tonight?" she asked demurely, not even able to look at him.

Just then the beginning strains of the waltz began, and she looked about, surprised. "Oh! Blast! Isn't it terribly against etiquette for me to have danced more than one number with you? I've missed our first dance entirely for running on! Did I miss any steps? I didn't even realize we'd come to a stop!" she said in a rush. He laughed his deep rich amused laugh into the violin's first beautiful tones and shook his head.

"Hang etiquette, Addy. I'll dance the night away with you and dare anyone to challenge me! And you've not missed a single step, my little forest sprite." Sweeping her into the first steps of the waltz, they swayed gently together, both enjoying the music, the moments together, and the feel of the other in their arms. Josiah inclined his head toward her, his head nearly touching hers. "Addy my girl," he said slowly, as though enjoying the words on his tongue, "I delight in being 'good to you' as you say for the same reason I asked your uncle for your hand." As the steps pulled them from each other, he smiled so warmly at her, his eyes golden in his mask, that she forgot to breathe. She couldn't take her eyes from his, and her heart beat a cadence in her chest that made her think she'd surely lift from the floor. Intertwined with one another, they moved effortlessly, their feet and hearts as one. As the waltz came to a close and he bowed to her and then she to him, he whispered over her ear, "It's because I love you, my darling. I knew you so quickly because my heart beats entirely for yours." At her sharp intake of breath and tremulous smile, his heart leapt. "Would you like to be seated a few moments?" Josiah asked her.

Eyes shining, she nodded and said breathlessly, "If you'll stay with me, Josiah. *Joe*," she murmured.

"I don't wish to be anywhere else," he said, a grin hitching the corners of his mouth.

As he brought her to his mother, however, Lady Joanna rose and put her arm through his asking to walk a bit. As Adeleine nodded at the silent question in his eyes, he asked if she'd like any refreshments. At first, she declined as good ladies were wont to do, but within seconds, with a quiet snort, she said, 'Oh, yes, *please*. I am *famished*.'

"Yes, m'lady," he said.

Lady Joanna smiled between them and said, "You two are the most beautiful here this evening. And your dancing,

I just can barely keep hold of myself for how lovely you are together!" Josiah met Adeleine's gaze with an almost fierce expression, eyes simmering, and she couldn't help the coquettish grin that melted across her face.

As they walked away, she realized she was all alone. The seats around her were empty, most everyone gone to the floor for a quadrille. Watching the dancers, she shook her head at the steps. A giggle escaped her as she imagined falling flat on her face for all the steps she'd have missed.

Like the first fine curls of smoke drifting from a fire, a spirit of fear filled the air about her. She felt chilled and choked for breath. A sensation of being watched overwhelmed her, and she found herself looking about the seating area anxiously. Seeing nothing but empty shadowed corners and candlelight flickering from the candelabras, she fought to allay her fears. Yet even as she tried, it coiled tighter and tighter about her.

Finally, Josiah came into view, and she sighed a relieved sigh. Rising to stand beside him, she smoothed her shaking hands on her skirts. "Your favorite, m'lady," he said, handing her the most sumptuous strawberry tartlet she'd ever seen. Unable to tell him she'd lost her appetite, she took a bite of the tartlet and drank the punch he offered her, then sat both down on their saucer in the chair she'd been sitting in.

"May we dance?" she asked, smiling up at him.

"But of course," he replied, taking her arm. Looking around the darkened area once more and seeing no one, she shook her head and took his arm. As he grinned so handsomely down at her, she felt herself begin to bubble over with delight at him again and left the fear behind her.

The night passed with several more sweet dances between them, a dance with Uncle Ben, and an auction for the charity in which Josiah bid a ridiculous sum to secure a seat at dinner with her. Billy and Iness came only briefly and were gone again, and she'd only seen her cousins enough to grin at them as they sailed past one another on the ballroom floor.

Finally, the ball came to a close with a last waltz. As they unmasked on the last strains of the instruments, she and Josiah gazed at one another with impassioned intensity. Something deeper had blossomed this night, and both knew it. Adeleine thought surely he'd finally kiss her right there on the ballroom floor. But at the last moment, he sighed deeply and bowed over her hand. Against all etiquette, indeed, in one deft movement he removed her glove to the palm of her hand and placed a warm, lingering kiss on it. She smiled into his eyes even as her heart burst into a million stars within her.

Later on the carriage ride back to Uncle Ben and Aunt Dottie's estate, she came to a realization. She was undeniably in love with Josiah ... but she felt she could not trust the God who'd seemed so cruel to her, to her family, that Josiah loved and trusted so fully. And yet she had begun to feel a burden within her since reading the portion of scripture in bed that night weeks ago. "Even while we were *yet sinners*, Christ *died* for our *sin*." Had this Christ then died for her very own sin even knowing she would one day resist him as she had? For the first time since Josiah had explained sin to her, she felt herself fully accept it to be true that she was herself a sinner.

She longed for peace after so many years of heart-ache. Still something within her fought against it. Lulled by the rhythm of horses' hooves and visions of being held in Josiah's arms, she drifted into a sweet exhausted sleep.

CHAPTER 32

$\mathcal{A}$deleine lay on the floor, a single candle guttering beside her. She felt the slip of tears from her eyes in the chilly air as they ran into her hair. The manor's door hung open, slack on its hinges, creaking as it swayed in the night wind. It cast ever-changing light and shadow across the dull wood floor, as though the dark and light danced a slow disjointed waltz. Her mother's voice cried out to God on the breeze, ringing with hope and belief through the night. Adeleine knew there was something she must do, yet the answer of what would not come. A feeling of fear grasped at her tightly and coiled around her, choking her. Suddenly, a gust of wind snuffed out the light of the candle, and she lay in utter darkness. The smell of death and decay filled her. Even the light of the moon had vanished, and she found it hard to draw breath into her lungs as panic charged through her.

Rousing herself from slumber, moving to shake herself from the years old' nightmare, Adeleine found she was unable to roll over. In desperation, she fought to wake, terrified of never waking. She started to shake her head to clear the remaining webs of terror from her mind and found she could not. Her head was in a vice, unable to move. She began to feel herself being propelled by she knew not what, her feet and toes aching and burning with their movement against a freezing cold floor. She felt an iron band around her ribs, squeezing the air from her, and realized her hair was hung on something, pulling so tight she felt stinging like fire through her temple and scalp. Struggling to open her eyes, she could make out nothing but darkness around her until her eyes focused on the few dim lights of the hospital corridor. She shuddered as awareness dawned on her, beginning finally to understand a man was dragging her down the hallway toward the dark belly of the hospital. The morgue.

She began to fight her assailant, digging her nails into the flesh of his forearm wrapped about her, and bucking her frame into him, nearly sending them both sprawling to the floor. He cursed into the silence as they crashed into a cart forgotten in the hallway. Jerking them upright and clutching her somehow tighter, he moved into an alcove and looked about feverishly. Craning her neck to see him as he faltered, she could just barely see the outline of his profile. She felt a chill envelop her as she began to recognize the man. His feral, gleaming eyes turned down at her, and just as realization set her mouth into a scream, he swung her around and slammed the side of her face into the unyielding stone wall. She heard a strange pop and felt a hot rush of liquid over her eye, and then blackness engulfed her.

*****

She was heavier than he'd anticipated, taller this close. He'd considered whether or not she'd fight, and thought not, as he'd intended to knock her out by pressure point if she did. After he'd heard the thud of bone against the stone wall and felt her body go limp, he'd made haste in throwing her over his shoulder, skittering and weaving about hurriedly like a cockroach to his place in the morgue.

As he'd watched her these long months, he could no longer fight becoming more and more enthralled by her. He'd become obsessed with longing to be close enough to touch her crimson gold locks and breathe deeply the lavender and honeysuckle fragrance of her. Melting into her room unseen was no longer enough; it could not satisfy the need to feel her skin, the warmth of her. He wondered what the aristocracy would think of him having been at the masquerade ball. He'd studied her the whole of the night, drinking her in like the finest of champagne. She'd looked ethereal, like something of dreams and legend. He'd fantasized of holding his fingers to the veins of her throat, to feel the surging of blood through her. He felt the languid flow of blackness unfurling through him. His eyes were cruel and glazed as the heat pooled in his belly. He held the girl against his chest for several long moments, swaying as though dancing with her, feasting on her unique scent and pressing his face to her throat.

He weakly tried to shake himself. This was not right. She was no whore, no filth. She was kind and good … and yet the darkness wanted her; it seethed and boiled within him as he stood holding her. He swung her legs into his arms and gently lay her on a gurney. He opened the buttons at her throat and took in her pearlescent skin.

His fingertips tingled as he stroked the silk of her neck. He suddenly choked on a sob as Caroline's face filled his mind. He braced his hands on both sides of the gurney, staring down at her. The steadily bleeding gash at her temple filled him with remorse. It just wouldn't do.

But even as he stared down at her, his eyes blackened, and his mouth curved into an evil leer. He gave himself over to it, the deep darkness, surrendering to the thrust of gleeful passion that rose from deep within. He raised the scalpel to the pale column of her throat and began to cut.

*****

Josiah put his palms to his temples, attempting to massage the tension from his head. He'd worked hard and long on his piece for the College this week. He found himself exhausted but grateful for new details and strategies that would serve to make surgeries safer and more successful. Rubbing his eyes and massaging his brow, he stood to prepare to leave. He tidied his desk, locking his written and hand-drawn and painted work in the safe. As he turned to grab his greatcoat and glanced at his father's pocket watch, he was astonished how the hours had flown. He'd stayed at the hospital hours past what was typical, tucked into his world of nerves, joints, and flesh. A great many of his notes and diagrams had beckoned him to his desk after his discussion with the probationers this morning.

His probationer. Adeleine ... oh, how he had enjoyed their time together these last two months. He rolled over in his mind again how Whitechapel and time shared together with her family had changed something so deeply between them. They'd laughed together again, discussed facets of life, of science, and so enjoyed the newness of being together unencumbered by pain or regrets. The masquerade charity ball nearly two weeks past had surely ignited the romance he longed for with her. Still he longed for her heart. And not for himself, as he perhaps had acquired it, but for the Lord above. This past Sunday, she'd drunk in the Word shared from the pulpit but hadn't shared any thoughts with him afterward nor at dinner with her family.

He dared not disturb their tender balance, their fledgling understanding of one another, and so he prayed hard for her and stayed ever open to her. Dear Billy, preaching on his corner across from the clinic, had shaken her further these last few weeks especially, it seemed. After her questions that first Sunday, she'd accompanied him to church, it seemed there was an intense battle waging in her heart. He could feel the wondering, the reaching, the search within her. He whispered to God for her soul now as he thought of her. "Lord, my God, open her heart, fill her mind. Give me your grace to reach her, Father, if that's what you'd have of me."

As he stepped from his office, he was startled by a sudden crash of metal down the hall. As it was so late, he couldn't think how a cart or gurney could come to be overturned at this hour. Laying his effects back in his office, he began toward the direction of the noise only to hear what sounded like the throaty beginnings of a scream. He started into a run, counting doors as he turned into the probationers' corridor. Adeleine's door stood open, and immediately, his breath left him. Bile rose in his throat, and he wanted badly to scream her name, to beg a response. But he fought to still himself, somehow knowing he mustn't. The murders over the last several weeks raced through his mind, choking him with fear.

Finally, he came to the overturned cart, his eyes surveying the scene for any sign of her. He saw no trace, but knowing there was an alcove just ahead, he tread softly and watched closely. His eyes had long adjusted to the dark having worked so late, and as he passed the alcove, he noted a strange mark on the whitewashed masonry wall. Stepping closer, his heart jumped to his throat as he saw the unmistakable color of human blood. Small drops had fallen to the floor, leaving a path of sorts before him. Quickly, he rushed back to the matron's door and knocked quietly but insistently. She opened the door quickly, and as his words tumbled out that someone had Adeleine, her eyes widened. "I heard something crash and was just about to see that all was in order, Dr. Cairns," she said even as he gripped her shoulders.

"Please get security. I am going to find her," he said as he pointed the direction of the trail of blood and lit into a run.

He couldn't believe his eyes as the spatter of drops led toward the morgue, and raced past them until he reached the darker corridor leading into the dank lowest levels of the hospital. Catching his breath as he eased himself down carefully, a pinpoint of light drew him toward the hunched figure of a man. Drawing closer, he swallowed hard at the scene, a thousand lurid nightmares galloping through his mind. Waves of horror at what he saw crashed into him, making him feel as if he couldn't trust his legs to hold him.

Adeleine lay still on a gurney, her face hidden from view by the man's back as he moved silently over her. He was … singing? His low voice sang some sort of lullaby over her. He stepped away, his back still to Josiah, to reach for a long blade at the table beside him. Josiah spared no second thought as he threw his robust, taller frame into the man's back. The man's face hit the table as they hurtled toward the floor, limbs twisting. Rolling and struggling, Josiah felt the sting of a blade through his waistcoat close to his hip and twisted away before the man could pierce him further.

Jumping to his feet and hoisting a stool above him, he hit the scoundrel in the side of the head as hard as he could. Still the man got to his knees, and turning his face to Josiah, he gave a ghoulish grin and lunged toward him again with the six-inch surgeon's blade. Josiah jumped back, and as he did, he bumped the gurney Adeleine lay on. As he stumbled, the man rose to his feet and lunged again, forcing Josiah back until the gurney tipped, and he felt Adeleine's body lurch over the gurney and onto the floor. As she gave a soft moan, joy and then rage flew through Josiah's body, and he kicked the man's shins and groin in quick succession. The man seemed possessed of evil, and even as Josiah plowed his fist into the smaller man's face, he hardly staggered. His fiendish grin stayed on his awful bloodied face even as Josiah landed blow after blow. Grabbing a heavy instrument from a nearby cart, he struck the man with an upward blow to the nose. "Jesus, help me!" he cried out as the crunch of bone finally stilled the devil. He slumped to the floor, his dazed eyes never leaving Josiah's face until they fluttered closed.

Voices and the sound of running feet came in a rush, and Josiah shouted and shouted until his voice was raw. He turned to Adeleine, shoving the gurney from between them, and gently turned her on her back. The sight of her in the darkness turned his stomach, nearly driving him to retch. Her face and throat were covered in blood; she dripped with it. He gathered her in his arms like a babe and turned to flee the dark morgue, screaming at the officer on duty and the others with him to bind the man crumpled on the floor and hold him, to call for the Yard. As he reached the next level of the hospital, the matron and two nurses stood waiting. "Help me, please!" he cried out to them. "I need light. I can't see her closely enough! I can't lose her. Please, God, don't take her from me!" he sobbed raggedly. He ran toward an operating theatre, with a steady stream of prayers pouring from his lips. He felt the wetness on his face and cared not. He could think of nothing but her precious soul, and her warm life's blood seeping onto his skin.

Once he reached the brightly lit operating theatre, he could hardly bear to release her to lay her on the table. As he tried, she opened her eyes, staring at him with such wild emotion he couldn't speak. Touching his face, she made to stand and he let her, but she crumpled to her knees before he could catch her. As if trying to clear her head, she shook it and grimaced in pain. Her husky voice wheezed out, "Am I living? I felt him cutting me … my head hurts so terribly … my throat, my … my throat!" She gasped, pulling her hand away from her throat awash with blood.

"You're alive, my Addy. I'm here. Let me take a look, my darling, please," Josiah said softly, earnestly. He began to try to lift her to her feet, but she pushed at him.

"No!" she ground out. "No, no … I must receive him before it's too late. I …" She looked at him wildly and swayed as she dropped to sitting splayed on the floor. She held her hand to her throat, and Josiah reeled at the blood she was yet losing. He dropped down to his haunches beside her, his hands poised to lift her.

"Please, let me examine you, Adeleine. You're losing too much blood, please—"

"No! I feel him! He came for me … He came." Her voice cracked, and her eyes filled with tears.

"You're safe now, Addy. I'm here. We're here with you," Josiah said softly, misunderstanding.

"No, no," she whispered. Her shoulders convulsed with emotion. She stared at the blood on her hands, holding them out before her.

"Jesus … Jesus!" she sobbed out. "You've let me live … I … I … I haven't believed. I don't deserve life. I don't deserve more chances. I've fought you so hard all this time. But I felt you with me. I felt your presence just now … I was so afraid of the darkness, the terrible pain, and I called to you from my heart, and you were there. Jesus, I believe … Take my sin and my disbelief, and cast them away. I repent. I know I need you, and you are all that I have been longing for … All these desperate years, it's been you, always you, seeking me out. Take me, Lord. Take my heart. I am yours. I believe, dear God. I believe …" The words had poured out in waves, a reverent cry from the soul.

Josiah watched her, mesmerized, unable to move yet feeling the tears streaming down his face. As she quieted, he watched a peace steal over her countenance as her eyes closed again that glowed with radiance, even through her blood and wounds. A soft smile spread across her upturned face. As he began to stand and reached for her, her head lagged backward, and he caught her just as she fainted dead away.

The room was silent though filled with nurses. Someone uttered, "God be praised." The matron clapped twice, and everyone flew into action. Josiah lay her gently on the operating table and pulled a chair just beside her head, turning his back to the commotion behind him. With his eyes never leaving her face, her bloody nightgown was whisked away. She was washed, covered; and superficial wounds to her hands, feet, and one arm were cleansed and bandaged. The matron whispered to him quietly with her hand squeezing his shoulder that Adeleine's temple, and the throat wound would require treatment quickly, rousing him from his despair. "She could speak and breathe, so there's no physical damage other than the depth of the throat wound and the persistent bleeding. The gash seems to have been to a lesser vein, but she's lost quite a bit of blood—though mostly from her head or throat, I can't really say. I fear the blow just here at her forehead may have injured the bone, as this hematoma is becoming pronounced. This laceration further toward the temple continues to bleed. We need your further examination, Doctor. We're ready to proceed at your word." Taking a deep breath to calm himself, he met her eyes and nodded, covering her hand at his shoulder with his briefly. It felt like hours had passed as he agonized over Addy's pale face and still form, and yet just minutes had passed instead. Precious minutes. Adeleine's ragged temple and throat were prepared for surgery and closing, and continued pressure applied to her throat to staunch the flow of her blood. He took his hand from where it had come back to rest in the hair atop her head, tucking strands behind her ear as he stood quickly. "Joe? *Joe?* Please don't leave me ... Don't go. I have to tell you ... I have to tell you I love you, Josiah. I love you," she whimpered softly.

"I'm here, my Addy, my girl," he choked out in desperate grief, not knowing if he'd hear the precious words from her again. "I'm here. I love you. Oh, Addy stay with me. Stay."

CHAPTER 33

The dock stank of filth, fish, and sweating unwashed bodies even in the cold. His lip curled in revulsion. What a lot of crawling, stinking maggots, he thought. Standing ready to board the ship, he brooded over the past several days and clenched his jaw in fiendish misery. He'd ever wanted to leave the wretched streets of London behind with their disparity of poor and rich, titled and destitute. It disgusted him, this place. In the Americas, he could become whoever he wished to be. Again. The thought of passing himself as a doctor trickled through his conscience.

His bashed and broken face ached in the cold. The doctor had been in a right rage that night. He'd fought back to kill, something driving him he couldn't explain. Still the doctor had finally knocked him out cold. Waking with daggers of pain through his head and nose, he'd crawled dazed through the dark to the undertaker's entrance. The idiot bobbies who'd stood chatting in the cold morgue paid no heed to his body. Perhaps the doddering fools had thought him dead. He'd been so close to being held and likely dragged straight to H division immediately, and no doubt quickly hung for his crimes against the filth of Whitechapel. Surely, the inspector would have had no doubt, not after what he'd done to Adeleine.

He'd thought on her again and again until he felt his skull would split. It had all felt so wrong, and yet he'd not been able to stop himself. Such beauty and elegance could never be his, he knew. The raging dark passions and his desire had become tangled past sorting, and he'd not been able to control the ravenous hunger. He had grown so comfortable sneaking into her room that entering while she slept had felt most ordinary. He'd watched her sleep every night since the ball until the sweat on his brow rose and the darkness raged in his very soul to see the blood flow from her. Bitter bile rose in his throat wondering over what had become of her. He hadn't dared return to St. Thomas'. Had she died? The bleeding had been more than he'd intended, and the ragged wound at her delicate temple had covered the side of her face with its seeping before his blade ever touched her throat ... Surely, the doctor would have saved her. He'd not cut her through like the filth in Whitechapel. He'd merely pressed the blade until he drew blood and then watched it blossom and ribbon round her throat, mesmerized. He'd sung to her as he watched, as he'd once sung over Caroline's still form. He realized with a shudder he didn't know what would have happened if the doctor had not interrupted. When he'd turned to grasp the long surgeon's blade, his mind had become so torn between Adeleine and his sweet sister and the disgraced harlots of Whitechapel that now he could not bring to mind what his aim had become in those last moments with her. Feeling another wave of disgust and remorse, he spat angrily at the ground and made ready to show his ticket to board.

The wench Mary Kelly filled his mind then. He'd gone to his lodgings immediately as he could, not knowing if the doctor or Adeleine would have recognized him and set the bobbies onto him. So he'd collected his few belongings, pieces of clothing, and his long-saved money and made his way to Whitechapel. He'd slept lightly through the early morning hours and into the afternoon in an abandoned tenement. When he awoke, he found water to painfully wash his face and went to the docks to purchase a ticket to sail immediately. At horrified looks toward his battered visage, he'd rasped out a false laugh and said "pugilism," lifting his shoulders as if in self-deprecating jest. Knowing looks replaced horror, and the fools got back to their own miserable business. Purchase of the ticket left him enough money to make his way in the Americas for some time. He'd wandered about Whitechapel for hours until he saw young Mary, or Marie, he cared not. A rage had suddenly poured into him that he'd never felt, not since Caroline's death.

Watching the whore move about in the streets with her pretty young face had put him into a fury, and all he could see was Caroline and Adeleine's sweet faces and in his heart knew she didn't deserve a face like theirs. Didn't deserve the life she took for granted with her squalid ways. It sickened him. He'd approached her calmly and asked if she had a place to bed down, though he knew she did as she'd left and come back several times in the past hours. It had finally grown quiet, and he could feel his blade burning in his chest pocket.

Still carrying his bag, he followed her to her one room lodging and started a fire in the grate. The silken blackness had begun to overtake him and instead of fighting against it, he welcomed it, settling it around himself like a warm robe. Setting his bag on one of the tables in the room, he partially undressed as she did. He could feel the black flames of rage licking the insides of his brain, his body. She lay across the bed, and hiding the blade behind his back, he went to stand over her. Before she could move or speak, he'd cut her throat through. Filled with fury over Adeleine, over Caroline, and drowning in hatred of her kind, he cut and he cut. He took everything from her that could be considered beauty in his maniacal disgust. He was utterly consumed with it and could not halt his frenzy. Gasping for breath, he finally dropped his blade, arms aching. As his vision cleared he took in all he'd done and felt nothing. Nothing at all, no completion, no thrum of finality.

The sudden emptiness left him confused, cheated. And so he was done.

He'd removed the clothes he still wore and burned them, burned everything save what would go with him on the ship. Cleaning his surgical kit instruments and carefully blotting his face and hands, he threw the scraps into the blaze. The fire was hot enough that he sweat from it even as he stepped several feet away. Turning to leave, he'd taken in his work once more. Disappointed at the absence of the darkness, he'd faded back into the night.

Having handed over his ticket, he took in the ship's decks and went to find his cabin. He despised having to share the tiny cabin with three other men, but passage to the Americas only took about a week now. Climbing into a top bunk, he settled his bag into the corner at his head. He lay back, clasping his hands behind his head and closing his eyes. He was filled with a deep sense of yearning, yet he'd long for nothing of London.

His heart seized in his chest, keening for the dark power that had forsaken him.

*****

Josiah leaned into the outside wall of the hospital, his long legs sprawled out in front of him. Reclining his head, he closed his eyes and relished the sun on his face and the sounds of the Thames beyond. His lower side twinged where he'd been pierced fighting the crazed devil who'd nearly murdered Adeleine. After he'd performed surgery on her, he'd removed his black waistcoat as he was drenched with sweat and was shocked to find himself bleeding. The matron herself had cleaned him up and stitched him closed. He ran his hand back through his hair and then down over his face. He blinked rapidly, finding himself in a daze of exhaustion and sorrow.

He'd prayed and prayed, staying at her bedside for days. The bruising that had taken over her face from the blows she'd received soured his belly. To think of what she had suffered seared his heart and near paralyzed his mind with helplessness. He'd imagined the tear at her temple was from the fiend smashing her face onto the brick wall and the hematoma from her fall to the floor from the gurney. He'd seen many a vicious trauma, many a slow agonizing death, and, indeed, many deaths from sudden incidents. He'd studied them, researching the causes and effects to further medical science. Never had he witnessed such harrowing injuries to someone he treasured … that he loved.

With Adeleine, he'd felt strangely frozen in fear, but somehow he'd proceeded in surgery on her. All that he'd researched over the years flew through his mind as he'd knit together her destroyed flesh and torn vessels bit by bit. He'd painstakingly opened the throat wound to get a clean visual of the fiend's blade penetration, relieved to find it minor over all. Still it was dangerous enough that he had to ligate the vein to stop its pumping out of her life's blood. The blow to her temple had opened a vessel, as well, that he'd closed in much the same manner. The knot on her forehead that had worried the matron had gone down in its swelling over the next long hours, but Adeleine didn't awaken. Her vital signs were promising, and her color began to return. She responded to her dressings being changed with quiet moans and movement of her head, yet still she slept.

Josiah had stayed by her bedside through that first morning to this fourth morning. Her uncle had come right away, sitting beside her and stroking her hand softly as he held it. He'd prayed and talked to her, and even sang her a silly children's song until his voice broke and he couldn't continue. He'd bowed his head and wept at that point and Josiah had felt his own tears coursing down his face where he stood in the corner of the room. As Uncle Ben stood to leave, he reached for Josiah and pulled him into a burly embrace. Pulling away, Uncle Ben had held him with a fierce gaze. Nodding to him, Josiah squeezed his shoulder as he made his way out.

Billy had stopped by the second night. He'd embraced Josiah as only a brother or father could, and he'd prayed for her healing. When Josiah had shared of her calling out to the Lord as he'd shared with Uncle Ben and that she had expressed that she loved him, the boisterous Irishman had shed tears and rejoiced. Much the same as Uncle Ben, Billy had held his gaze with intensity. He then hugged him again, and was gone.

He fully realized their thoughts. He felt Uncle Ben's broken heart. He felt Billy's relief over her redeemed soul. But he knew they'd thought she'd surely die. The head wounds had been enough, and with her not waking, the chances grew slimmer by the hour of her being herself if she did wake. Of course, the loss of blood alone had been enough to take her. There were truly no promises, and he felt himself hanging only by the most tenuous strand of hope.

His mother had come just this morning, which had somehow been that much harder to bear. She'd come up behind him where he sat on a stool close to Adeleine's side, looking into her face. His mother had bent over him, wrapping her arms about him and resting her head on his shoulder. He'd felt his composure shatter, and she held tightly even as he'd brought his hands to his face and sobbed. "Sshhh, ssshhh, my dear boy," she'd murmured. "The Lord holds her. He is in control yet. Don't give in to fear or doubt. No matter the storm, the Lord holds all things together." She'd come to stand beside him then, resting her hand atop Adeleine's chestnut waves. "She survived an epidemic all alone. I have faith she'll survive this too." Turning to smile at him, he saw the tears brimming in her eyes as well.

"Stay with her a little while?" he'd choked out. She'd nodded and encouraged him to get some air. He'd grasped her hand and stood, bent to kiss her, and made his way to the outside walkways.

Looking over the water and up to the sky now, his voice broke as he cried out, "Would you take her away again, Lord? I pray you won't … please … Father God, please give me grace to bear it. Please help me understand …" Drawing his knees to his chest, he brought his hands to his face as his shoulders convulsed in grief. "Please save her Lord, please bring her back to me," he gasped softly. He let himself weep in sorrow and fear, in frustration and hopelessness. He'd found his usually steady faith unraveling as the days had worn on, knowing full well the odds were against her. Fearing he hadn't done enough or found her quickly enough pierced his heart with guilt and doubt.

Running his hands over his face again, he let out a beleaguered sigh. A voice coming from down the walk caught his attention after several moments. Realizing his name was being shouted by a nurse, he jumped to his feet and ran to meet the girl, who he realized was a probationer. "Dr. Cairns, please come quickly! It's Adeleine!" The girl's flushed cheeks and breathless speech sent a bolt of terror through him, and his legs quickly outpaced hers. Making his way to Adeleine's room feeling as if through quicksand, he was vaguely aware of many people standing about the bed. He moved them all aside as he reached it and came to an abrupt stop.

Sitting propped up with a dozen pillows, her hair flying and waving about in fiery chaos, sipping water and wreathed in smiles was his Addy. "Addy, oh, Addy, my girl!" he cried out, losing his legs and hitting the stool hard. He realized his mother sat across from him, smiling and holding the water Adeleine sipped.

Lady Joanna offered, "After you went to get a breath of fresh air, I gathered her hands and began to pray. When I finished, I opened my eyes, and she lay gazing at me with that sweet smile on her face. She said she was so thirsty, so I asked for help, and here we are."

Curious and somewhat shocked, Josiah asked, "What did you pray?"

"Well …," she started, smiling and tingeing a bit pink, "I begged the Lord to bring her back to us. To you, Josiah." At that, Josiah gave a watery laugh, pushing his hair back and shaking his head.

"You and me both, Mother," he said thickly. "Praise God," he whispered. "Praise God."

He himself gathered Addy's hands then, thrilling at the feel of her fingers twining with his. As he looked into her eyes, he saw hope, and joy, and something deeper. "Are you in any pain? Do you feel drowsy or weak?" he asked earnestly. She sighed and looked about the room.

"I feel as if I've had the best sleep I've had in fifteen years. I also feel as though that old stallion of Papa's threw me into the rose gardens again." Relieved at her wit, Josiah chuckled fondly at the old memory. She'd been bruised and scratched and nearly trampled that summer long ago, and, indeed, he'd been the one to pull her from harm. Her mind seemed keen. "I do feel a bit weak, Josiah," she murmured, her eyes gone serious. Josiah stood and asked that the room be cleared, save his mother and the matron.

With the ladies' help, Adeleine was brought to standing, and Josiah observed as the matron put her through several movements to gauge her balance, perception, and acuity. She did well on all, but it was obvious she was weakened from the loss of blood and would likely bear the lingering symptoms of concussion for some time. As they made to get her back into bed, Josiah made a hasty determination and situated himself to be seated in the bed first. The matron and Lady Joanna gasped with laughter at him and, ignoring his antics, helped Adeleine into his waiting arms where she curled onto her side against his chest. He sat back against the pile of pillows and gathered blankets about her. Lady Joanna departed to send a messenger to the Ashtons, and the matron departed to collect broth and tea for Adeleine.

Alone with her, holding her, Josiah asked just above a whisper, "What do you remember, Addy?"

Taking a long slow breath, she replied, "Waking up to being dragged toward the morgue … having my head thrown into the wall … feeling the excruciating pain of him cutting me and knowing I was going to die." She shuddered deeply, and when she spoke again, her voice broke into a cry. "The blackness was so overwhelming and intense, and all I could think was that eternity would be that way separated from God. I felt searing pain at my throat and warmth on my face and then heard terrible crashes and noises. I called to Jesus, and then I was falling. When I woke again, I was with you, and I felt I couldn't stay conscious. I knew I had been fading in and out. I tried to stand but fell to my knees on the floor, and, suddenly, it was all so clear … I was somehow alive and had another chance to repent and receive Jesus, and I wanted so badly to do so. And I did—I did—and I felt the most beautiful peace when I'd cried out to him, when I trusted and believed. I remember more pain and knowing I was losing consciousness again ... And then I woke up to your mama praying so sweetly over me." He held her tighter and tenderly kissed the top of her head over and again. He openly wept, reaching to hold her face gingerly with his hand to his chest. She grasped his arm, understanding finally what had lain between them. She wanted to say so much, for she knew she couldn't fight to stay awake much longer. Especially not held in his arms, with his fingers running through her hair.

"Do you know this is four days later? That you've slept this long? You've given us a desperate fright," Josiah said emotionally, his voice raspy.

"Why, this isn't the next morning?" she said in a hushed, somewhat alarmed tone. Adeleine's mind started putting the details together as a nurse and, in truth, found herself to be shocked. She well remembered the blood covering her hands, just knowing she'd soon die. The searing conviction in her heart had cried out to her with urgency, and she'd finally lain down her fighting and been freed. She wondered at the Lord's steadfast love for her, at his forbearance of her stubborn heart. She was grateful to the Lord God, indeed, for he had saved her—in body and in spirit.

When his mother returned and the matron returned bearing broth, tea, and biscuits, Josiah gently rose from the bed with her in his arms, then lay Adeleine back against the pillows. He covered her again with blankets as she shivered, being removed from his warmth. He held her tea and broth cups for her as she drank, dabbing her mouth when she was done. She gave a soft giggle and said teasingly, "Good doctor, 'tis *you* who is nursing *me*." His affectionate smile was the last thing she saw as she slipped back into a deep sleep.

Hours later, the afternoon sun cast long beams and golden shadows across the floor. Josiah sat by her sleeping, his head in his folded arms on Adeleine's bedside. Hearing his name called softly in the quiet room, he fought to open his eyes. He felt gentle fingers running slowly through his hair and felt his heart swell. "Addy," he said, as though it were a caress.

"Josiah," she called again. He opened his eyes, and finding her eyes on him, he gazed back tenderly. "Yes, m'lady," he murmured sleepily.

"Did you save my life?" she asked. He sat up, resting his head on one hand with his elbow on the bed. His other hand reached to touch her face, his fingers tracing lightly over her cheek. He looked into her eyes and suddenly dropped his face into his hands, overcome with emotion. Fighting to keep his composure, he returned his eyes to hers.

"I was so afraid I'd not done enough, Addy," he cried. "I was outside this morning when you woke, begging God to give me grace to understand if I lost you again," he said, his voice breaking. "I performed a ligation in both your throat and here at your temple. Those finally stopped your bleeding. You had a hematoma here, and we were afraid your skull was injured, but the swelling began to lessen this last couple of days. You'll surely have a long road of it the next several months and need a good deal of rest as the injury to your head heals," he said, trailing his fingers over her face as he explained. He pulled his shirt away from his side to show her his own stitches, reddening her face and bringing a warm laugh from her. She began to speak again, and her voice caught.

"We're a couple of ogres after all, are we not, Joe?" she said, looking intently into his eyes.

"That we are, but, Addy my girl," he said, mirth filling his warm voice, "you should see your face!" As they laughed softly together, they both became silent, gazing at each other with longing in their eyes. He pulled her shoulders to him then, and she leaned into his arms gladly, her head over his shoulder and one arm twining about his neck. She marveled at his strength and bravery, and he at her softness and spirit. Holding her tightly as he dared, he rocked her gently. "I love you so, my Addy. I always will."

She smiled tremulously through her gathering tears, tightening her arm about him. She felt a precious belonging held in his arms and had to tell him. She had to tell him what was in her heart for him. She knew so deeply and resolutely it was time.

She said shyly, "Joe, I remember something else. Something else that came over me that night that I had to say." He felt his chest tighten as he eased away to meet her eyes, wondering if what he'd longed to hear again from her lips was what she spoke of. He gave her a soft nod and brought her hand to his cheek.

"Please tell me, Addy. I long to hear of it."

Taking a deep breath and meeting his eyes, she said softly, "I … I love you, Josiah. You've ever been my dearest dream. And I'm here with you … to stay."

The end.

EPILOGUE

*S*ong of Solomon 8:6-7

Place me like a seal over your heart, like a seal over your arm. For love is strong as death; its jealousy unyielding as the grave. It burns like blazing fire, like a mighty flame. Many waters cannot quench love, rivers cannot wash it away.

Adeleine lay awake in the silvery light just before dawn, tucked warmly into her bed at Uncle Ben and Aunt Dottie's home. Snow was gently falling this Christmas morning, swirling on the wind and settling onto the window panes. Stretching her limbs, she smiled thinking of sharing the holiday with her uncle and aunt once more, and her smile broadened as she thought of Josiah and Lady Joanna being with them. Her cousins wouldn't be able to join them today for visiting their extended families. Nevertheless, joy flooded her heart as she sighed contentedly into the stillness. Oh, what precious changes to her life had been wrought this year.

Snuggling down into her covers, she whispered to herself the twenty third Psalm she'd memorized, pondering the truth of each line in her own life. It had touched her so deeply when she came across it in her old Bible.

The LORD is my shepherd; I shall not want. He maketh me to lie down in green pastures: he leadeth me beside the still waters. He restoreth my soul: he leadeth me in the paths of righteousness for his name's sake. Yea, though I walk through the valley of the shadow of death, I will fear no evil: for thou art with me; thy rod and thy staff they comfort me. Thou preparest a table before me in the presence of mine enemies: thou anointest my head with oil; my cup runneth over. Surely goodness and mercy shall follow me all the days of my life: and I will dwell in the house of the LORD for ever.

She thought of the waters in Bourton, and of the sweet life she'd had with John and Christine. She considered how the Lord had kept her safe from harm in so many ways … indeed from evil and a horrible death nearly two months past. He'd redeemed and restored her soul, and certainly goodness and mercy had been with her all the days of her life, and continued today. The pure peace and contentment she felt in Jesus was like nothing she'd ever encountered. She could see so clearly now how every facet of her life reflected God's goodness and presence. Every moment, every joy or trial, even sorrow, had been given purpose by the One who held all things together. He had not been cruel; no, he had sought to win her out of darkness and bring her to his light. She realized now that simply having faith that he would hold her, no matter the storm, gave her the strength and hope to continue on. She closed her eyes and thought of her mama and papa, and the hope she had now that they'd had, for one day she'd walk alongside them with the Lord above. She thought of Papa's last words to her, and whispered her thanks that the Lord had indeed been with her, waiting for her heart so long. She blinked away the bittersweet tears that had begun to fall at the thought of their dear faces, and determined to go back to sleep.

Just as she began to roll onto her side to ease back into slumber, there came a faint tapping on the door. She was surprised to see Molly poke her head in as she quietly called "Yes?" Molly's smile was full of merriment as she softly exclaimed "M'lady, you have a gentleman caller." Adeleine sat bolt upright and said "Surely you jest? Why, it's barely past dawn!"

"Nonetheless, your Dr. Cairns awaits you in the foyer." Molly grinned and waited to help Adeleine ready herself, telling her she must dress warmly. At Adeleine's bemused expression, Molly smiled widely, pointing to the window. Adeleine threw her legs over the side of the bed and hurried over to the glass. She gasped as she saw a gleaming, familiar mount standing in the snow with a beautiful sleigh sitting behind her.

Turning back to Molly hastily, she cried "What shall I wear?" but Molly already had her arms full with a warm winter frock, stockings, cloak, and gloves. As Adeleine quickly washed and got into her clothing, Molly took her brush in hand. "How do you feel, m'lady?" Molly asked gently. "Fairly well. The headache lingers day by day, but less so in the morning," Adeleine replied. "I'll just tie back the front with ribbon, then," Molly said.

But Adeleine was hardly able to think on it for her mind reeling about. Josiah downstairs at practically dawn? What was he about? And the sleigh …and that horse! Feeling Molly finish her hair, she rose quickly. Her thoughts were flying so furiously she simply stared wide eyed at Molly for several beats. Gently placing her hands at Adeleine's shoulders, Molly turned her about and steered her toward the door. Adeleine stepped into the hall and headed to the stairway silent and seemingly in a daze. Molly couldn't help but chuckle quietly, delighted at Dr. Cairns' plan shared with everyone late last evening.

Hearing footfalls above, Josiah turned from his nervous pacing and gazed up at Adeleine as she descended the stairs. He felt the familiar swell of his heart as he studied her. The bruising had finally faded from her face, her color looked wonderful, and the headaches were no longer as severe from her concussion. He took in her gently styled hair, all but completely loose down her back, her coppery waves dancing in the dim lighting. As she came to stand before him, he felt her eyes searching his face.

"Good morning, Addy my girl," he murmured with a grin. Her lips parted in a tender smile as her eyes met his. As she gazed up at him, he took her cloak and gloves from her arm and brought the cloak to swirl about her shoulders. Pulling the cloak's hood up over her head, he allowed his fingertips to graze her cheeks. He didn't miss the shiver that ran through her at his touch, nor her trembling in excitement to leave the house. He held her gloves out to her and she pulled them on. Taking her hand, he began for the door just as Molly hurried in with an apple. "For that beauty," she said with a knowing smile. Josiah thanked her warmly, and seeing Adeleine fairly fizzing with anticipation, he quickly ushered her outdoors.

Breathing in the icy air and delighting in the falling snow, Adeleine giggled happily as she stretched out her arms and spun in a slow circle on the walk. She'd not been totally confined since her release from hospital, but she'd certainly not been out of doors often, if at all. Josiah's emotions gripped him at her exuberance. The morning was going just as he'd hoped, yet he still found himself nearly breathless with nerves.

He followed her then as she made her way over the snowy walkway to stand before her horse. Gently she blew into the horse's muzzle, tilting her head to the side as she waited for the horse to respond. Adeleine's eyes filled as she watched her mare paw the ground and nicker, and she gave a tearful laugh as the fine Arabian Jewel tossed her head and nuzzled her nose into her lady's middle. The mare then seemed to pull her into an embrace with her neck outstretched over Adeleine's shoulder. Adeleine wrapped her arms about Jewel's neck and trailed her fingers through her mane, reaching to scratch her ears. Josiah laughed softly at the scene the two of them made and handed Adeleine the apple from his pocket. He watched her whisper and coo and chortle at her beloved horse with a sweet delight. Drinking in her treatment of the cherished animal, he felt his love for her deepen yet again. As she turned and looked up at him, the twinkling in her brilliant green eyes set his heart racing. The deep red of her cloak contrasting with the snow was so striking that he couldn't take his eyes from her.

"Josiah, how can this be? I don't understand," she asked, her voice husky. He felt himself beginning to come undone at her tears, happy though they were, and shook himself. "Come sit with me," he replied after collecting his wits, once again taking her hand. Helping her into the sleigh, he carefully tucked blankets about her as he took his seat. Once they were settled, he gave the reigns a gentle flick of his wrist. The little mare pulled the sleigh wonderfully, and Josiah gave a happy chuckle. "John said she was a strong little thing, but I didn't believe it." He watched and waited, both anxious and amused, for her to take the bait.

"Why, she is a wonderful strong girl!" she said indignantly. Just then her face blanched. "John! How could you have spoken to John?" she cried, clearly astonished. They'd never even met! Oh, how she ached for John and Christine both. "Why, he and his lovely Christine arrived just last night as your houseguests," he said brightly, hardly able to contain himself. "I'd hoped to have a special announcement to share at breakfast this morning, you see, and so Uncle Ben invited them for a fortnight or thereabout."

As her mouth gaped and her forehead drew together in disbelief, he called out merrily, "Ah, here it is!" The sleigh came to a stop beside a quiet city square festooned with cheerful ribbons and greenery. Holiday wreaths hung on gas lamps that twinkled in the falling snow. Adeleine sighed with quiet joy as she took in the beauty of it all. Josiah helped her out of the sleigh and walked a few steps with her to the center of the square. Realizing suddenly that Josiah no longer stood alongside her, she whirled about, only to find him on one knee just behind her. "Joe! Whatever are you-" but he sweetly cut her off.

"Adeleine," he began softly. "Fourteen years I grieved never spending another Christmas with you. Oh, how I longed for your laughter, your eyes. Our merriment." His eyes began to shimmer with moisture, and she felt a wave of elation about to break over her. "Having you back this year has touched my heart, knitting back together more than I ever realized was broken." Her mouth dropped open as he pulled a familiar carved box from his pocket. She brought her right hand to her lips as he took her left hand in his.

"My lady, my darling. My beauty …my dearest friend." He paused to take a deep breath, and as he continued his voice wavered as his eyes filled. "My life has only ever been complete with you in it. Adeleine Eleanor Ashton, would you permit me the honor and joy of being your husband? Would you gift me the pleasure of your laughter every day for the rest of my life? Would you marry me?" He held the box out to her, popping open the lid. There inside the box lay her Mama's delicate filigree wedding band, and her Papa's more heavy band alongside it. Choking back a sob, she fell to her knees before him.

"Oh, Josiah! How is this possible?" she cried. Tilting up her chin to meet her streaming eyes, he replied "Uncle Ben found them in your Papa's bureau many years ago. He came to think they were taken off for you to have if you lived and they passed when the pox came. He wanted us to have them after I'd asked him for your hand." Her lips trembled, but she broke into a radiant smile. Placing her hands on either side of his face and holding his eyes, she laughed "My dear doctor, I thought you'd never ask!" Throwing her arms about his neck, the hood of her cloak fell away and her hair swirled around them on the wind. His face broke into a smile, and he laughed softly at her sweet teasing.

Pulling her into a close embrace, he ran his fingers through her snowy hair and gently tugged a lock, waiting for her response. With a chuckle she said, "My Josiah.

Always my dashing rascal!" She brought her face to rest in the curve of his neck just below his ear, drinking in his delicious spiciness. "My answer is yes, of course. Yes, Joe. Yes!" she trilled excitedly. He pulled away to study her eyes, and what he saw there pulled at his very soul. My Josiah, she'd said. Surely his heart would burst this day, he thought.

Kneeling together there in the snow, with snowflakes in their hair and overwhelming joy in their hearts, he brought his lips to hers in a poignant kiss. She tightened her arms about his neck, bringing them closer, and reveled in the feeling of being loved by him. The sensation of his lips capturing hers was like nothing she'd ever felt, and she thought she'd swoon with the intensity of it.

Finally breaking the sweet kiss, he stood and helped her to her feet. Gazing down into her glowing eyes, he teased with a grin "I told you I'd have an announcement for breakfast." Returning the heat of his gaze, she smiled coyly at him. She took his hand and playfully made as if to waltz with him. He took the first few steps with her, then lifted her off her feet and spun her in a circle. Holding her against him, he brushed his lips over hers once more, savoring her nearness. He could scarcely believe she'd accepted his proposal and never wanted to let her go. Never wanted to be further than a kiss away from her ... Before he utterly lost himself, he set her down carefully. Grasping her hand, he bowed over it as he watched her. He pulled her glove below her wrist and kissed it roguishly, waggling his brows at her. "M'lady, your sleigh awaits."

She let out a cascade of giggles as he began to playfully dash away from her then, and he burst into laughter as well. Returning to her side, he tucked her hand into the crook of his elbow. Returning them to the sleigh, Josiah intertwined his fingers with hers and sat down closely beside her.

"Addy my girl, what do you say we return to the manor for breakfast and read Dickens to the little ones? To everyone we love, as they should all be there by now." She gaped at him in surprise. Her heart began to thrill at the thought of being together with all of her loved ones, for now she fully understood his meaning. "Will they really all be there?" she asked.

"Oh yes, my love! The Pierces, your aunt and uncle of course, your cousins and their families, mother and I ... why, I believe even your matron is to stop by today to wish us well," he said teasingly, winking at her and waggling his brows again. "What do you say? Are you ready to be introduced as my bride to be?"

"Only over my morning chocolate," she answered saucily, her eyebrow raised at him. His rich baritone laughter spilled over her again, warming her to her toes. Filled with delight she could not contain, she melted into his tender embrace as he led Jewel back home, excitedly looking forward to the day-and forever-with him.

*****

Across town, the widow Lady Lauren Wesley struggled against the handsome man she'd let into her heart. She'd been brought out of her slumber by him pulling something about her neck, and he wouldn't let her go. Surely he knew she couldn't draw breath. Surely he couldn't mean to hurt her. Even as her vision blurred and she saw bright spots of light, then red blackness, in her heart she longed just to be held by him.

Coming Soon

---

*Interrupting
Cadence*

PROLOGUE

*E*ibhlín stood kneading dough at sunrise for the household's daily bread, lost in her thoughts. She smiled softly remembering her darling Stiofan, caressing his name within her heart. She could scarcely fathom him having been gone these two years past. She felt her eyes mist as she thought again of him being taken on the raging sea. He'd loved it so, the sea. It had called to him with its waves, its foamy spray. No man's job was without peril, she knew, but the sea was perhaps most cruel of all.

She'd married Stiofan her seventeenth year, and they'd had two wonderful years together, though much of it he'd spent at sea to earn a living and save for their future. In his absence, she'd served under one of the finest cooks in all of London. It had given her needful experience and led to her hire here by referral. She thanked God again for the family who'd kindly taken her in just months after Stiofan's death, for surely she'd have starved without them. The hard earned money had gone so quickly, with the rent suddenly gone higher and higher, putting merely surviving out of possibility. Lord and Lady Wittingham had been good to her since hiring her on, and truly she was content. Even in her servitude, they were fine and upstanding, generous, never belittling her.

Suddenly she felt hands at her waist and gasped in indignation. Turning fiercely, she thought to slap the scoundrel, but his lighthearted chuckle and the spark in his eyes mollified her. Somewhat. The young groomsman had shamelessly flirted for months, and spent much time charmingly trying to pull the closely guarded secrets of her heart from her. Still she would not take her heart from her dearly beloved husband, and so she would not return his advances. And indeed she held herself to moral goodness, as she'd not disgrace herself nor the family she worked for. Nor her husband's memory.

"Get out of my kitchen, ye no good welp!" she scolded. "Ah, I do love that fire in your bonny tongue, mistress *cook*," he drawled. She nor anyone else could tell if he was truly a Yank or just played one well. He'd attempted her name time and again, but couldn't pronounce it's Gaelic roots with any finesse, nor the more English version. The fool! She'd finally told him to cease trying. He annoyed her in truth, but he was pleasant to the eye and indeed amusing. Laughter with her Stiofan was what she missed most sorely. Still the fellow gave her some bit of unease, a nervous spirit; a strange sensation of fear. Something akin to stories of old about lurking monsters back home in Ireland. She shook it off and gave him a day old crust and bit of cheese and shooed him out, aided no doubt by the kitchens filling with her help for tonight's ball.

The hours passed quickly in creating pies, pastries, and sweet meats, platters of cheeses and fruits, three soups, two lavish dinner vegetables, and savory roast pork and beef.

As the army of serving staff carried each course of the meal out to the waiting guests, she felt exhaustion begin to take her. There was naught left to do but clean, and then she could rest.

Alone in the huge kitchens quite suddenly it seemed, she felt a sneaking sense of being watched and held her breath, straining to hear any unwarranted sound. She heard nothing, yet chills rippled through her. Walking to the servant quarters hallway, she poked her head in but saw nothing. As she turned about, the groomsman stood just before her.

A wolfish smile spread across his face and he seemed altogether a different man as she took him in. His hair was combed impeccably, not windblown, and his attire far too fine for a groomsman. His eyes seemed ablaze with ferocity, setting her nerves burning in alarm. Something was horribly amiss. As she stood searching his face, he took her in his arms tightly, too tightly. She stood stock still in the metal bands of his embrace, awaiting an opportunity. Looking down at her, he said perfectly with a casual air "Eileen, how I've longed to hold you so." At her astonished gasp, he chuckled and said "Oh, I play the fool well, *muirnín*. Disarms most chits, but not you. No, my wee beauty. You must have really loved your mongrel Irishman." At that, she stomped his foot hard as she could and struggled free of his grasp.

As she turned to flee, she was vaguely aware of a flutter of wide ribbon over her face. She heard it snap tight and felt it encircle her neck. She fought to tear at his hands with her nails but they were just out of her reach; to stomp at his feet but he'd pulled her upward so her toes barely reached the floor. Quickly too weary to struggle, she went limp against his body. He leaned over her shoulder, pulling the ribbon tighter still. As she began desperately fighting again to draw breath, he murmured into her ear. "I've grown tired of my charade here. Playing the servant turns my stomach. I'd rather find something more refined, more engaging to fill my time and ease my boredom. But I'll have you first, sweet lass. You've kept me waiting so very long, and I'll not wait longer.

I do so love a pretty girl tied with a pretty ribbon."

Of Historical Note

Gloucestershire, England is an historic county dating back to medieval times, with mention in the *Anglo-Saxon Chronicle* of the 10th Century. Filled with rich history and abundant in antiquities, it is the ancestral home of the author's paternal lineage as far back as can be traced. Bourton on the Water is a village within Gloucestershire lying along a valley and among the hills of the Cotswolds. Brimming with fascinating history and lore, it dates back to medieval times as well, and beyond. An ancient Roman road, centuries old buildings and bridges, and traditional Cotswolds architecture of limestone walls, stone roofs, and steep gables give Bourton on the Water an idyllic storybook charm to this day. The smallpox outbreak described in this novel is based on the 1895-96 epidemic that resulted in 434 deaths. Two earlier outbreaks, in 1858 and between 1873-75, took a combined total of 220 lives. While there were many advocates for early means of vaccination, there were many against it as well. Isolation hospitals for the confinement of infected individuals were inadequate in their design, unattainable financially for many, and therefore ineffective to stop the spread of disease. The 1895-96 outbreak of smallpox reached epidemic proportions as it spread among children in schools, then home to home.

Edward Jenner of Gloucestershire (1749-1823) is remembered internationally for his devoted determination in research, scientific study, writings, and medical advancement of modern day immunology. This doctor from the country known for his innovative work toward the eradication of smallpox himself underwent variolation against the disease as an eight year old boy.

Florence Nightingale, "The Lady with the Lamp", and pioneer of modern day nursing opened her Nightingale Training School at St. Thomas' hospital in July of 1860. Nursing students were referred to as *probationers*, and they were under the direct supervision of a nurse of good standing and long tenure referred to as *matron*. The matron's assistants were referred to as *sisters*. St. Thomas' hospital has ancient ties as well, going as far back as 1106. It was the site of the first English Bible printing in 1537, and its operating theatre built in 1822 stands today as a museum. Though moved and rebuilt, St. Thomas' remains an operational hospital, and the nursing school lives on today as the Florence Nightingale Faculty of Nursing and Midwifery at King's College in London. Nightingale's passion and groundbreaking work in regard to nursing changed views of the profession worldwide. Formerly there was minimal if any training or professionalism, and the vocation was mocked and belittled, even by beloved author Charles Dickens. While mortality rates shifted little toward the end of the Victorian era, it was a time of sweeping medical advances all over the world. From Germany to France, from Louis Pasteur to Joseph Lister, infection and it's causes were coming to be more fully understood. Prevention of illness by sanitary means, new treatments, and new procedures became key in the art of healing. Florence Nightingale's work was part of a wave of change that became the catalyst for incredible progress in the twentieth century.

In this time of dawning medical understanding, there was a burgeoning increase of population in England. Municipalities were overrun and overwhelmed with waste, petty crime, and the responsibility to meet basic human needs such as clean water and burial of the dead. Victorians perceived illegality as a lower class problem, and indeed lived an existence not typically burdened by violent crime. Policing had become more refined and professional since middle of the century, and Londoners enjoyed an overall feeling of safety even as they devoured sensationalism in the news about the most trivial matters. Meanwhile, forensic pathology was in its infancy, and generally detectives were ill received and thought to be intrusive or unnecessary.

It was into this fray the murderer we've come to know as Jack the Ripper made his existence known 135 years ago.

About the Author

Born longing to live in another time,
A. M. Swinson holds a lifelong love of
history–the good, the bad, and the macabre.
Walking the halls of the anatomy
department of a teaching hospital as a child
cemented her fascination for forensics, and
spawned her obsession with the psychology
of history's criminals.

A survivor and a fighter, her most vibrant passion is to share with others how there can be hope and healing after heartache through faith. She dearly loves mentoring teens in their personal faith journey, in fearlessly sharing the Gospel, and toward excellence in the written word for God's glory through school journalism. She is affectionately known in her circles as "the wordy girl."

Wife to her high school sweetheart and mom to a miracle, she is an adoring dog mom, devoted music lover, MS warrior, and tireless advocate for women and children.

Made in the USA
Middletown, DE
05 May 2023